Enthralled

ISBN: 0615808921
ISBN-13: 9780615808925

TO: Frankie
Thank you for being
my go to guy!
Enjoy.   Rebecca S.

Enthralled

Rebecca S.

2013

Acknowledgements

First and foremost I would like to thank my number one supporter my husband, Ezequiel. Thank you for your words of encouragement and for believing in my dream. I am a true believer when someone can dream your dream magic can happen. You are my happily ever after. Thank you to my two amazing children Nicholas and Sophia. Nicholas since the moment you were born you have been my ray of light. You always amaze me with your charm and you can always bring a smile to my face. Sophia you have absolutely changed my life the moment I found out I was having a baby girl. You are the sweetest little girl any mommy can hope for and just hearing the sound of your voice makes my heart swell with pride. To my very first fan Teri Delallo, thank you for pushing me to keep writing, showing the enthusiasm to make me keep going, and for making me believe that I am good enough. To Ryan Soto, thank you for being so supportive. Only you can come over my house every Thursday night, let me read to you out loud chapter by chapter and still be fabulous. To Sergeant Michelle Romero, thank you for your words of encouragement all the way from Afghanistan. You are not only my best friend, but my hero and I salute you. To Al Martinez, thank you for your support and good wishes. You are one of the most genuine people I know and I am lucky to call you a friend. To Sigrid Martinez, I can't believe all along you were my Scarlett in disguise. Having a childhood friend still in your life in adulthood says a lot. Thank you for your support and for letting me boss you around for the day, a girl can definitely get use to this. To Raymond Rodriguez, thank you for your amazing work on my cover and graphic design. You have truly captured the essence of what I was looking for. You are a true talent. To Juan Sanchez "Bubu Chulo", thank you for the amazing makeup work, no one could have nailed it better. To my readers, I welcome you. I welcome you to take time away from your everyday life, become enraptured into a world full of danger, wonder, and excitement. I hope to see you moving from page to page leaving you wanting more and before you know it you find yourself completely utterly enthralled.

"The only person you are destined to become is the person you decide to be."

— Ralph Waldo Emerson

Prologue

The old man poured himself a glass of Scotch, knowing it would most likely be his last. He took a steady sip and enjoyed the old familiar burn of the liquor in the back of his throat. My God, how long had it been since he'd promised his dear sister he would change his life around, live a life for the good? Twenty years? He set the bottle down and looked around the small apartment he'd resided in for the past few years. *So this is where it ends.* His mission was done. He'd protected the girl's identity for as long as he could, just as he promised his sister he would. He brushed back his grey hair with his hand and took off his glasses, rubbing his eyes. They were on to him; his old age was making him careless and forgetful. He walked over to his window, stared out at the dark sky, and inhaled the thick air. It smelled of the death that awaited him. The air shifted around him, and he knew without turning that he was not alone.

"Didn't take you long to find where I live," the old man said, turning around to face the evil before him.

Piercing blue eyes stared at him, studying him as if trying to read his thoughts. "You have made it very easy for me, old man. Let's skip the small talk. You know why I have come. Where is the girl?"

"Let me guess: if I tell you, you will let me live." The old man chuckled, took another swig of his Scotch, and set the glass down on the table.

"Either way this will end badly, old man."

Before the old man could utter one more word, the intruder was before him, grabbing him by the throat and holding him against the window. His feet dangled in the air as the glass cracked against the weight of his body. The man bared his fangs as his piercing blue eyes turned dark. He set the old man down, but his hand remained at this throat.

"Her name, old man. Now," he growled.

Gasping, the old man let out a laugh, looked into his attacker's expressionless face, and uttered what he knew would be his final words. "She soon will be ready. She will be your doom."

The old man never even had a chance to scream. At least death came quickly. The intruder dropped the body, disgusted. He hated humans and all they represented. *Everyone wants to be the fucking hero!* The killer wandered about the old man's tiny apartment. He opened draws, looked under the mattress, scanned the whole apartment, and came up with nothing. Walking back toward the old man's body, he looked down at the Scotch on the table. *What the hell?* he thought and finished it.

As he set the glass down, he noticed a picture in a black wooden frame, perhaps of the dead man's wife when she was younger. She was beautiful. Long, pale blond hair framed an oval face with striking green eyes. He picked it up and noticed there was weight to it. Breaking the frame with his bare hands, he found a paper folded and taped to the back of the picture—a name and address in Latin. *Gotcha!* He walked over to the window and stared at the sky.

The time had come to put an end to the prophecy of the girl with the strength and power to lead the war against the undead, the girl born from a vampire and a human. The prophecy was thought mere legend until one of the ancients saw her in her dreams—the child that was born. That was twenty years ago. Now they were closer than ever to ending it all, even before the girl would know of the great power she held. He personally didn't give two shits what happened to mankind. He was paid handsomely to see the job done, and no one could get a job done better than he could.

Ian looked down at the paper with the name on it. The old man had made it easy for him…too easy. It was as if he wanted to get caught. *What did the old man mean she will be my doom?* Ian chuckled. *I will be her doom, and she will wish she was never born.* Crumpling the paper and tossing it to the floor, he jumped out of the window and landed on his feet on the ground ten feet below. He walked out into the cold night. He would remember the name Scarlett.

chapter

ONE

"Scarlett." He whispered my name so softly I wasn't sure I'd really heard him.

He leaned down and kissed me. Not your sweet lovey-dovey kiss but as though he wanted to devour my very soul. I could not help but respond with feverish need, my mind screaming for me to push him away but my body and heart screaming for him not to stop; the feel of his lips against mine was clouding my senses and, most of all, my judgment. He put my hands behind my back and held me still to his assault. I moaned, letting him take complete control of me. My body was not my own but now his. His lips started to trail to my neck. Lifting his head he looked up at me. His steel blue eyes turned to black, he released a growl, and fangs protruded from his mouth. I stared, stunned. I could not speak.

"You are mine," he said and bit down on my neck.

I woke with a start, heart racing, my hand touching the side of my neck, where I could still feel his lips.

"Holy shit," I mumbled, out of breath.

Rubbing my eyes I sat up in bed. These nightmares were getting worse, more vivid. It felt so real. Looking at the clock by my nightstand, I saw it was 7:30 a.m., not even time to get up for work yet.

"Oh well. Might as well start my day early," I mumbled to myself.

Huffing and puffing I got up and walked to my bathroom, the best place in my small but cozy apartment. Pink walls and a French-style bathtub; nothing better than to soak in a hot bubble bath after a long day at work at the boutique. Brushing my teeth, I looked at myself in the mirror, grabbed my contact case, and put my contacts in. I needed contacts for my poor vision but would use them regardless. I was born with heterochromia: two mismatched eyes, one light brown and the other green. People did tend to stare, so two brown eyes it was.

I walked over to my closet and selected a white collared shirt and black slacks, accessorized by the vintage designer belt I bought at an estate sale, and donned my favorite blue pumps. Back at the mirror, I applied my makeup and my favorite lipstick: pink a la mode. Grabbing my keys and purse, I did a last-minute check of my apartment and went out the door to catch the bus.

It was cold outside, and the fallen leaves stuck to my heels as I walked toward the bus stop. Waiting with others at the bus line was not ideal, but I was saving up for a car. My beat-up old Volkswagen Jetta had bit the dust. I was sad to let her go, but the poor thing just wouldn't start one day.

Everyone from teenagers to the elderly filled the bus, and of course there was Sally. Sally was the type of person you just wanted to bake cookies with. As funny as that may sound, it was true. A sweet lady, she wore her graying hair wrapped in a bun and had a warm, friendly smile. She volunteered at the local library and was always on the morning bus kindly holding a seat for me.

"Hey, Miss Sally. How are you doing this morning?" I asked, smiling at her.

"Scarlett, dear, I am well. How are you?" She asked, moving her bags and making room for me.

"You know, same ol', same ol'. Still waiting for my billionaire so I don't have to take the bus anymore," I said, giving Sally a wink and a nudge.

Sally laughed. "Oh, honey, I'm surprised you don't have suitors lining up at the door."

I let out an exaggerated sound. "No, I can't say I have any suitors at all," I said, laughing.

"It will happen, honey. When you least expect it."

I smiled in response. A few blocks later, I reached over and dinged for the bus to stop. I said my good-byes to her and made my way out. Downtown Westport was busy as usual with morning commuters driving to work, and, with Christmas coming up, it was going to be a busy day. I stopped at the coffee shop next to the boutique. There was nothing like a nice coffee and warm croissant. Inside the café, the smell of coffee hit me quickly. College kids and your morning early birds filled the place. Looking at the clock on the wall, I thought about leaving, but thought what the heck. I definitely would need the coffee if I was going to be pulling off a long shift at the W. I ordered a caramel latte and a croissant, grabbed it to go, and walked across the street.

As I entered the boutique, Mr. W himself greeted me. His name was Walter, but he liked to be called Mr. W. A skinny, outrageous, demanding African American man, he never took no for an answer and made his way up in the industry with his keen eye and boisterous attitude. People admired him, and if they didn't, they at least respected him. He was one of the top designers in Connecticut and often went to Fashion Week in New York, where he even hosted a few after parties. I started working at the W through Jewels.

I got the job right on the spot. I literally walked in, and he looked me up and down and told me that I would do. I found it difficult at times to work with him, but I knew that deep down in that fashionista heart of his, he meant well.

"Scarlett, darling," Mr. W said, kissing me on both cheeks.

"Hello, Mr. W," I said with a smile.

"Darling, darling, you are looking fierce. Please tell me those are my slacks."

"Of course they are. I would never go and buy elsewhere," I said, cringing as I walked away. I bought them on sale from our competitor.

"So I heard something from a little birdie," Mr. W said while looking at his perfectly manicured nails.

I walked over to the register and set my bag down. "Have you now? And what did this little birdie say?"

"Darling, why didn't you tell me it is going to be your birthday in two days?"

"Oh my God. Did Jewels tell you? It's not a big deal," I said, fixing the jewelry on display.

When I didn't get a response, I looked up to find him staring back at me open-mouthed.

"You are turning twenty-one! Darling, that is a big deal. We are going to throw you the best soiree, on me!"

I took a deep breath. I hated large crowds. "No, no. Please. I don't really celebrate birthdays. It really is no big deal," I said hurriedly, thinking of a way to get out of it.

Mr. W looked at his nails again and then back at me. "Scarlett, do you like your job?" he asked very seriously.

"Um, of course I do," I said, looking a bit confused and wondering where this was leading. Knowing Mr. W as I did, I knew he was going to get his way no matter what I said.

"Then that settles it. We will have our soiree in two days. Gypsy themed at The Red Door, VIP for the best darling." And just like that, Mr. W sashayed back to his office, leaving me speechless.

"Fuck!" I mouthed.

After my shift ended at 6:00 p.m., Jewels came waltzing in to start her shift. She wore a grey blazer, a beautiful animal-print scarf around her neck, and black slacks, her long blond hair pulled back in a ponytail, showing off her beautiful features.

"Hey, you," she said innocently.

I had known Jewels many years, and we had become great friends. We met when we were partnered up in a design class and instantly clicked. She was your all-American girl: blond, blue eyed, and looked good in anything. I guess you could say she took me out of my comfort zone. Where I was shy and stayed away from crowds, Jewels was the opposite. She loved to be the center of attention, and everyone loved her. She was compulsive and sometimes would say the most outrageous things. Let's just say she had a way of rubbing off on people, especially me.

"Hey. Why did you tell Mr. W my birthday's coming up? He wants to throw this big, over-the-top party that I don't even want to go to! You know I hate parties," I whispered, crossing my arms.

She walked behind the counter, set down her purse, and turned back to me with a very serious look. "Listen, Scarlett, you don't even go out. All you do is work. It's time to go out and have a little fun. Don't you think?"

"Umm…that's for me to decide! And anyways, who's keeping track?"

"Everyone."

"*Everyone?* Seriously?"

"Scarlett, we just all feel that you should loosen up. Sometimes you can get a little uptight," Jewels said looking away.

"Me? Uptight?" I knew that sometimes I kept to myself, but that didn't mean I was uptight. Maybe my being guarded was giving people the wrong impression. *I am so not uptight.*

"To put it mildly…yes."

"Don't put it mildly."

"OK. You want to hear not mildly?" she asked, looking around to make sure there were no customers around.

I nodded.

"Take the stick out of your ass. There, I said it. God, that feels good. Let me say it again: take the stick out of your ass." She stared at me wide-eyed, waiting for my reaction.

I looked away. She was right. There was no point in denying it: my attitude was not just guarded, and I could be a little uptight. I let out a deep breath and reached over for my purse.

"OK. Well, maybe you're right. But I'm still not sure I want this big party. You know it's not my scene, Jewels."

Jewels came over to me and gently touched my shoulder, her eyes concerned. "Listen, I will let Mr. W know you don't want anything big, just something mellow," she said, trying to reassure me.

"Mellow is not in Mr. W's vocabulary," I said, thinking of the gypsy theme he had in mind.

We both started laughing. I could never stay mad at Jewels. She always meant well and had my best interest at heart. I looked at the clock: 6:30 p.m.

"Shit, I better run," I said, grabbing my keys. We said our good-byes, and I rushed out the door.

It was freezing out as I walked as fast as I could to the bus line. The bus was always late, so I thought maybe I would get lucky. It was supposed to come around 6:20 p.m. As I made it closer to the bus stop, I saw it waiting. I broke into a run trying to get to it as fast as I could, but it was difficult in six-inch heels.

"Wait!" I yelled, but it was too late. The bus drove off leaving a pile of grey smoke in its wake.

"Shit, shit, shit," I said angrily to myself, almost stomping my feet like a child.

Taking a deep breath, I reasoned with myself. *OK. From here it's a couple of blocks to my apartment. No big deal.* As

I made my way home, many cars passed on the street, most likely heading home or rushing to downtown trying to make their dinner reservations. Christmas lights lit the streets and people rushed back and forth with their shopping bags. As I crossed the street, I got the feeling someone was watching me. I looked around quickly, almost bumping into someone in the process. Mumbling my apologies and shaking my head at my stupidity, I still couldn't shake the feeling.

The hairs on the back of my neck started to stand, and I knew for certain someone had eyes on me. I clutched my purse tighter and picked up the pace. Finally reaching my apartment complex, I started rummaging through my purse for my keys. There's nothing worse than a big bag you can't find anything in. But then the bag was designer and on sale, so who was I to complain? I heard a little whining sound and looked down at my doorway, and there sat a puppy at my door. He rushed over to me as if he knew me, tail wagging, jumping up and down barking.

"Oh my God. Who are you, little guy?" I bent down and petted him, scratching him behind the ear. He was a Beagle with light brown and black fur with little white spots and the softest brown eyes. He whined some more, licking my palms.

"Aw, aren't you a sweet little thing. Where's your owner? Huh, cutie?" I asked looking around.

Picking him up, I noticed two things: he has no collar, and he was definitely a boy.

"Well, buddy, let's go inside. OK? You must be cold and hungry." He rewarded me with another lick to my hand.

Opening the door to my apartment, I looked back outside. I didn't see anything, but I still felt someone's eyes on me. I shook my head. *I must be really tired.*

The person dressed in black walked away, making his way deeper into the shadows as the girl entered the apartment with the dog. The girl stood looking out into the darkness as though aware he was there watching her. She had sensed him as soon as she began walking when she missed the bus. That was good. The change was soon coming. They had gotten the call of her location and stood ready, ready for the war they were all destined to be in with their leader. They had remained in hiding, waiting for this day to come, and now they were days away from seeing the prophecy come to fruition.

He saw her in a vision. She was to be their hope, their salvation. Just like her father, she would be a true warrior, ready to fight for the cause, to avenge. She would be driven and she would succeed, but it was going to get dirty. The queen always played dirty; that was the name of her game. He turned and started walking in the other direction. Grabbing the cell phone out of his pocket, he made the call to the X's. Walking a short distance away, Con held the cell phone to his ear, waiting for someone to pick up.

"Hey, he's in. She did not make me, but I know she sensed me. She is close to her change. We need to make our move fast," he said. After listening to the response, he hung up.

Walking faster, he went deeper into the shadows; he glided through, careful not to be seen, his powerful body moving tenaciously. Instantly he vanished, as though the darkness had welcomed him in.

"OK, little guy. Home sweet home. Well, at least temporarily, until we find your owner," I said, closing the door behind me.

I turned on the lights, feeling a little more secure now that I was inside. There was no place like home. I set the puppy down, and he looked up at me as if waiting to be given the grand tour.

"Well, since you're going to be my temporary room-mate, let's show you around. This right here is the living room. You are not allowed to poop or pee here, or anywhere indoors, for that matter. Let's move on to the kitchen."

I walked with the puppy right at my heels.

"This is the kitchen. We eat here," I said sharply to him, letting him know I meant business. "OK. This right over here is the bedroom." I pointed to my closet. "This right here is my closet. You, little guy, are not allowed in this closet. If I find a scratch, bite mark, or slobber on my Jimmy Choos, you, my friend, are out." I bent to meet the puppy eye to eye. "Capisce?"

The puppy cocked his head to the side and yelped, stamping his little paw to the floor.

"OK. Who are we kidding? They're not real Jimmys, but you get my drift," I said, scratching his ear.

He trotted over to the corner of my room and lay down, closed his eyes, and started drifting off to sleep.

I got up and made my way to the bathroom. Taking off my shirt and pants, I dropped them to the floor and reached over to start the shower, leaving it on hot to steam up the bathroom. I removed my contacts and makeup. Standing in front of the mirror in nothing but my bra and underwear, I looked myself over in the mirror. Pulling my hair behind my ears and putting my shoulders back, I looked at my real self, the person I tried to hide with contacts and makeup. What I saw was a girl with oddly colored eyes too big for her face, skin too pale, and hair in desperate need of cutting. Lifting a strand, I did have to admit I loved my hair. Neither curly nor straight, it was a happy medium.

Rolling my eyes at myself, I hopped in the shower. Letting the warmth of the water hit me, I closed my eyes as I let it relax my achy muscles from a long day of work. Feeling cleansed and refreshed, I hopped out of the shower and wrapped a towel around myself. I peeked in my room to check on the puppy and found him still fast asleep. Poor thing was probably exhausted, most likely out all day looking for shelter. Tomorrow morning I would make a few phone calls to the local animal shelters to see if anyone had called in a missing pup.

In my bedroom, I opened the bureau drawers slowly and quietly, dropped my towel to the floor and put on my underwear and an oversized T-shirt. I tiptoed to the kitchen and opened the fridge. It was practically empty. *Geez, I really needed to stop ordering takeout.* Closing the fridge frustrated, I went into the cupboard and took out the peanut butter. Shaking my head, I realized I was out of bread. *Oh, well,* I said to myself. Grabbing a spoon out of the drawer, I got a spoonful of peanut butter put it in my mouth, and leaned against the counter thinking to myself, *I will go grocery shopping tomorrow.*

Totally unsatisfied I put the spoon in the sink and turned off all the lights, being as quiet as I could not to wake up my new roommate. Pulling the sheets back, I got in bed, shifting a little so I was in the right position. Before I dozed off, I thought to myself, *Wonder if puppy would like the name Hugo?*

chapter

TWO

The room was dark except for a light by the fireplace. We lay on the floor, clothes scattered everywhere, the need for each other so strong we hadn't made it to the bed. We'd just finished making love, and he was gazing at me adoringly, his hand smoothing my hair away from my face. He leaned down slowly and kissed me. My body once again on fire for him, breaking away from his kiss, I rolled on top of him, holding his hands above his head. He let out a growl and I looked up at him, arching my eyebrow and giving him a lustrous smile. I leaned over and trailed kisses from his chest to his neck and worked my way back down, this time with my tongue, never letting my eyes leave his, my tongue lapping on him as though he was a sweet candy I could not get enough of. He let out a groan and arched his lower body upward, letting me know how aroused he was. I smiled again. I loved being the aggressor. I let go of his hands, and he quickly rolled on top of me. Moving my head to the side and arching my neck, I silently begged him please to drink from me. He tilted my head back, his finger-tips lightly caressing my face.

"Say it," he growled looking deeply into my eyes.

I knew what he meant. I was his, body and soul. I was deeply in love with this man, as he was with me.

"I am yours. Forever," I whispered meaning every word.

"Forever," he whispered back, putting his forehead against mine.

Lifting his hand he gently bit his wrist and brought it to my mouth. I drank from him. His taste was pure ecstasy—so sweet. His blood consumed me. He consumed me. I could not get enough of him.

My alarm clock sounded, waking me from my dream. With a start my hand went to my rapidly beating heart. *That felt so real.* I licked my dry lips and took a deep breath, sitting up. I leaned over turning off the clock, frustrated with it. Swinging my legs from the bed, I was greeted by Hugo. He ran over to me barking, jumping up on my leg.

"Hey there, Hugo," I said with a smile as I bent down to scratch his ear.

He stopped jumping, sat on all fours, cocked his head to the side, and looked at me curiously.

"Hey, buddy, I was born with the name Scarlett. Trust me when I say you can handle the name Hugo."

I got up and walked to the bathroom to brush my teeth and wash my face. I grabbed my contacts and put my left contact in. It was completely foggy. Grabbing my eye solution, I cleaned it out and put it back in my left eye. Blinking rapidly, I still could not see out of it.

"What the heck? I just bought these," I said aloud. Hugo stood in the doorway watching me.

Taking out my contact, I realized I could see clearly—clearer than I ever had before. Walking into the kitchen with Hugo trailing behind me, I picked up a bill and read the small print. Dropping the bill onto the counter with a dumbfounded look, I walked over to the living room. Finding the remote control, I turned on the television and stood as far from the screen as I possibly could. What would have been a big blur just the night before, I saw now as clear as day. Rubbing my eyes I focused again on the television. Still clear.

Going to look out the window, I saw everything as I'd never seen it. Opening the window, I put my head out. The cold wind hit my face, but I was too freaked out to notice. I could read street signs a few feet away. Everything was so much clearer than before. Pulling my head back in, I closed the window, totally confused.

"OK. This is very strange. I've never heard of eyesight just improving on its own. Have you?"

I looked at Hugo, who only yawned in reply.

I headed back to the bathroom and applied my makeup and curled my hair in soft waves. Applying my lipstick, I looked again at my eyes, really hoping people wouldn't stare. They could be a little intense even for me.

"Oh, hell with it," I said at the mirror, combing my fingers through my hair to loosen up the curls. I actually liked what a saw.

I tucked a white shirt into my black pencil skirt and put on my favorite navy blazer with white polka dots. Having a seat on the bed, I rolled on my nude stockings. I walked over to the closet and put on my fake Jimmys. Standing in front of the mirror, I was satisfied.

"Whoa! I look hot. Don't you think, Hugo?"

He gave a soft whine as if bored.

"OK. Let's go for a quick walk, and I will check out this little shop to see if they have some dog food."

I grabbed my purse and keys. Hugo was right behind me, and I noticed he hadn't made a mess yet. What were the odds that I just had a smart pup?

We both headed out of the apartment complex and walked over to the shop, one of those little mom-and-pop shops that had a little of everything. I noticed a sign: "No Pets Allowed."

"Hugo, you wait out here, OK? I will be just a second," I promised him, walking inside.

Grabbing a basket by the doorway, I went right to the pet section. I didn't know what to get. There were all different kinds of dog food assortments—turkey and bacon, ham and bacon, beef and bacon—so I got all of them, putting a can of each in the basket. I got the other things I needed, paid the cashier, and headed out, looking down at Hugo, who was patiently waiting for me.

"OK. I hope you like bacon," I said as he followed me back home.

Hugo let out a growl, and I looked down at him.

"Well too bad, buddy. This stuff costs a fortune." Rolling my eyes, I started walking faster, knowing I had to catch the next bus.

Back in my apartment, I filled up the fridge, left food and water out for Hugo, kissed him good-bye, and hurried to catch the bus.

The bus was already at the stop taking in the last of its passengers, closing the door, and starting to drive off.

Shit. Not again! "Wait!" I yelled, waving my hand to get the driver's attention.

He didn't hear and started to pull out. That's when I took off running to catch up, pure adrenaline kicking in. I picked up my speed, surprising myself at how fast I was in heels, dashing and swerving through the crowd like I was running a marathon. The bus stopped at the stoplight, and I made it just in time, pounding on the door for the driver to open up before the light turned green. He jumped, startled, and opened the door. As I paid the man, I noticed I wasn't even out of breath.

Making my way to Sally, who was holding a seat for me, I sat down. As I said my hellos to Sally, I felt as if everything was turned on high. Everything seemed so loud. A teenager with a pair of big headphones on sat a few seats away, and I could every word of the rap song playing. The bus came to a stop, and a man walked on. While paying, he accidently dropped his coins on the floor. I heard them drop as if it was right by my ear, causing pain. I winced, closing my eyes.

"My dear, are you OK?" Sally asked, touching my shoulder.

That's when I realized I had my hand over my ears and my eyes closed. Taking my hand away from my ears, everything seemed to be back to normal. Just like that, the high volume was switched off.

"Yes, yes. I'm OK. Sorry. I just feel a migraine coming on," I said, reassuring her.

"Oh, dear. Drink some hot tea. It always helps with my migraines."

"I will. Thanks."

What the hell just happened? I wiped the sweat from my brow. This day was getting stranger and stranger.

Eight hours into my shift, the sun was beginning to go down. It was almost time to lock up the boutique. While I had downtime, I called four local animal shelters and came up with nothing for Hugo. Looked like me and the little guy were stuck together. Leaning over the counter, I looked out the window, watching people passing by. A young couple holding hands came by, and I couldn't help but stare.

When was the last time I'd had a relationship? There was always the occasional dating here and there, but nothing serious. I found myself looking at the couple longingly, feeling very much alone. When was the last time I'd been kissed? I had so little experience when it came to sex, I began to wonder if I'd even made it to second base. I'd always had plenty of guys asking me out, but I could never let anyone close. It just didn't feel right...with the exception of the man in my dreams.

God. To feel that intensely for someone really would be a dream. I rubbed my eyes and let out a deep breath. Being shipped off foster home to foster home probably didn't help matters. I learned quickly to keep to myself, and being ignored was something I dealt with on a daily basis. There had been no birthday celebrating, Christmas tree decorating, or white picket fences. I learned to shut myself off from the world, never wanting anyone to get too close. I always felt different, and my foster parents sure as hell didn't make me feel wanted. All they wanted was that monthly check they would collect from the government, and as soon as I was eighteen, I got out as fast as I could, never looking back.

I was curious, as all orphan children are. Who were my birth parents? I went as far as going to the adoption office hoping they could help me find my birth parents, but their names were a total mystery. Not wanting to be found, they'd left me with nothing but my name. I wondered if they thought about me as often as I thought of them. There were so many questions unanswered. Why did they give me up? Did they love me?

"Scarlett, get a grip," I said angrily to myself, wiping down the counter to busy myself. That's when I got the feeling I'd felt the day before, when I was walking home. The hairs on the back of my neck started to stand. I looked up even before the bell on the door sounded. A beautiful, tall, African American woman walked in. I smiled, greeting her.

"Hello. Welcome to the W. Can I help you look for something?" I offered, walking over to her.

The woman smiled as I approached her, and my uneasiness intensified. As I stood before her, I had to look up a little. *She must be a model,* I thought. She wore her hair braided up and had glowing dark skin, dark brown almond-shaped eyes, and ruby red lips. She was stunning.

"So you are the one. I have heard so much about you, but I had to come see for myself," she said with a hint of an English accent, looking at me as if she knew me.

"Umm…I'm sorry. Have we met before?" I asked, nervously tucking my hair behind my ear.

"No."

"Oh, OK. Did you get a referral? We have a lot of models that come in. Mr. W just came out with his new winter collection that I am sure you will die for." I selected a white silk blouse and pulled it from the rack. "This would look great on you," I said, my senses on full alert. Something wasn't right.

"Scarlett, I am not here to buy a blouse," she said, cocking her head to the side.

"You know my name. Who are you?"

"My name is Zayah; I am here to give you a warning. And I know you sense something is wrong. That's very good. The change is starting for you."

"What warning? What are you talking about?" I asked, putting the blouse back as fast as I could and heading back to the counter, putting as much distance as I could between myself and this crazy woman. I quickly looked at the doorway, expecting Jewels to pop out and scream, "Gotcha!"

"Scarlett, you are in danger. The war is soon upon us. The change will happen tomorrow, and people will come after you. We can protect you, but you are going to have to listen and understand. I want you to come with me before it happens because once it does, all sorts of hell is going to break loose, and they will ensure that you are dead," she said with deadly calm, putting her hands behind her back.

My eyes grew wide and my mouth gaped open. OK. This was no joke. This bitch was crazy. *What the hell is she on?* I swallowed and took a deep breath.

"Zia…or Zayah…or whatever your name is, I don't know what your deal is, but you better leave now before I call the cops."

"The cops won't help you," she said, shaking her head.

I said nothing, just stared at her, waiting for her to make her move. I sized her up. *I can take her, I think.*

She smiled at me. "You're brave, Scarlett. Tomorrow will be the day. We will watch and wait, but make no mistake: the change will happen, and when it does we will be right by your side, to fight and die for you if we must." With that she turned toward the door.

Staring at her retreating back, I could not stop my curiosity. I called out, "Who's 'we'?"

She looked back at me and simply said, "The X's," and walked out the door.

I quickly walked around from behind the counter, locked the door, and put our closed sign up. I looked out the window but didn't see her. *Where the hell did she go? The X's? This lady is on some serious drugs,* I said to myself, shaking my head. I walked back around the counter and took down the register, counting the money to make sure everything evened out for the day. Putting the money in the safe, I went back up front, got my purse, and turned off the lights. I walked to the door and set the alarm, waiting for the beep before I shut the door behind me. It wasn't as cold out as it was yesterday. I saw the bus coming to a stop and thought, *What the heck. I'll walk home.*

Making my way through downtown, it was quiet, the sound of my heels stomping away. I felt this chill run down my spine and the hairs on the back of my neck stand again. I walked a little faster. I looked back and saw no one behind me. As I turned back around, a man in a ski masked dressed in black stood in front of me, surprising me. Before I could utter a word, he grabbed me by the arm and shoved me into a tight alley and pulled me behind a dumpster so no one could see us. I tried to scream, but he covered my mouth before I could let out a sound. He slammed me against the wall so hard I lost my breath.

"Make any noise, bitch, and you'll get cut," he whispered holding a knife to my throat. I felt the cold blade scratching against my skin.

I nodded, breathing heavily, his hand still on my mouth.

"Get her purse, yo," someone else whispered.

There was another guy in the alley. The one holding the knife snatched my purse out of my hands and handed it to the other guy. He searched my purse, took out my wallet, and dropped my purse to the ground.

"What the fuck? This bitch only has forty bucks," the man hissed, looking up.

The man holding the knife smiled at me, a sinister smile. He ran the knife down the front of my shirt, popping two of my buttons. I cringed in disgust.

"It's OK, dude. She can make it up in other ways."

The other man laughed and started touching himself. "OK, man. Let me go first."

I felt a ball of anger rise in me, making my hand ball into a fist. Out of nowhere, as though I were someone else, I kicked him right in the balls. As he bent down, howling with pain, he dropped the knife to grab himself, and I kneed him in the face. He fell down, completely knocked out. I stared down at him, unable to believe I had just knocked out a guy twice my size. Completely distracted, I forgot about the other guy. He grabbed me by the hair and backslapped me, splitting my lip, and shoved me to the ground.

"You're going to pay for that, bitch!" He yelled over me.

As he made a grab for me, we heard a noise that almost sounded like a growl. He turned toward it, and before I could see what was happening he was thrown against the wall. He screamed out in pain but was shown no mercy. He didn't have a chance against his assailant. He took several punches to the face before he went down. Hearing steps coming toward me, I tried to get up but fell over. *Damn heels.*

My savior grabbed me up roughly. I winced from the pain, my eyes closed. His hands went around my neck tightly as if to snap it. I gasped, my fingers going around the hands at my throat. He was cutting off my circulation. Opening my eyes wide, I met the stare of steel blue eyes, the eyes from my dreams. His eyes widened, beautiful eyes that looked deeply into mine, and he slowly loosened his grip. His eyes dropped to my lips, and I unconsciously licked them, tasting blood. His eyes turned dark.

"You," I whispered incredulously.

He let go of me as if I'd burned him. He seemed as shocked as I was. Did he know me? He stared at me for what seemed like forever, and as quickly as he had come, he left, running into the darkness.

I started to go after him, wanting to call out for him to stop, but just then the men started to groan. Quickly grabbing my purse from the ground, I sped out of the alley. I ran all the way home, tears running down my face. What the hell was going on? I got to my apartment. Not waiting for the elevator, I ran up the steps, taking two at a time. At the door, my shaky hands dropped the keys before finally opening it. Once inside I closed the door, locking it quickly behind me and leaning my back against it. I felt myself sliding down to the floor, relief washing through me as I thanked God that I was OK. Hugo came running over to me barking. He laid his head on my lap as if sensing something was wrong.

"I'm OK, buddy," I whispered, gently touching his head.

Those bastards were going to rape me and God knows what else. Maybe I should have gone straight to the police and filed a report, but what was that going to do? I hadn't even seen their faces. If it wasn't for my savior, who knows what would have happened. *My savior, the man from my dreams,* I thought to myself. There was something different about him. There was no gentleness to his eyes; there was coldness there. My God, how could that be? Was it possible? As my tears faded and clarity began to set in, I started to remember something about my savior, the one from my dreams: he had fangs.

chapter

THREE

Queen Ezarbet stood at the window looking out at the night sky as what her foreseer had just told her sank in. It was a beautiful night, with the stars shining perfectly in the dark sky. It would have been romantic if she believed in romance. The foreseer had just told her something she did not want to hear. The prophet was safe and had already made contact with the X's. Queen Ezarbet took hold of her goblet and took a sip, her anger starting to build. The foreseer stood behind her still talking, but she heard no words. *The prophet will end the war.* She smirked. *Never.*

She turned to the foreseer, eyes pitch black.

The foreseer squirmed beneath her stare.

"Are you saying you see this prophet ending the war and defeating me?"

"Queen Ezarbet, I meant no such thing," he said, shaking his head.

The queen arched her eyebrow and moved closer to him, smiling all the while. "What did you mean?"

"I simply meant..."

The queen put her hand through his chest and took out his heart, dropping it to the floor, and watched as his body turned to ash, loving the look of agony on his face. Walking away from the pile of ash, she resumed her place at the window as if nothing had happened. She yelled for Abel, her soldier as well as her lover. He walked in, looking down at the black ash that had been the foreseer. He bowed before approaching her.

"My queen," he said softly.

Turning toward his voice, she looked upon her lover who had been by her side since she took reign. His face was beautiful except for the hideous scar that ran from his eyelid down. He wore a fitted vest that showed off his bulging muscles nicely and jeans. A sword hung at his side. He was always ready to do battle. He was loyal to a fault. He was like a dog always needing attention, always seeking approval from his master. He had become a pebble in her shoe in many ways, but she knew she could trust him to see the job—any job—done.

"We will need another foreseer, and make sure this one is loyal to its queen," she growled.

He stood waiting for her to say more, but she turned, dismissing him.

"Yes, my queen. Of course," he said, bowing again before walking out the door.

Turning back to look out the window, she thought of all the cards she had set in place. *Scarlett,* the queen thought to herself and smiled. *I will rip out her beating heart and eat it with her followers watching. They will all be brought to their knees bowing to me as their queen.*

Hugo let out a yelp of pain as I accidently rolled on top of him.

"Oops! Sorry, buddy. I forgot you were in bed with me," I groaned, lifting my face off my pillow. Rolling onto my back, I looked to over him. After the previous night's ordeal, I put Hugo in bed with me. I just didn't want to be alone, and for some reason it felt right to have him there with me. I probably had the deepest sleep I'd had in a long time. I watched as he found a more comfortable spot on the bed, careful to stay away from me. He actually looked pissed that I'd disturbed him from his slumber.

"Geez, I said I was sorry. I'm not used to having a man in my bed," I said, laughing.

Hugo cocked his head to the side.

I got up and headed to the bathroom. I went to the mirror to examine my lip, which had been split and puffy the day before. It looked fine. I saw no trace of the events that took place yesterday. I was not even the least bit sore. I pulled up my pajama pants and looked at my knee that was scraped yesterday. Nothing. No scrape. No bruises. *OK. Weird. Maybe I'm going crazy. Maybe yesterday didn't even happen. And maybe, just maybe, I didn't see my savior with fangs.* Putting down my pant leg, I walked out of the bathroom. Hugo quickly sat up and looked at me as if he was worried.

"Hugo, today I am off of work. And guess what? It's my birthday. My boss is having a birthday party for me, and I'm going shopping," I said with fake cheerfulness, trying to forget what had happened.

Determined to have a good day and not think about the day before, I got dressed as quickly as I could. Putting on some comfortable black yoga pants and a fitted purple sweater, I found my pair of UGG boots and put them on. After making sure Hugo was fed, I went outside with him. The weather was not too cold out; the sun was shining. Hugo went about his business, and I brought him back inside.

"OK, Hugo, honey. Mommy has to go, but I'll be back." Wrapping an animal print scarf around my neck, I bent down, picking up his little body and nuzzling his fur against my nose. Giving him a quick kiss, I set him down. Closing the door, I felt a little sad leaving him by himself. I couldn't believe how attached I was to Hugo already, but then we had a lot in common. We were both abandoned, left alone to fend for ourselves. Heading out of the elevator, I stepped outside. The weather was great—bright and sunny with a nice chill.

Making my way through the street, I decided to walk, my steps slowing as I reached the alley where I was attacked. I slowly stepped into the alley, half wishing and hoping I would see my steel-blue-eyed savior. But there was no trace of him. It looked as though nothing had taken place here. I wondered what had happened to the men. *I bet they'll think twice now before they ever attack a helpless woman again.*

Leaving the alley disappointed, I headed toward downtown to my favorite salon. Walking in, I spotted Fernando. It was a chic unisex salon with very upscale clientele. There was usually a six-month wait to get an appointment, but Mr. W could connect you with anyone. Fernando was the best. A Spanish man with dark, shiny hair slicked back into a ponytail, he always wore a red silk scarf. If fabulous had a picture in the dictionary, it would be of Fernando. He was the only one I would let touch my hair. Before I could ask the receptionist, who was wearing designer eyeglasses and had her platinum blond hair cropped to the side, giving her a couture look, if he was free, he saw me and rushed over, giving me air kisses on both cheeks.

"Scarlett, mi amore! Happy birthday! Mr. W already filled me in! Party at the Red Door, gypsy theme. He told me to give you the works, as if you need it," he said, his voice thick with his accent. He rushed me over to his chair.

I laughed. *Really, Mr. W, the works? He would say something like that,* I thought to myself. "Yeah, seriously," I said with fake confidence, waving my hand.

"Mi amore, but look at you! You are bellisima: beautiful! You must know that!" he exclaimed, kissing his fingertips.

I looked at the mirror with him, and I swear it was as though I was seeing someone else. Of course I always thought I was pretty, but what I saw now was a beautiful woman. My lips looked fuller, redder; my eyes looked very bright, and yes, mismatched, but very exotic; my long hair, naturally highlighted red from the sun, framed my pale skin. I looked at myself feeling beautiful for the first time— not caring that I looked different, but embracing it.

"OK, Fernando! What should we do?" I asked, giving him full trust. He was a professional, after all.

"I want to keep your length, so we will trim and put your hair in soft waves so it will frame that beautiful face. Makeup we will do after. I am thinking smoky eye, red lip. Classic!" he exclaimed excitedly, his eyes shining brightly.

I took a deep breath. *Red lip. OK. What the hell?* I nodded in agreement and let him get to work.

Three hours later he turned my chair. *Holy shit!* The girl in the mirror was not me. This girl was sexy. Soft waves cascaded down my back and framed my face. The red lipstick made my lips looks even fuller. My eyes stood out seductively. I could not take my eyes off of myself.

"Mi amore, you like?" Fernando asked, knowing full well what my answer would be.

"I love it. You're a genius," I said, hugging him and air kissing him on both cheeks, being careful not to smudge my makeup.

We said our good-byes, and I made my way over to W boutique. I opened the door to find Jewels standing at the counter.

"Oh my God!" she yelled, rushing over to me.

I laughed trying to be modest, but inside I was beaming.

Mr. W came out to see what the commotion was about and stopped dead in his tracks, mouth open.

"Darling, Darling! You look fabulous," he said, sashaying toward me giving me more air kisses.

"Thanks, guys," I said, smiling and blushing.

"Darling, I have a present for you," he said as he turned, heading to the backroom.

"Aw, you didn't have to get me anything," I called out to him, shaking my head at Jewels. She shrugged her shoulders as if she didn't know anything, but I saw a twinkle in her eyes.

Mr. W came out holding a square white box with a big red bow, smiling from ear to ear like he was giving a child a present for the first time. *Weird. I could never envision Mr. W as Santa Claus.*

"Darling, I made this just for you. Don't open it until you get home. Just wear it to your party, and if you don't have it on for your party, consider yourself unemployed," he said, handing me the box.

I laughed and then realized he wasn't laughing. "Thank you so much, Mr. W. I'm sure I will love it," I said, giving him a cheeky smile.

He stared at me sharply and sashayed back to his office. *Oh how I love him.*

Jewels and I looked at each and burst out laughing.

I entered my apartment, closing the door behind me, and before I could turn, Hugo rushed toward me barking. Smiling down at him, I put my gift and purse down on the counter.

"Hey, honey," I said, bending down to pick him up, petting him gently.

It was great to come home to someone. With him in my arms, I went over to the window and looked out. The sun was starting to go down. I shivered; I couldn't shake this strange feeling I'd had since leaving the W. Hugo peered up at me, his soft brown eyes looking worried. I gave him a quick kiss on the nose and set him down. As I stood back up, I felt an ache in my stomach. Pressing my hand against my stomach, I felt another hot rush.

"Ahh!" I gasped, feeling my knees begin to buckle.

Hugo started whining at my feet.

"I'm OK, buddy," I reassured him.

I stood still for a minute, waiting for the pain to come again. No pain came, but I still felt a dull ache. I shook my head and walked to the bathroom to start the shower. I took off my clothes and got in, careful not to get my face and hair wet. Out of the shower, I put on my robe. I grabbed my gift from the counter and set it on the bed, nervous to open it. As I paced back and forth in front of the bed, the big red bow was taunting me. Letting out a huff, I untied it and opened the box. Inside lay a very low-cut, white, sexy dress. It was strapless with a deep V, the fabric pulled together in a ruching detail, and it was quite short. *Oh my God. I cannot wear this.*

I opened my dresser drawer and put on a lacey white thong. Removing my robe, I slipped on the dress. I walked over to the mirror and was again amazed. This was not me. *Who is this?* The woman I saw before me was sexy and confident. The dress hugged in all the right places, the cut in the front—low, yes—showing off just the right amount of cleavage. I turned around. *Whoa!* My ass and legs were looking great too. Going into my closet, I grabbed my silver heels with tiny rhinestones on them, sat on the bed, and put them on. I went back to the mirror and touched up my makeup. I did a final check and looked over to where Hugo lay.

"Well, what do you think?" I asked, turning to him, pulling my shoulders back as though I were modeling.

He cocked his head to the side and let out a bark as if approving.

I smiled. "Good answer."

Turning back toward the mirror, I heard a horn honking. I ran over to the window and saw it was the driver Mr. W had sent to pick me up.

"Shit. He's early."

I grabbed my clutch and made sure my ID and keys were in it.

"OK, Hugo. I have to go, but Mommy will be back," I said, giving him a quick pat.

I headed out the door, the cold air hitting me, making my teeth chatter. I couldn't believe I'd decided to go out without a coat, but I knew the club would be hot inside and didn't want to wait in line for coat service. A man stepped out of the black Town Car and opened the door for me. I took a seat and put my hand to my stomach, taking a deep breath. *My nerves must me getting to me.* The dull ache in my stomach was getting worse. I could not shake the feeling that something was going to go terribly wrong tonight.

chapter

FOUR

After Scarlett left the apartment, I quickly jumped off the bed, going into a sitting position as I transformed from puppy to man. Transforming was easy, as soon as you became used to it. I looked out the window, careful so she wouldn't see me. I watched as she got into the car, and the car sped off into the cold night, heading in the direction of her new life. I thought back to the time before getting here, before the X's, the time before fate drew Scarlet, the X's, and myself together.

My hands were sweaty from nervousness. I quickly rubbed them off on my jacket. The magic that I spelled was used to find the aging guardian that was given to the prophet at birth. It wasn't just the magic that worked; it was as though the guardian summoned me, leaving a trail of light that beckoned me to follow. I went up the steps slowly, purposely taking my time. Reaching the apartment door, I hesitated before knocking, pausing with my fist at the door. This was it. I was about to know who the prophet was. Did I want to know? Was I really the one chosen to protect her? Before I could knock, the door swung open. There stood a small, aging man with gray hair and glasses—John, the guardian.

"Well are you just going to stand there or are you going to come in?" he asked grumpily, opening the door wider for me and walking away.

At a loss for words, I stepped inside and closed the door. He had a neat apartment, small but comfortable for one person. The furniture looked used but in good condition. Turning I followed him toward his kitchen area, where he stood with his back turned, pouring himself a cup of coffee.

"Do you want some coffee?" he asked, looking back at me.

"No, thank you," I said, standing awkwardly by the table. I noticed a picture frame on the table holding a photo of a woman, his sister Celine, the mother of the prophet.

"Well, have a seat then. I want to enjoy my coffee," he said, turning to stare at me as he drank from his cup.

Sitting down I wondered how this was supposed to work.

"I guess you want to know why I have summoned you, huh?" he asked, looking at me over the rim of his cup.

I said nothing; the aura around him was foggy, and I sensed he wanted to talk. He was seeking something. Closure?

"You see that bottle over there, son?"

I looked down at the table again and saw a bottle of aged Scotch sitting a few inches away from the picture. Next to the bottle sat an empty glass looking like it was just waiting to be filled.

"I haven't had a drink in twenty years. I keep it next to her picture to remind me of the reckless person I once was.

That's how long I have been a guardian. You change your life for the good. It's a choice. Do you understand what I am saying?"

"Yes," I said quietly, knowing full well what he meant.

"My sister came to me when I was drunk, drunk like a stinking pig, and told me she was with child. She said she needed my help. Me, her only brother, who was never good for nothing but getting drunk; she needed me. She believed in me. I guess I always believed in the supernatural, but there it was, shoved in my face. She told me of the prophecy, of the child she carried that would change the world. I knew I had to make a choice. I made the choice to be what my sister believed in."

He paused for a moment, setting his coffee cup on the kitchen counter. I could tell his emotions were getting the best of him.

"I took the child like they said, but those bloodsuckers were on my tail. I had to make a move, a bold move, but I knew it would throw them off. I took the baby to a church during the day and left her with nuns and took off. The only thing I left was a letter stating what her name was. I knew it was what her mother would've wanted. It was easier to travel without a baby, you see. I always kept tabs on her, and thanks to the X's, she was well protected. She became the ward of the state. Did she have the ideal childhood? No. Did she deserve better? Yes. Scarlett wasn't happy with her situation, but it was for the best, to keep her safe. I guess you can say it is character building," he said, softly taking off his glasses and rubbing his eyes.

Scarlett. I now knew the name of the prophet. John continued, putting his glasses back on.

"Now she is of age, and if you hadn't notice already, I am old. What protection can an old man give?"

I didn't answer him; I saw sorrow in his eyes, regret.

"My time is up. That is the one thing I have to say I envy about those damn bloodsuckers. They have nothing but time. You are the real guardian, but I bet you knew that already, didn't you?"

"Yes." I slowly nodded.

He nodded as well and walked over to his bedroom. He came out after a minute, holding a silver box that I was sure was once beautiful. He slowly took a seat across from me, put the box down, and slid it over to me, his old, wrinkled hand looking frail against the box.

I looked at him questioningly.

"This is from her father. He wanted it given to her when she came of age. You will see that she gets it after her change. I will make you vow to me, just as her father made me vow. You must promise me that you will take care of her, protect her at all costs. Not just from those bloodsuckers but from herself. Though she did not know of me, I have come to care a great deal for her. She is part of my sister, after all."

"I promise you I will protect her with my last dying breath," I said, meeting his stare.

He nodded as though satisfied. He got up once again and walked to his kitchen counter, opened one of the drawers, and took out a manila envelope. Again, he sat across from me and slid the envelope toward me. I opened it, trying not to let him see how anxious I was at finally knowing who the prophet was. Inside was a five-by-seven picture of a woman with mismatched eyes, pale skin, and long, dark hair. She was breathtakingly beautiful. I knew right away this was Scarlett.

"On the back of this is her address and the location where the X's are hiding out. They are good vamps, friends of her father. They are expecting you. Meet with them first to come up with your game plan."

"Of course, but I have to ask you something first. What do you know of the other half of the prophecy?"

He smiled at me. "People sometimes play on the wrong side of the field. They don't see the bigger picture. All I can tell you as her guardian is to let fate play itself out. She will need you not only as her guardian but as her friend. She has a long journey to walk, and it will be a bumpy one. When she loses all hope in herself and in humanity, you will have to be the one to keep her centered. She will need you more than you know. In the end it will all work itself out, but the end is very far away," he said. He got up from his seat slowly and turned his back on me, silently dismissing me. He stood at the window staring outside.

His cryptic message did not sit well with me. I got up from the chair and took hold of the silver box, finding it heavier than it looked. Walking toward the door and opening it, I took one last look at the old man. It was as if he knew his time was indeed up. It was as though time stood still for him and he was sensing his own death. It surrounded him. I could smell it in the air. I walked out of his apartment and couldn't help but feel sorry for him.

And now I was with the prophet. Having seen her gasp with pain, I knew her change was quickly approaching. Although she didn't know it, her life would forever be changed. Meeting her in person, I saw her aura of power and integrity, so much so that she was streaming brightly with a glow. She lived her life simply, your average girl with a feisty attitude, but there was a kindness to her that I knew she would lose as soon as she became aware of the dark world. It had a way of changing you. Looking around her apartment, I thought of what it would be like to live a normal life. To get up every day and work a nine to five, to worry about bills, getting married, and having children— all the things I would never get to experience and that she would most likely experience with dread. Just as I, she was fated to beat the odds and prevail at whatever cost. She would either rebel against her destiny or embrace it, and I would be there every step of the way with her.

Letting her go to her birthday party alone was a risk, but taking John's advice wholeheartedly, I knew I had to let fate play itself out. I had to trust that she would be safe.

Taking one final look at the apartment, I left, heading down the stairs of the apartment building and out into the cold night. Keeping my head down, I walked the streets, putting my hands in my pockets to keep them warm, heading opposite the direction Scarlett had gone. I looked up briefly to the sky and noticed a full moon. Stopping in my tracks, I looked at it, huge and stained red. I closed my eyes quickly and opened them and the color was gone. Death was coming. It was time to get down to business. Today was the day. The war had begun.

chapter

FIVE

The limousine driver opened the door for me. The Red Door was packed with a long line of people waiting to get in. I walked past them to the doorman and gave him my name as Mr. W had instructed. He looked at me and smiled, his eyes going up and down checking me out. Grabbing his clipboard, he looked down his list and let me in. The crowd let out a sigh of frustration at still having to wait out in the cold. He wished me a happy birthday and told me my VIP section was upstairs.

The club was full of people, the bright red lights and art deco décor making it a very vibrant place with high rollers and celebrities partying it up. The huge bar held only the top liquor brands, and scantily dressed women worked bottle service. I started to feel nervous as I headed upstairs. *I could just turn around and head home. No one would even know*

I was here. Tell everyone I got sick, but Jewels's voice kept popping into my head.

"Take the stick out your ass. Take the stick out your ass," the nagging voice repeated.

So I sucked it up and marched on. At the top of the stairs, everyone saw me and shouted, "Happy Birthday!"

I did a fake surprised face and started laughing as everyone rushed toward me. Breaking through the crowd surrounding me, Jewels handed me a drink. She looked beautiful, her gorgeous blond hair pulled back tight. She looked very dominatrix in a strapless black leather dress that showed off her amazing curves. Mr. W sashayed toward us wearing a fitted all-black suit and a black bejeweled mask with rhinestones of all colors, taking the gypsy theme he had planned to the extreme.

"Scarlett, darling, happy birthday! We have a show for you, and we have a fortune teller!"

"Show? What show?"

Jewels took my hand and made me have a seat. She grabbed the chair next to mine and sat beside me.

Suddenly the VIP area went dark and all that could be heard was the music playing downstairs. I leaned over to ask Jewels what the hell was going on. That's when bright gold lights illuminated the room, and I heard the sound of bells ringing. Four ladies came through dressed beautifully, each wearing a black midriff top and a lavish hot pink wrap with a gold pattern. They wore gold headdresses with bangles and ankle bracelets, adding sound to their movements.

A man in a blue getup carried a drum of some sort. He began to tap the drum using his hand, and simultaneously the women began to move in unison to the sound of the beat. Using the bells in their hands, they created a beat together with the drum, their midriffs ticking and swaying to the sound. The crowd cheered them on, clapping to the beat. They were fantastic. I felt myself begin to loosen up and join the clapping. I looked over to Jewels, and she gave an innocent shrug of her shoulders. Rolling my eyes at her,

I couldn't help but smile. Leave it to Mr. W to go above and beyond. The women ended their routine with a bang, moving their hips fast to the music and stomping their feet. When they finished they received a standing ovation, the crowd screaming "Bravo!"

"Let's get your palm read," Jewels said as the crowd began to break apart.

"What? No thanks. You really believe in that stupid stuff?" I asked.

"Come on. Please tell me you're not scared. Besides, it's for entertainment."

Before I could say anything else, she dragged me by the hand and ushered me into another part of the VIP section. A heavyset older lady sat alone at one of the tables with a drink her hand. If Mr. W had told her to play up on the whole gypsy theme, he was definitely getting his money worth. She wore a black sweater with a long floral skirt and a matching headscarf wrapped so it covered her hair. She looked up at me and signaled me to sit down.

"OK. Here she is," Jewels said cheerfully, pushing me forward and turning to go.

"Wait. Where are you going? Aren't you going to sit with me?" I asked.

"I can't. You have to be one on one. She says she can pick up other people's energy," Jewels said, backing away. She says this as if she is now a psychic expert.

"OK, fine," I said, rolling my eyes at her. I looked down at the teller, who was staring at me intently, and realized I was coming off as a bitch.

"Sorry about that. Hi," I said, having a seat.

"Hello. I am Drina," she said with a thick accent.

I just smiled at her. This was more than awkward. How do you tell someone they are full of shit without it coming off as rude?

"Give me your hand, please," she said, opening her palm face up.

I place my hand over hers, face up, and watch as she begins to go over the lines of my palm. I shivered, feeling tickled by her touch.

"Your name is special. Your birth mother gave it much thought. The color of red," Drina says, looking closer at my hand.

My breath catches at the mention of my birth mother. How would she know something like that? No one knew I was an orphan but Jewels.

"You will find the love of your life…or better yet, he will find you," she said, breaking into my thoughts. "You are going through a change." She looked closer at my hand, her eyes blinking rapidly as if she was not seeing right and then widening with fear. She let go of my hand, dropping it as though scared she was going to catch something from me.

"This cannot be. The prophet standing before me," she hissed, getting up so quickly she almost knocked over the chair behind her.

"What?" I asked, confused.

"You," she said, pointing her finger accusingly. She stood pointing at me for what seemed forever. Then she walked off, heels stomping away angrily. I stared after her, my mouth wide open.

"Oh, my God. What did you say to the Gypsy?" Jewels asked, rushing over with a drink in her hand.

"Nothing. She's nuts," I said, getting up from the table.

"Well why did she leave pissed off?" She put a hand on her hip and looked at me accusingly.

"I swear, nothing. She is off her rocker, OK?"

"Well she told me some great stuff, but she was kind of scary," Jewels said, laughing.

"What did she say to you?"

"She told me that I would meet my match, someone as stubborn as I. We will save each other. As if I need saving, right?"

I laughed. I couldn't picture anyone as stubborn as her.

Drina stood in the shadows of the club watching the two women joke with each other. Her eyes kept straying to the one named Scarlett. Before reading her palm, she had sensed something special about her. She had an aura she'd picked up on as soon as she made eye contact with her, but reading her palm, she started to dig in deeper. She saw her future, her own damnation, the prophet, the one that would lead the end to world order. It could not happen.

Heading out of the club, she dug into her pocket taking out a cell phone. She knew exactly who to call. Keeping her head down, looking behind her periodically, she began to dial. Of course she was loyal to the queen. You had to be stupid not to be, and she was no fool. Dialing the number, she waited patiently for someone to pick up.

"The prophet is here," she said.

Jewels handed me another drink. Taking it from her hand, I eyed it suspiciously.

"What's this?" I asked, looking at the pink drink.

"Who cares," she said, looking a little tipsy.

I laughed, shrugged my shoulders, and took my first sip. It was cranberry and pineapple with something else. Its taste was fruity and delicious. If alcohol tasted like this, I could drink this all day. I hoped it would ease the pain still dwelling in the pit of my stomach. Jewels grabbed me by the hand, and we walked over to the bar. She leaned over to the bartender, who was not looking at her but at her breasts.

"Hey, honey, can you get me and my friend two shots of tequila," she said flirtatiously, knowing full well that he was taking a good look at her attributes.

"You got it, sexy," he said, making our drinks. He set two shot glasses in front of us and started pouring the tequila.

"On the house, gorgeous," he said, winking at Jewels.

"Thank you." She lifted one of the shot glasses and saluted him before handing it too me. She picked up the other off the bar and held it up, put her finger in her mouth, and let out a huge whistle. The crowd fell silent.

"To one of the best people I know, Scarlett. Happy birthday. I love you," she toasted, clinking her shot glass with mine.

I looked down at the drink for a second. *What the hell?* I was done with playing it safe and always worrying. It was time to live and live in the moment. I knocked it down, the taste burning the back of my throat, watering my eyes and making me gag.

"Holy crap," I said, putting the glass down.

"Come on. Let's dance," Jewels shouted over the music.

She grabbed me by the hand, and we headed downstairs to the packed dance floor. Jewels took me to the middle of the dance floor, and we began to dance. Turning away from her, I looked up and there he was—my savior. He was upstairs at the banister looking straight at me. I looked back to get Jewels's attention, but she was nowhere in sight, getting lost in the crowd. I turned to where my savior had been, and he was gone. *Shit.* I went back through the crowd trying to find Jewels, but with the bright lights flashing, it was hard to see. I started to get caught up in the hypnotizing music and began to dance again, feeling light headed, my body warming from the liquor. I closed my eyes and just let my body move to the music.

I was totally lost. I ignored the feeling of pain that was building much worse in the pit of my stomach. I sensed my savior was there, watching me again. Opening my eyes, I saw him, standing in front of me on the dance floor. Not saying one word to me, he grabbed me roughly by the arm and I helplessly followed him through the thick crowd. Seeing a doorway, he took me to a more private area of the club and shoved me into the room. I turned and looked at him.

"It's you," I whispered, shaking my head.

I studied him. He had to be the sexiest man I had ever seen. He was tall, blond, and lean, wearing a black V-neck shirt, leather jacket, and black pants—with steel blue eyes I could get lost in.

He studied me back, desire clear in his eyes.

"Are you just going to stare at me?" I asked bravely, standing a bit straighter. I felt so warm, as if in a fever. The liquor must've been giving me a set of balls.

As I was about to say something else, he moved closer to me, so fast I didn't have a moment to react. He shoved me into the far wall of the room and kissed me, taking me by surprise. I opened my mouth to let out a gasp, and he took full advantage of that, working his tongue in, mating it with mine. God help me, I responded back with the same velocity, shoving my hands through his hair to bring him closer to me. My body was tingling from head to toe. I had never been kissed like this; it was as if my body was on fire for him, just him.

He growled in response, his hands all over me. He put his hands behind my back and grabbed my ass, bringing me closer to him and putting his knee between my legs. I moaned, feeling myself start to grind against him, the lower half of my body having a mind of its own. I felt his hard erection against my belly; his hand went under my dress, lifting it. His cold hands against my bare skin made me shiver. He moved from my mouth down to my neck, kissing and licking me, his tongue leaving a sweet trail. I felt his teeth graze against my neck and moaned with delight.

"Please," I said, grabbing his head.

I wanted more. What that was I wasn't sure. My senses were all haywire. I start rubbing myself more urgently against him.

"Please what, Scarlett? Please fuck you?" he asked, looking up at me, his hands now at my hips holding me still.

I licked my lips, stunned. Oh, my. No one had ever talked to me like that.

"Yes," I whispered, licking my lips.

That's when I felt a pain in my stomach so powerful it knocked me to my knees. I groaned, holding my stomach, tears stinging my eyes. *What the hell is happening?*

"Shit! The change is happening," he hissed, grabbing me roughly up by the arm. I was forced to walk after him, stumbling.

As we made our way back to the dance floor, the hair on my neck stood to full salute. I was following my savior through the thick crowd when out of nowhere, this huge man grabbed me by the arm, turning me toward him. I let out a scream as I looked at his face, eyes dark as night and fangs protruding from his mouth. He hissed at me. My savior growled and shoved me behind him as he and the other man—or whatever he was—squared off. Before I knew it, my savior grabbed the beast by the neck and twisted, breaking it. At this point it was pure chaos in the club with people screaming and pushing each other out of the way. I felt myself being grabbed again, but this time it was Zayah.

"Scarlett, come with me!" she yelled, pulling me toward the fire exit.

I looked back at my savior and saw him fighting against three more men. I had the overwhelming urge to go to him and help.

"Don't worry about him; he can take care of himself," Zayah said.

The pain came again, knocking me to my knees, and I let out another scream. *Oh my God, what is happening to me?* Zayah helped me up, wrapping my arm around her neck. We walked as fast as my legs would let me, Zayah carrying most of my weight.

Outside I heard sirens and people screaming, but I was in so much pain I couldn't keep my eyes open. I felt like my insides were being torn apart.

"Come, Scarlett. We must get you to safety," she said as a black SUV pulled up.

Opening the rear passenger door, she tossed me in like I was a sack of potatoes.

"Drive!" she said to the two men in front, climbing in beside me and closing the door.

At this point I was groaning in pain, my body shaking uncontrollably.

"Is she going through the change?" one of the men asked.

"Yes," she said quietly.

chapter

SIX

The car came to a stop. The door opened, and one of the men gently picked me up and carried me into a building, my head hanging limp. I tried to open my eyes again, but the pain was overwhelming all my senses. He lay me gently down on a bed, and I felt the bed sink with someone else's weight. Someone was sitting beside me, placing a wet cloth on my forehead trying to bring down this fever that was overtaking my body. I let out a whimper, my head tossing and turning, my breath coming out raggedly. This pain was going to kill me. I was sure of it. Another wave of pain hit me, and I let out another scream, my body arching upward off the bed, and I felt strong hands on my abdomen holding me down.

"Is it supposed to be painful for her?" I heard one of the men ask.

I didn't hear the response. My eyes rolled into the back of my head as another bolt of pain came. I felt myself lift from my body. I looked down at myself, weakened, and everyone around just began to fade. I was not in pain anymore. Looking around I realized I was not in the same place; I was in a different time, a time that I was not from. This was the past.

I was in a castle with a woman with long blond hair and delicate features who seemed to be working as a servant. She was young, maybe in her twenties. I walked behind her and watched as she made eye contact with a man dressed in armor. He was very attractive, muscular with long, dark hair. The hairs on the back of my neck stood in warning. He was a solider of some kind. He seemed to take notice of her but looked away from her just as quickly, but I felt his eyes straying toward her. She went about her duties, entering one of the quarters. The attractive man who'd followed her with his eyes was there in the room with her.

"Edrick, you shouldn't be here. It is dangerous. If the queen should find out…" Her worried voice trailed off as he came to stand before her.

"Tell me you don't feel the same for me, Celine. Tell me you don't feel this fire burn deep inside you for me. Tell me you are not in love with me."

I looked at the woman named Celine, watching her face as she tried to deny her feelings for this man. I didn't need to hear her reply. It was evident in her eyes that she was in love.

"I love you," she whispered to him softly.

He grabbed her in an embrace and they kissed. I wondered why it was such a big deal. They were in love. Why would the queen find out, and why would it matter? Was it because she was a servant girl?

As I looked on, I seemed to spin into another area of the castle grounds as though fast-forwarding through time. Edrick and Celine were talking quietly. It was night out, and they were standing under a willow tree, the stars shining on them romantically. They were meeting in secret. Celine was not in her servant getup but wearing a beautiful sheer pink gown with long sleeves. She looked beautiful, almost angelic. Edrick wore the same armor he had on last time, but his hair looked longer. Waving my hands, I tried to get their attention but they did not see or hear me. They were holding hands, and Celine looked happy. No longer was there doubt in her eyes. I watch as he bent down on one knee and kissed her belly. She appeared to be in the early stages of pregnancy. She smiled down at him lovingly, gently touching his hair. They looked happy at the prospect of expecting. I smiled at them.

"We will leave here, I promise," he said to her.

She nodded, trusting him. She was worried, though. Although she hid it well, I sensed it. She put her hand protectively on her growing stomach, and he put his hand over hers.

Then my world spun again and before I knew it, I was on the run with them. What the hell was going on? They were packing everything as fast as they could, jamming clothes into suitcases before heading out into the night. Celine was heavily pregnant now. It looked like she was due any minute. They made their escape by car to a wooden home, where a man who looked to be maybe her brother welcomed them in. His name was John, and his breath smelled of liquor. He assured her everything was going to be OK. I looked at her face and I knew she knew differently. Edrick stood quietly in the home and seemed very somber, as if he knew what was to come and was accepting it for what it was. With the sun about to come up, he told Celine he had to leave. I watched as he walked over to her and embraced her, being careful of her belly.

"I love you," she whispered to him.

As he pulled out of her embrace, I saw tears in his beautiful green eyes.

"I love you too," he said. He put his hand on her stomach and bent down, whispering something I couldn't catch to the unborn child. He went over to the bags Celine had packed and took out a beautiful silver box. He turned to John.

"John, this is for you to give to my daughter when she becomes of age," he said, handing him the box.

"How do you know it's a girl?" John asked, taking the box.

Edrick smiled a smile that didn't quite reach his eyes.

"I just know. I also know that you will take care of her. Farewell, my friend," he said, giving John a hug.

He left before the sun came up, and Celine cried the whole time. Shortly after his departure, her pain began. *Holy shit! She's going into labor.* I wished there was something I could do. I'd never witnessed a birth before. She was screaming in agony and drenched with sweat. Luckily it was a quick labor that her brother assisted her with.

"It's a girl!" her brother shouted, wrapping the crying baby in a towel and handing her down to Celine. I slowly walked over to her and her new child. She was crying, staring down at the baby in awe. I looked at both and felt myself getting teary-eyed. *So this is what it's supposed to look like when a mother sees her child for the first time.*

"Your father was right: you are so beautiful. Look at you, you are absolutely perfect. I love you so much," she whispered, tears running down her face as she softly kissed the baby's tiny fingers. The baby made a cooing sound in response and opened her eyes. They were mismatched, one green eye and one light brown, very much like my own. My heart stopped. What were the odds?

Her brother looked at the child and smiled sadly. "What shall you name her, sister?"

Celine looked back down at the baby, a sadness now taking over her beautiful features. "I shall name her Scarlett."

I let out a gasp, my hand flying over my mouth. No. This couldn't be! Was this my mother? The man named Edrick my father?

He took the baby from her, and she cried harder. I put my hand to my mouth, crying with her.

"It must be done, Celine. This was the plan from the very beginning," he said gently to her.

She nodded her head.

"Yes, I just did not realize it would be this hard. Please take care of her, John, and take care of yourself," she said, wiping away her tears.

"Of course, sister; I promise you," he assured her.

She looked one last time at the baby longingly, wishing for more time, for a better future. I heard Celine's scream of frustration and agony as John walked out the door with her baby, carrying it protectively under a blanket.

Night came fast, and I watched as Celine prepared herself as though she knew what was to come next. Why had she let John take me? Where was Edrick? I wished there was some way I could communicate with this woman who I now knew as Celine, my mother. I heard cars surround the lodge, people running toward the door and breaking it down with a loud boom. Soldiers came rushing in, grabbing her by the arm and forcing her out of the home. I watched them tear the home apart looking for something. They sniffed the air and found the bloody rags and sheets that John had hidden. I yelled for them to let her go.

They took her back to the castle and put her in some kind of chamber. The door opened, and I saw my father being shoved into the room, his face bloodied and battered. My mother started crying when she saw him. He fell to the floor wounded. She tried to rush over to him, but the guards held her back. A man with a hideous scar on his face entered after Edrick. He wore armor and held a sword in his hand. He walked toward my father with a smirk on his ugly face. I heard the door open again, this time held by one of the guards. A woman walked in, and I held my breath. There was something very sadistic about her. She had long red hair and eyes black as night. She wore a red silk gown with spaghetti straps; it was cut very low, showing off her cleavage. On her head sat a gold crown.

"You will bow to your queen," the man with the scarred face said, shoving my father to his knees. My father fought against him.

"Never," he growled and spat in the man's face.

The man punched him, sending him to the ground, and kicked him in the abdomen with his booted foot. I winced, closing my eyes and again wishing there was something—anything—I could do.

The queen laughed and clapped her hands as though enjoying the show. She smiled at the man with the scar like he was a pet who'd done right by his master. Her laugh was a laugh I don't think I will ever forget.

The other soldiers rushed forward and brought Edrick to his knees, holding him still. The queen came forward to stand in front of him.

"Tell me, Edrick, where is the baby?"

He looked toward my mother. She looked back at him, nodded her head sadly, and mouthed the words "I love you." He turned back to the queen, his eyes black, and for the first time I noticed he had fangs.

"She is safe and far, far away from here. The only regret I have is not being alive to witness your death at the hands of my daughter," he hissed.

The queen grabbed the sword from the man with the scarred face and, in one swift move, sliced my father's head off, turning him to ash. My mother and I screamed.

My mother is crying, her head hung in defeat, when the queen approaches. "Celine, where is the baby?" she asks patiently, as though talking to a dog.

My mother looked up at the queen, anger and courage flashing in her eyes. "I will never tell you. You cannot make me talk."

The queen smiled and grabbed my mother's face, her fingers digging into her flesh.

"*No!*" I screamed.

"Really, now, stupid human, you should never say that to a hungry vampire," she hissed at her.

She forced Celine's mouth open and made a grab for her tongue, leaned forward, and bit down, ripping her tongue out. I screamed again. She grabbed Celine by the hair and brought her bloodied face close to hers.

"I am going to make your daughter suffer, and I will eat her heart!" she said as she put her fist through my mother's chest before dropping her lifeless body to the floor.

I woke up screaming and out of breath, sitting up from the bed. Zayah, sitting right by my side, brought me in for a hug. My body shook with the pain of everything I'd just witnessed.

"They loved me. They really loved me," I whispered, tears rolling down my face.

"I know," she whispered, gently stroking my back.

It seemed like forever Zayah held me, gently rocking me back and forth as one would a child. Taking a deep breath, I got a hold of myself and wiped my face. I pulled away from her and looked around. Where was I? I noticed we were not alone; there were people in the room with us. All men—really, really huge men.

"Who are you?" I asked nervously.

"We are the X's." The man with the dark skin spoke first and as he did, they all began to go on one knee before me—all except one. In the corner stood a man with red hair and the palest of skin. He avoided my stare, his face taking on a look of distain. He looked pissed by the whole situation, folding his big arms stubbornly across his chest, his stance making it very clear that he did not want me there.

I swallowed looking back at the dark man. "And who am I?" I asked softly.

The dark man raised his head, his eyes revealing with full certainty that what he was about to say to me would change my life forever.

"You are our leader."

chapter

SEVEN

Ian grabbed the beaten ancient by the neck and hauled him outside the club. He took one final look over his shoulder and saw Scarlett being safely whisked away by one of the X's.

"You will never get away with this, Ian," the ancient named Alec said trying to pry Ian's strong hands off of him.

Ian was much older than Alec, whose power was minimal compared to Ian's great strength. Ian laughed. Alec was turned at a young age, no more than eighteen years old. He started off as a sentinel and was turned by the queen. Unlike other vampires, he was not built with a huge physique. His hair was cropped to the side, and the clothes he wore were not those of a soldier but a human. He had on tight jeans and a silver, collared shirt, as if he'd been partying in the club before all hell broke loose. Ian didn't understand why Alec was recruited as a soldier to begin with, but the queen did many things that no one understood. Taking him deeper into an alley, Ian slammed him against the wall making him wince with pain.

"Who says I am trying to get away?" Ian asked, cocking his head to the side, daring this young vampire to challenge him.

"The queen will find out about your treachery. You will die with the prophet," Alec said, stuttering with fear like the loyal lapdog he was to the queen.

Ian smiled coldly and moved as if he was going to hit him, making Alec flinch in fear. "You give our dear queen a message for me," Ian said slowly, bringing his face closer to Alec. "You tell her if she wants the prophet, she has to go through me first. Tell her I have become bored of the game we are playing, and now I play by my rules."

He backed away from Alec, choosing to let him live. Alec wasted no time in running in the other direction before giving Ian one final look and taking off into the night. Ian turned and headed the other way, hearing the police and ambulance sirens in the background as the bright lights flashed.

"*What the fuck just happened in there?*" he asked himself.

He had never lost control. *But this woman, Scarlett*, he thought, disgusted. He'd had an opportunity twice to kill her, and he could not. One look at those eyes, those damn eyes. Even the sound of her voice was a turn on. Grinding his teeth, he made his way down the busy street, keeping his head down. He inhaled a deep breath, trying to find her scent. Her scent enveloped him—the scent of lavender. He sensed her. She was near and safe. No longer with him but with those damn X's. *Fuck!*

Morning sky was coming soon. He would wait, and he would have words with Scarlett. He had just declared war on his queen, and he meant what he'd said. If she wanted Scarlett, she would have to go through him first. She had just gone through her change. Now more than ever the queen would want her dead at all cost. Alec would give her the message, and there would be hell to pay. She would send more of her men; he had no doubt about that. At least she was with the X's. For all their faults, he knew they would protect her. Ian thought back to the old man, and his words shot back at him: *"She will be your doom."*

I looked over to the men and Zayah. This couldn't be real. *I must be dreaming.* I rubbed my eyes again.

"Does that mean I am a vampire?" I asked, my tongue going over my teeth to feel for fangs.

Zayah spoke first. "No. You were born human. Your father Edrick was a vampire, and your mother Celine was human. But you inherit special powers that come from your father. You have the strength of a vampire. You see, you are the first of your kind."

What the hell am I? I wondered. *An alien?*

"OK. So I'm human."

They all nod.

"And you guys are ancient vampires?"

They nod again.

"And these other ancient vampires want to kill me because I am a prophet that you guys read about in some book. Are you sure you have the right girl?"

Zayah grabbed my hand; her hand felt cold against mine.

"Scarlett, we know this is a lot for you to take in, but you witnessed it yourself in your change. This is real."

"Do you know how crazy this all sounds?" I yelled at them. They all looked away, unable to find the right words to ease my hysterics.

Taking a deep breath, I tried to calm myself down. Having left the confines of the bedroom, I started to look around at my surroundings. It was a warehouse, but it looked more like a training camp. A huge blue floor mat lay spread out across the floor with exercise machines and boxing bags on one side of it. On the other side stood a glass case holding swords of all shapes and sizes.

"What is this place?" I asked, my eyes going wide.

"This is where we will train you," Zayah said.

"Train me? For what?"

"For the war that will be raging between humans and vampires."

I was stunned. War between vampires and humans? The only war I knew about was between countries. What the hell was going on?

"You guys are vampires. Why are you on the humans' side?" I asked.

"We believe in balance and peace," Zayah said. "This world order is about domination and destruction."

"What does this prophecy say I do?"

"The prophecy states that a child will be born from one male vampire and from one human female. This child will become of age and with this age will hold great power. A new era is coming, a coming of evil, a coming of war. A queen will rise. Sides will be taken. Rules will be broken. The prophet will lead in the war of the undead.

The queen, I thought to myself, *the woman with the evil laugh and the pitch black eyes, the woman that killed my parents.* I started to tear up, but I got a hold of myself. "Why does being born from a vampire and a human make me special?"

"Vampires do not breed. You are the first of your kind," Zayah repeated.

I just stood silent. First of my kind? That made it sound like I was a new endangered species. I looked down at my clothes: a white T-shirt and some black tights. *Oh, my God. Hugo! What if those ancient fucks got Hugo!*

"Listen I have to go home. I have to get Hugo," I said, looking for the closest exit.

"Of course," Zayah said. She began putting on her jacket.

I stopped her. "No. I want to go by myself. I'll be fine."

"That's not a good idea," the dark man said to me. "What if you come into danger? We need to be there with you."

I stared sharply at him. "Listen, I appreciate your concern, but I'm a big girl."

He looked down as though he knew he'd crossed some kind of line. "Of course," he said awkwardly, coming to stand by Zayah. He stood a little too close. Were they an item?

Zayah reached into her jacket and handed me a cell phone. "All you have to do is press this code, and Con and I will be right at your side."

"OK," I said, nodding.

Con reached into his back pocket and handed me a knife. I looked down at it. It looked so big in my small hand.

"Knife to the heart," he said, taking my hand with the knife and placing it against his heart.

"Um…yeah, sure. I got this," I said with fake certainty, putting the knife in my back pocket.

They both led me to the door. Before I left I looked at them both. I needed to know something. "Who's the man with the steel blue eyes?"

Con spoke before Zayah could. "His name is Ian. He was sent by the queen to kill you."

I walked the two blocks from the warehouse to my apartment in a daze, my mind running in circles. Between the change, finding out about my parents, and vampires existing, I was tempted to check into the nearest hospital. It began to rain. I raised my face and welcomed the cold wetness. It began to turn dark as well. I walked even faster to my apartment. I didn't bother using the elevator; taking the steps two at a time, I was anxious to get in, but my senses started to take over, making me cautious. The hairs on the back of my neck began to stand. I slowly walked to my door. Someone was in my apartment. I was sure of it.

Vampire, a voice whispered in my head.

Checking on the knife in my back pocket to make sure it was in place, I slowly put the key in the lock and opened my door. I walked slowly into my living room, closing the door behind me and turning on the lights.

"Hugo," I whispered.

No answer.

I walked into my kitchen first. Nothing looked out of place. I went into my bedroom, and there waiting for me sitting on my bed I found Steel Blue Eyes, Ian, my savior, my enemy. I let out a gasp. We stood staring at each other for a long time, the energy between us unmistakable. He spoke first.

"Who's Hugo? Your lover?" he asked, staring at me intensely, his voice thick with a hint of an English accent.

"Are you here to kill me?" I asked, ignoring his question. I reached into my back pocket, taking out the knife, my hand shaking, holding it out away from me toward him, my heart racing.

"Put that away before you hurt yourself," he said softly, a warning look in his eyes.

"You didn't answer my question," I said.

He got up from the bed slowly, his big body crowding my bedroom. Swallowing I took a step back, ready to attack if he stepped toward me. Before I could even blink, he was in front of me, making me gasp with fear. He slapped the knife out of my hands and shoved me hard against the wall. He grabbed me by the arms, his face close to mine, and laughed.

"You are the prophet? A fucking weak human? You won't last a day," he snarled at me. His eyes went black, and his fangs, long and vicious-looking, protruded from his mouth.

I felt a surge of anger rise in me, and before I knew what was happening, I put my hands on his chest even before *he* could blink and shoved him so hard he flew to the other side of the room, hitting the bed and flipping over. I gasped, looked down at my hands, stunned, and ran as fast as I could for the door. I heard a growl behind me, and I reached the door, I felt his hands at my waist pulling me back. He picked me up effortlessly and headed toward the bedroom. I tried to let out a scream, but he covered my mouth with his hand.

I brought my hand over his and bit down on his hand as hard as I could. He let out a grunt. I elbowed him in the stomach, and he let me go. Turning on him quickly, I started swinging and kicking at him. Catching my swinging fist easily, he tackled me onto the bed, his body falling heavily over mine, making me lose my breath. He lifted my hands above my head, trying to hold me still.

"Get off of me, you asshole. What did you to with Hugo?" I yelled at him, trying to twist and kick him off of me, no longer fearing him but just wanting to hurt him in the worst way.

"Hold still, damn you," he growled at me, and I stopped moving. He stared deeply into my eyes. "Listen to me. I want you to relax. Will you do that for me?" he said softly. As I stared deeply into his steel blue eyes, I saw his pupils dilate. What the hell was he doing?

"And I want you to drop dead," I hissed at him, starting to fight him off of me again.

His head tilted in wonder, and he looked taken aback for a moment.

"Interesting," he said. "Your eyes glow when you're angry and when you are aroused."

I stopped fighting and looked at him again—really looked at him. His eyes were pitch black, and he had a lean face and chiseled jaw. His face showed light stubble, and his hair was so blond it almost looked white. He was still the hottest man I'd ever seen. My memory strayed back to the club, to what we started there. I felt my face begin to flush with desire for him. His eyes darkened further, and I knew he was thinking the same thing. It was time to finish what we started. It seemed as though my body wouldn't have it any other way.

He let go of my hands, and I reached up and pulled his head down, kissing him hungrily. He responded with a growl and put his fingers in my hair, molding his body further onto mine, and he shifted his legs so that he was lying between mine. He broke our kiss, making his way to down to my neck. I moaned, feeling myself arch upward to grind myself against him. He growled again and leaned up, grabbed my shirt by the front, and ripped it in two. I gasped trying to grab my shirt together and cover myself, but he would not be denied. Lifting my arms above my head, he started kissing down to my breast, put my nipple in his mouth, and sucked generously while his other hand began to tease my other breast. I moaned and started thrashing my head. He took my nipple between his teeth and grinded himself harder against me, making my body pulsate with need.

"Please," I started begging him. I didn't know what I needed, but my body was reaching for something.

"I know," he said.

He let go of my hands and pulled down my pants, along with my panties. I didn't even have a moment to feel shy. He took off his shirt, and I couldn't help but stare, my eyes going wide. He was sculpted like a Greek god. Not one ounce of fat. He got up and pulled off his pants. He was wearing no underwear. My mouth gaped open. Oh, my. I swallowed so hard, I could have sworn he heard me. He smirked at me. He was big, too big. Before I could start freaking out, he was over me again kissing me. The feel of his body against mine was heaven. Our bodies were like fire and ice that melded beautifully together. He made his way down again, palming my breast and pinching my nipples with his fingers. He started kissing my belly, swirling his tongue around my navel. I was quivering, my desire reaching new heights. I began moaning, trying to bring him back up to me.

"I want to taste you," he said.

"Taste me? As in my blood?" I asked, lifting my head to look down at him, my eyes going wide with fear and curiosity.

He smirked. "I could do that too."

He bent his head, opening my legs wide and kissing me in the most exotic place a man could. I let out a gasp of surprise. Feeling his wet tongue on my clitoris, I let out a moan and shoved my hand into his hair holding him to me.

"Don't stop...oh, please..." I begged him, my voice trailing off.

My body was no longer my body. It was his. He sucked at me and used his tongue in so many devious ways. I felt a finger enter me, and my body began to quake and my toes curled. Something was happening, and I couldn't control it. I moaned again, but before I could grasp it he was up over me again.

"You taste so good," he said kissing me, his tongue battling mine, and I could taste myself on his lips.

He positioned himself above me, and I felt his cock entering me. I let out a gasp. *Oh, no. He is too big.*

"Ahh...wait a second," I moaned, trying to get him to stop. The first feel of him inside me was overwhelming.

"Jesus, you're so tight," he grated out between clenched teeth.

Showing me no mercy, he rammed into me, filling me completely. I screamed from the burning pain, tears stinging my eyes, my fingers clawing his back. He stopped for a second and looked down at me in surprise, desire leaving his eyes, replaced with anger.

"Fuck," he said, breathing heavily.

But his body began to move, thrusting in me gently. I grabbed onto his arms and looked up at him. His eyes were closed and his face was turned away from mine. My body helplessly started to respond back. I moaned, feeling this buildup again beginning in my lower body. He growled and began to move faster, pounding into me, the bed creaking from our weight. I started to arch my hips, meeting him thrust for thrust. I threw my head back. My body was starting to sing, and I felt this hot, sweet rush come over me and spread throughout my body making me scream—this time with sheer pleasure. He pounded into me further and let out a groan, spilling himself into me.

Unlike the man in my dreams, he didn't hold me lovingly afterward. He pulled out of me roughly, making me wince from pain, and rolled away from me. We both were breathing loudly, trying to catch our breath. I could hear my heart pounding in my ears. He sat up from the bed and grabbed his pants off the floor. I sat up too, trying to cover myself as best as I could with my ripped T-shirt and bringing my legs up. He pulled on his pants; I looked away shyly. I couldn't look at him. *I just fucked my enemy*, I said to myself. *The one sent to kill me. What kind of prophet am I?* He put his T-shirt over his head, bent down to the floor to pick up his jacket, and zipped it up. Walking to the doorway, he looked back at me as if nothing just took place between us, totally emotionless.

"Next time bring protection when you go out into the night," he said, closing the door behind him.

chapter

EIGHT

"A virgin, a fucking virgin," I said to myself angrily.

I rushed out of the apartment as fast as I could, my body craving something other than her body. It craved her blood. I needed to feed and feed now. The need to go back into that apartment and feed from her was overwhelming. It took all my power not to do so. Spotting my car down the street, I got in, my fingers tightening over the steering wheel, and sped down the street right through red lights, going on the prowl, not caring who it was. My need to feed was overwhelming; my body clenched from the overwhelming need of it. No time to be picky.

Spotting a woman on the corner wearing a tight red dress, gold hoop earrings, and stockings with a run in them, I came to a stop next to her and rolled down my window. She walked over, a big smile on her face for her first customer of the night. If she only knew. Leaning in, she smiled again, her teeth showing signs of decay. Her makeup was heavily done.

"Hey, sugar. You need a date? It'll be fifty bucks, and I'll give you the night of your life," she said.

"Get in," I demanded quietly.

She hopped in eagerly, and I drove to the nearest alley.

"Get out," I said, opening my door and walking around my car with my head down.

"OK, sugar. Mmmm. You look good, sugar. Foxy gonna treat you real good," she said, getting out of the car.

I could smell the liquor on her breath. She was probably in her early thirties but looked much older. My thirst needed to be quenched and now. She would do. When I looked up, my eyes were pitch black, fangs protruding. She looked at me stunned, and then pure terror set in as she saw the evil in my eyes. She turned to run, but I was quicker. I came to stand before her, grabbing her by the throat and cutting off any sound she could make.

Tilting her neck to the side, I took my first bite of her, not caring that she winced in pain. I took great pulls of her blood. Her taste was not satisfying at all. Her poor health from years of drug use was evident in the taste of her blood. I could not help but picture mismatched eyes and pale skin. Taking greater pulls of her blood, I stopped, lifting my head. I sealed her bite mark with my tongue and released her, disgusted. She was in shock, her face going pale from the loss of blood. I roughly grabbed her and looked deep into her eyes.

"A customer was supposed to meet you here, and he never showed up," I said, entrancing her.

"He never showed up," she repeated, dazed.

Letting her go I walked around my car, opening the door and getting in. Scarlett was engraved in my head. Her innocence did something to me. *A virgin! Fuck. She responded as if she had experience.* It took him by surprise—a fucking human that confused him beyond belief. But she wasn't full human, was she? She had beautiful glowing eyes and could not be entranced. What was she? *She showed great power when she knocked me on my ass. Soon the queen will know of my betrayal, and there will be hell to pay.* I smirked.

"I always do love a challenge."

I woke up to the bright sun in my face. Rolling over on the bed, I closed my eyes feeling a dull ache in the lower half of my body, the remembrance of what took place last night. The images were still there: Ian's face, his hands and mouth all over my body. I just had sex with a stranger who wanted me dead. I could not believe everything that had taken place here in my apartment on my bed; my savior or my enemy? The Ian from my dreams was different. The Ian in my dreams was gentle and loving. This Ian was dark, cold. My feelings, on the other hand, were the same. I wanted him still, if not even more. And how the fuck would I explain Ian to the X's? *"Um...yeah, well, remember when you told me about Ian being sent from the queen to kill me? Well I decided, no, he's not going to kill me. He just wants to fuck me."*

Rubbing my head I felt the dull throb of a headache coming on. I sat up. Where was Hugo? Ian sure didn't know who the hell I was talking about. He'd actually looked a little pissed when asking me who he was. I smirked. *Good.* Getting up from the bed, I made my way to the bathroom, looked in the mirror, and touched my lips. Remembering his kiss, my body began to get warm and my cheeks flushed. His touch was still there, as though he'd branded me. *I don't look any different though. Don't they say you look different when you lose your virginity?*

Shaking my head, I turned on the bath water, grabbed my scented chamomile and lavender bubble bath, and poured it in. Watching the bubbles rise, I removed my clothes and put my foot in first to test the water. Satisfied I got in and let the warmth of the water relax me. I let out a breath of ecstasy from the feel of the water. Leaning back I closed my eyes and tried to clear my thoughts of Ian, the X's, and the prophecy. I felt myself start to doze off and sink in the water. Letting my head slowly submerge, I opened my eyes in the water and felt myself drift. I drifted to some place far away, to a time I wasn't from.

I was in someone's home, a mansion. Following the sound of voices, I walked over to the next room, a living room with beautiful furnishings. I watched as two women, both very beautiful with red hair and emerald green eyes spoke softly to one another. One was dressed very provocatively wearing a designer, fitted, red sleeveless dress. Her long hair hung loosely in soft waves. The other wore jeans and a black sweater with her hair pulled back in a ponytail. They were identical twins, but there was something different about each of them. The one dressed casually is pleading, almost begging her sister.

"No. You mustn't. I plead with you, sister. Please do not do this. To use magic and upset the balance is wrong. I won't stand by and let you do this."

The other sister smiled. There was something not right about her. A dark presence surrounded her. She lifted her hand, sending a flash of white light at her sister, who flew back and was held against the wall, the white light holding her still. The girl let out a scream of shock, her eyes going wide with fear.

"You think to stop me? No one will stop me. I think it is time to pick a side, sister. You stand with me or against me."

"Sister, please," the trapped girl said slowly.

"Poor Flora. Do you doubt me and my great power? This will work, and when it does, you will be the first to bow before me." She left the room, her magic releasing Flora. As the door closed, Flora slumped to the floor crying.

Then I seemed to be taken elsewhere. I was at a celebration, a wedding. People stood gathered around the couple, congratulating them—a king and queen celebration. *Vampire!* my mind screamed. The girl with the red hair and dark presence around her was wedded to the vampire. Everyone was there, congratulating the happy couple. I spotted my father, Edrick, standing in the corner all by himself. I went over to him and saw him quietly watching someone. I followed his gaze to Celine. Dressed as a servant, she was offering drinks to the guests. *Is this where he first met her? What was a human doing surrounded by vampires? Did she know of the danger?*

I wanted to learn more of the forbidden couple, of the couple I now knew as my parents, but my vision has other plans. It took me to the sleeping quarters of the groom and bride. I was with them on their wedding night in their private chambers. She looked beautiful. Her dress was silk, and she wore a long cathedral veil with her bejeweled crown, her long red hair flowing down her back. She almost looked innocent. I watched as she drank from her goblet, her devious eyes focusing on her husband.

"My husband, you know of our arrangement. You promised," she pouted seductively. She put her goblet down and walked over to him, determination in her eyes.

"Of course, my love. I've thought of nothing else since I have become enthralled," he said as he gathered her in his arms and pulled her into an embrace. He kissed her at first, and she pulled away. Taking her veil off her head, she pulled her hair to the side, arching her neck and moaning. His eyes turned pitch black, and he let out a growl. He bit her, drinking from her. After a few gentle pulls of her blood, he released her, bit his wrist, and put the fresh wound to her mouth.

"Yes, darling. Drink from me. You are mine," he said, rubbing her hair, gently coaxing her. She drank from him quickly, taking great pull of his blood as though starved for it. He threw his head back, eyes closed, pleasured by this. She finished drinking, turned from him, and began to chant words. I watched as she turned from human to vampire, her fangs growing long and sharp. The king had no idea what was taking place. She walked over to the table and handed him a goblet, smiling at him lovingly. He drank, put the goblet down, and had a seat, removing his crown. I watched as he finished his drink, his eyes glazed over, and he dropped the goblet. He put his hands to his eyes, rubbing them, and looked as if he was about to pass out. The queen smiled at him again.

"Poor, poor king. You should be very careful who you trust," she said, laughing.

"What…what have you done?" he asked, slurring his words.

He tried to get up and fell back down, slumping in the chair, paralyzed by the spell she had him under.

"Done? This is nothing compared to what I have planned. You were merely a piece to my puzzle," she said, walking slowly toward him.

"You…you won't get away with this," he stuttered.

"Oh, but my love, I already have," she said, laughing at him again.

She yanked his head roughly to the side and drank from his veins. He let out a grunt, powerless to move as she began taking huge pulls of his blood. His black eyes began to roll back as she had her way with him. She drank and drank until she sucked him dry. She turned, and I saw her face. Her eyes were pitch black. *I know that face. It's Queen Ezarbet.*

Then I was brought to a different place, a more present time. Queen Ezarbet was talking to a female vampire named Maylina who looked like a soldier. She was tall, she wore her hair pulled back tight, and she wore gear with a sword held by her belt. She looked emotionless, very cold, much like Ian. The queen began descending the stairs of her castle. It was dark and moldy with spider webs everywhere. I followed her down the steps, wondering where the hell she was leading me. It was even darker in the basement; it smelled of death. There were several closed doors down there. She walked over to one of doors on the far side of the basement and started speaking through it.

"Ian has betrayed us. Looks like he has become enthralled with our dear prophet. I have need of you. You know what must be done."

Silence followed her as she walked away. Who the hell was she talking to? I looked at her retreating back and slowly, cautiously walked over to the heavy door with a big lock on it. I peeked through the heavy bars, and gleaming red eyes stared back at me.

I sat up from the water with a start, gasping for breath, water splashing everywhere. *How long was I out?* Getting out of the bathtub in a hurry, I put on my robe, not bothering to dry myself. Outside the bathroom, I paced back and forth and placed my hand on my head, my thoughts racing. *I have to call the X's.* I retrieved the cell phone from my pants pocket and flipped it open to put in the code. I paused, looking at the time. *Shit!* It's 4:00 p.m. I looked out the window and saw the sun still shining brightly, taunting me.

"OK, OK. I'll just wait." I told myself out loud, slamming the phone shut and setting it on my bureau. I sat on the bed and looked at the clock, willing it to go faster, not certain of anything anymore.

But I knew two things for certain, and my stomach dropped with dread: the beast with the red eyes most certainly was going to try to kill me, and Queen Ezarbet was a witch.

☯

I looked out the window again at 6:30. The sun was finally starting to set, and I was really tempted to give it the finger. I made a grab for the cell phone to reach the X's. As I began to dial the code they gave me, I heard a scratching sound at my door. My heart dropped and my breath caught in my chest. I looked around for the knife Con gave me. It still lay on the floor where it had landed when Ian slapped it out of my hands. Picking it up I, crept toward the door. I felt the blood leave my face, and my hand began to shake as I clutched the knife tighter, my knuckles going white. *Vampires are not allowed in without an invitation, isn't that right? That's what the movies say.* Then I remembered Ian came in without an invitation. *Fuck!* I walked to the door and peeked through the peep hole—nothing. Only silence followed. I stopped breathing, waiting. Then I heard a bark and more scratching.

"Hugo!" I yelled, dropping the knife and unlocking the door.

"Hugo! Oh, thank God. How did you get out of the apartment?" I asked him, tears stinging my eyes, overjoyed that he was OK. He barked and jumped up and down my leg. As I picked him up and kissed him, he seemed skittish. He started to growl ,and I let him down out of my arms.

"OK, buddy. You must be starving," I said, turning to go back inside, not noticing the man quickly approaching.

He pushed me inside and closed the door. I fell to the floor with a gasp, dropping Hugo from my arms. Turning I looked up at the man. He was huge, wearing dark pants and a leather jacket. He had long hair and eyes black as night—one of the ancients. The hairs on the back of my neck stood.

"You're the prophet? A measly human female?" he asked, laughing. As he laughs, I see his long fangs.

Why does everyone keep saying that? I felt an anger surge build up within me. Before I could move, Hugo let out a growl and bit down on the ancient's ankle, his body looking so small against the ancient. He let out a hiss, grabbed him by the tail, and flung him off. Hugo hit the wall, letting out a yelp.

"You son of a bitch!" I yelled, charging at him with all my might.

I tackled him to the floor and started punching his face, my fist making contact with his nose. He began bleeding profusely and let out a growl. I growled back. My rage overtaking me, I became someone else. He grabbed me by the hair and pushed me off of him. I tried to stand, but he was quicker. He kicked me in my side. I let out a scream, holding myself. He spat blood onto the floor.

"You're no fucking prophet!" he yelled as he yanked my head back, bringing me to my knees.

Before he could utter one more word, from the corner of my eye I saw Hugo transform into a man. He whispered something and lifted his hand, and a blue light beam shot out of his palm, hitting the ancient. The ancient flew back against the wall, held still by the magical blue light. I saw the knife on the floor and crawled toward it, picking it up.

"You will die, human bitch! The queen will be victorious!" he yelled, blood from his nose running down his face.

I cocked my head to the side, my anger flaring. I was getting really sick of hearing that shit. Gripping the knife tighter in my hand, I slowly stood, my eyes narrowing. With all my might I flung the knife at him, aiming straight for his heart. He let out a scream, and his face turned black, but not before registering a look of surprise. His body began to shake and smoke came out of his ears and mouth. He began to fade, becoming nothing but black ash. I looked on, shocked. *Holy shit. I just killed someone. Holy shit! He just turned to ash.* My hand flew over my mouth, and I let out a gasp, feeling lightheaded.

I felt a hand at my shoulder trying to comfort me. A man's voice spoke to me, but I couldn't hear the words. I turned toward the man who saved me. He is tall and lean, wearing a hideous long black trench coat and black pants. He looked to be about my age or just a little older. He was very attractive but needed a hair cut in the worst way. And those eyes, those familiar soft brown eyes—Hugo's eyes! He spoke to me again, but his voice was starting to fade out. He became a big blur. I closed my eyes and did what any normal, rational person would do. I fainted.

chapter

NINE

I found myself in the castle again, this time in her bedroom. A big canopy bed made with mahogany wood sat in the center of the room, sheer red lace hanging from the top; her duvet comforter was gold and cream with a jacquard pattern. She sat in front of her beautiful gold vanity brushing her long, lustrous red hair. Queen Ezarbet appeared to be expecting someone. I watched as she applied red lipstick and pinched her cheeks, trying to bring color to her pale skin. She was dressed in a silk black sleeping gown with beautiful sheer lace at the bodice. *Who the hell is she trying to look sexy for?* I looked at her disgusted, wishing I could launch myself at her. The door opened, and we both looked over. *Ian!*

"They said you were in here," he said as he closed the door, eyeing her.

The queen smiled seductively, turning from the mirror, the long slit of the gown exposing much of her leg. I looked at Ian and I saw I wasn't the only one who noticed. She stood and approached him seductively. I cringed.

"Yes. I have a mission for you. You are to seek someone for me, a human girl."

"You have your pick of human girls here. What makes this one so special?"

She paused. I could tell she didn't like to be questioned by anyone. I could also tell Ian didn't give a flying fuck what she liked.

"It is said she may be the prophet," she said, arching her eyebrow, awaiting his reaction.

Ian looked away as if bored. I watch him and my heart sinks, dreading the deal he will be making with the devil.

"The prophet? I thought she was merely a bedtime story," he said.

"No. You will find her and kill her for me," she said as she leaned into him, her lips near his, her black eyes filled with want for him. Her hands reached up to his neck, and she brought his head down for a kiss.

The vision seemed to fade, flinging me from the past into the future. I was fighting, engulfed in a battle. We were in a castle that looked medieval in decor. There were two stair cases on either side of the huge room, with a long balcony that had men running down eagerly ready for battle. My heart skipped a beat in terror. I didn't look like myself at all. This woman was fierce and showed no sign of fear that I felt now. My hair was tied up into a ponytail, and I wore a leather jacket and black pants. The X's were at my left, Ian to my right, fighting by my side. He kept looking at me, making sure I was safe. I axe-kicked the ancient in front of me, sending him flying back. Another ancient came at me with his sword, and I easily blocked him with my shield. I kicked the sword out of his hand and broke his neck with my bare hands. My eyes glowed, my adrenaline reaching new heights. *Get the queen!* my mind shouted. *Where is she?*

I looked up and there she was, standing at the top of the staircase. This was it, my chance at retribution. We made eye contact, and she cocked her head and smiled evilly at me, waving at me, taunting me. I made my way to her, running. I heard Ian scream, telling me to stop. I kept running. The queen, beginning to chant, lifted her hand, and I watched as a sword came flying at me. Before I could react, Ian pushed me out of the way, taking the sword to the heart. I screamed and held him as he fell to the ground. I was crying, begging him not to leave me and telling him that I loved him. I heard the queen laugh as Ian turned to ash in my arms.

I gasped, waking up in a room I didn't know, and sat up. *What the hell was that? Another vision?* I heard people talking loudly, arguing. I got up and opened the door. I was in the training building again; the X's were there. As soon as they heard me, they stopped talking, all staring at me as if I had two heads. Hugo stood in the corner, but not Hugo my puppy, Hugo the man.

"Hugo!" I yelled, running over to him and hugging him tightly.

For a moment he was stunned, but then his arms wrapped around me, rubbing my back, comforting me. Someone let out a cough. Pulling myself away from him, I looked over at the X's. Zayah walked over to me, her eyes full of concern.

"Scarlett, we need to know what exactly happened," she said.

"Before I answer any of your questions, I want to know exactly what the fuck is going on." I looked back at Hugo. "What are you?"

I took in his features: big, soft brown eyes; lean face with a straight nose; very good looking.

"I am your guardian. I have been with you since your first guardian died. It is said in the prophecy that you will be protected at all cost by your guardian," he said so softly that I barely heard him.

Guardian, I said to myself. Then I had a flashback of him chanting and the bright light that shot out of his palms, holding the vampire still.

"Are you a witch?"

One of the X's let out a laugh, and Hugo looked offended.

"No. I am no witch. I am a warlock," he said proudly.

"I thought that was the same thing," I said, confused.

One of the X's let out a laugh again. Hugo looked pissed now.

"No," he said, shaking his head.

"Did you have a vision?" Zayah asked. When I didn't answer right away, she asked again. "What did you see in your vision, Scarlett?"

Prying my eyes away from Hugo, I rubbed my forehead. I could still feel the dull pain of a headache. *Visions? So they are not dreams. They were visions: the queen, Ian.* My heart dropped. I walked a little away from them with my head down, trying to collect my thoughts. Con came to stand by Zayah. Five more X's stood staring at me. I didn't know any of their names yet, but they were in my vision, fighting by my side, willing to die for me. *Their leader.* I took a deep breath.

"I don't know how to explain it. It's like I can see the past. Then I fast-forwarded to the future. At least I think it's the future. At this point I just don't know anymore."

Zayah and Con looked at Hugo.

"Scarlett, you have a great ability," Hugo said. "You are a foreseer. Your father was a foreseer. You are able to see the future. But you are unique. You are able to see the past as well."

I swallowed.

Hugo came toward me and touched my arm, his eyes shadowed with deep concern. "What did you see?" he asked gently.

"Queen Ezarbet is a witch," I said. "She drugged the king and killed him."

Zayah let out a hiss, her eyes blackened, and her fangs protruded from her ruby red lips.

"There's more. There's this thing, this creature with red eyes that's going to come after me. She has it in the basement. He is going to come after me," I said, purposely leaving out the part to do with Ian. Things were complicated enough.

"Creature with red eyes," Hugo whispered.

I looked at him. He knew what I was talking about. I felt he knew way more than he let on.

"Hugo, what is it? He's not a vampire, is he?" I asked.

He looked away for a moment, deep in thought. He looked back at me and shook his head. "No, he is not. He is a beast, also known as a werewolf."

My mouth gaped open. What the hell? Was I in a book of fairytales and make believe? Vampires, witches, warlocks, and now werewolves? I couldn't keep up anymore. *Lions, tigers, and bears. Oh, my!* The X's started speaking in unison, all talking over one another. I put my hand again to my forehead, all the chatter bothering me. I began to feel the pain of the headache increasing. I had to get back to my apartment and call the W. *Holy shit. I'm supposed to be in work this afternoon. What if the ancients look for me there? What if Mr. W or Jewels gets hurt?* I couldn't bear the thought of them getting hurt because of me.

"I have to go to work," I said abruptly.

They all stopped talking at once. The X with the red hair came forward. I had to look up at him. Big Red was a name that suited him. He was huge and had green eyes and a muscular physique. *Is it me or are all these guys hot?*

"You cannot leave. It is not safe anymore. The life you once led is over. Now that we know of the wolf, it is not safe for you in the daylight," he said, looking at me as though he hated me.

Life that I once led? "Listen, this prophet has bills to pay. I have to work!"

Big Red looked stubbornly at Hugo. "You need to tell her," he said.

Oh, God. I didn't think I could take any more surprises. "Tell me what, Hugo?"

"Come with me," he said, not awaiting my reply. I silently followed after him, staring at the back of his black trench coat.

He let me walk into the room first and closed the door behind us. Walking over to an antique wooden bureau, he opened the drawer and took out a box. He took it over to the bed and had a seat. I sat silently beside him, wondering what he was going to show me. The box looked familiar. Where had I seen this box? It looked to be an antique, once silver and beautiful and now tarnished with age. Very gently he opened it, revealing an interior lined with navy blue velvet. It had a few things inside. First Hugo handed me a paper folded over in four ways. I look at him, a question in my eyes.

"Read it," he said softly.

Nodding, I unfolded the paper very gently; it was on very old stationary and looked as though it had been sitting in the box for a very long time. I looked down and realized it was a letter—a letter written to me.

Dear Scarlett,

As you read this, you will be of age and will know of the great responsibility you now hold. It is with great sadness that your mother and I will not see the beautiful woman you have become. Know that it took great sacrifice to let you go, but we knew what we must do and trusted that you would be kept safe. The moment I was told that Celine was with child, I knew that you were going to be special. You see, I dreamt of you even before you were born, and I loved you with every fiber of my soul. You are part of me as well as your mother, who loves you just as much as I do. You will have an amazing gift, a gift that will do good for this world that will soon become dark. You will be the light. You will be the salvation. You are halves of me and your mother. I am a foreseer, someone who is able to see the future, which you will inherit from me. I have seen many springs and winters and I have left you not without. Your guardian, John, your uncle, will give you everything you need. The X's will be your alliance. Trust them as I have trusted them. Know that everything that I have done was for you. Be the great leader you were meant to be.

Your Father,
Edrick De Laurentiis

The tears running down my face clouded my vision. I now knew why the box looked familiar. It was the box he handed to John in my vision, before he took off into the night. *Edrick, my father, he wrote this before I was born. He loved me; he died for me. I now know my real name: Scarlett De Laurentiis.* I wiped my eyes.

Hugo handed me something else, a little blue book. It looked like one of those savings bond books. I opened it and was stunned. $670 million was in the account. Coughing, I quickly closed it and looked up at Hugo. He nodded. I opened it again. The account was in my name. *It's mine... all mine.*

Hugo handed me a black velvet jewelry box. I opened it to find beautiful diamond chandelier earrings. My breath caught. I took one out of the box, holding it up with my fingertips, moving it from side to side and watching it twinkle in the light. Like any other woman with diamonds, I was mesmerized by its beauty.

"They were your mother's. Your father bought them as a gift to her," Hugo said softly.

I felt myself tear up again placing the earring back in its box, sadly putting it away.

"What did my father do for a living?" I asked Hugo.

He looked away from me before answering. "He worked for Queen Ezarbet," he said softly.

I clenched my teeth, feeling my anger build up. Then I thought of something.

"Where is John, my uncle? He was my guardian. Why are you now my guardian?"

"He was killed," he said, looking me straight in the eyes.

"Killed?" Who killed him?" I asked, dreading his answer.

"Ian."

chapter

TEN

Hearing Ian's name from Hugo's lips made me sick, along with a feeling of something else. Something I could not name. What was Ian's game? He was sent to kill me. He killed my guardian, my uncle. Why didn't he kill me? And what did my visions of him before I met him mean? In my vision we carry on this affair like two people in love with one another, the type of love you see in the movies and hear about in stories. I was in love with this man from my vision. *But how the hell can I love this cold, calculating person in my reality?*

Hugo must have noticed my expression. "There is still so much to explain. Soon everything will be clear to you," he said gently.

I looked back down at the bank book. *Holy shit.* I wasn't just rich; I was filthy rich!

"It's all yours to do with what you wish. Your father planned ahead before you were born. No more fake Jimmy Choos," Hugo said with a smile, reading my thoughts.

I looked at him again and smiled. He remembered my shoes. That says a lot about a man. There was this kindness to his eyes, but with this kindness came a haunted look, a look of experience. Who was Hugo?

"How did you become my guardian, Hugo?"

He took a deep breath, his eyes again taking on a haunted look. "Well, for starters, my name is not Hugo. It's Henric."

"Henric?" I asked, squinting.

"Yes."

"I am sorry, but Hugo sounds more of a warlock name."

He arched his eyebrow. "And you will know this because?"

I shrugged, and we played the staring game, seeing who would let up first. I started batting my lashes at him, and he cracked a hint of a smile. We both started laughing. I stopped laughing when I thought of something—something so embarrassing that I flushed with anger from head to toe.

"Oh, my God. Did you see me naked?" I asked, tossing the bank book to the side and getting up from the bed, looking at him accusingly.

He looked down, embarrassed himself. I could see the faint hint of pink clawing up from his neck.

"It's not as if I have never seen a naked woman before, but if you must know, no. I played the perfect gentleman," he promised, looking up at me.

"OK. I believe you, Hugo." I said his new name purposely, daring him to object. Turning my back and walking toward the door, I caught a glimpse of myself in the mirror. As I walked toward it, my mouth gaped open in shock.

"What the hell is wrong with my eyes?" I asked, blinking quickly, trying to make it go away. *My God.* Was I seeing things? My eyes were bright, as if they were glowing. I looked a bit freakish.

"That is the vampire side of you. When your emotions run high, your eyes will glow. You will have to learn to control them," Hugo said, coming to stand behind me.

Control them? How the hell do you control the other half of you? So that is what Ian meant before we both totally lost control with one another. Great. Now I had mismatched eyes and they glowed to boot. What else was I going to have to deal with? Would I need to drink blood? Just the thought made me want to throw up. I needed to get out of there, to feel just a little bit normal.

"Listen, I need to get a few things from my apartment, and I have to tell give my job a story about why I'm leaving; I at least owe them that. Besides, they're probably worried sick about me," I said, looking back at him in the mirror.

"OK. We will let the others know; I will go with you," he said, walking toward the door.

"Wait. You never answered my question."

He looked back at me, his eyes guarded again.

"How did you become my next guardian?"

"I was named in the prophecy with you."

Before I could ask any more questions, he walked out the door. *Named in the prophecy with me? Why?* I would have to ask him more, when we were alone again. I felt a chill go up my spine. Big Red was right: the life I once led was over.

We walked side by side to the W boutique as the sun began to go down. The weather was windy, and the air smelled of the rain yet to come. Even though I said I didn't feel different, everything seemed different. My senses seemed clearer, on full alert. I glanced over to Hugo as we walked. He looked so out of place. He still wore that long black trench coat and black boots. When the time was right, we were going to have to discuss his attire and the haircut he needed so badly. Jewels stood behind the counter when we entered. She looked up as she heard the door open.

"Scarlett!" she yelled, rushing over and hugging me. "My God. We were so worried about you! You disappeared from the club after that big fight broke out, and then you don't show up for work, and..." Her voice trailed off as she looked over to Hugo, who stood by my side, her big blue eyes going wide.

"I'm sorry, Jewels. I should have called. A lot of things are going on right now. Can you do me a favor and just let Mr. W know that I have to take a leave of absence? And thank him for everything," I said.

"What? What the hell are you talking about? And who the hell is this?" she said, pointing her finger at Hugo, her cheeks going red with anger.

"Jewels, calm down; I can't explain it right now."

She walked over to Hugo, standing in front of him. She looked small next to him. With her index finger, she jabbed bravely at his chest.

"Calm down? Calm *down*? Listen, asshole, I don't know what you have Scarlett involved in..."

Hugo looked down at her, caught her finger, and mumbled something, making Jewels trail off in what she was saying. A dazed look came across her face, and she looked at him with ease.

I walked over to her and touched her arm. "Um, Jewels, are you OK?" I asked looking over to Hugo questioningly.

"Yeah. So you want me to tell Mr. W that you have to take a leave of absence," she said, smiling at Hugo and me.

"Um, yeah, that's what I need to do."

"OK. Sure, hon. I'll let him know. No biggie," she said, shrugging her shoulders and waving me off.

I looked at her, confused by her sudden change in mood. I gave her a quick kiss on the cheek, and we said our good-byes. We walked out the door, and I couldn't help but look back. Would this be the last time I saw Jewels? The last time I would be in the W? I felt a chill creep up. It was starting to get cold. I pulled my jacket closer to my body.

"Good-byes, I suppose, are difficult," Hugo said gently.

"Yeah, and don't think I didn't notice what you did back there," I said, playfully nudging him.

"I don't know what you're talking about," he said with fake innocence.

"You did something to Jewels."

"I put her in a trance state; it will go away after an hour. She was panicky. There is nothing worse than a panicky female."

I burst out laughing.

"She is a spitfire," he said, shaking his head.

"You don't know the half of it."

We made it to the corner where my apartment complex was, and I started to feel the hairs on the back of my neck stand. Something was not right. Hugo grabbed me by the arm, bringing me to a halt.

"We can't go in your apartment."

I nodded, and we quickly headed in the opposite direction and went into the nearest alley.

"Someone is following us," Hugo whispered.

I had a sick feeling in the pit of my stomach. Something whipped by us quicker than lighting. Before either of us could react, Hugo was grabbed by his collar and flung through the air, his grip releasing me. He fell back a few feet away, hitting the floor hard.

"Hugo!" I screamed. The shadow whipped around again. I turned, ready to attack, my eyes glowing.

Standing before me was Ian, his eyes not steel blue but black. I felt out of breath, my heart racing. He started to walk toward me; I hesitantly took a step back, not knowing his intentions. Before I could ask him, a flash of blue light beamed out at him, sending him flying back against the wall. I looked behind me and saw Hugo holding out his palm, his magic holding Ian against the wall.

"Fucking witch! Let go of me," Ian growled.

"He's actually a warlock," I corrected him.

Ian looked back at me, his stare so intense it shut me up for a moment.

"Why are you here?" I asked softly. "I know the queen sent you to kill me. Why didn't you kill me?"

"Damn if I know," he said.

Hugo released him, and Ian stood before him, meeting him eye to eye. I was scared Ian was going to strike Hugo at any moment. Hugo on the other hand seemed unfazed by his deadly stare. If anything he looked almost amused.

"If I ever see your hands on her again, I am going to kill you and enjoy it," Ian hissed menacingly, his long fangs protruding from his mouth.

Hugo stayed silent, assessing him.

What the hell was his problem? He had no right to talk to Hugo this way, let alone stake his claim on me.

"Listen," I said, "I don't know why you did what you did, but thanks, I guess. We don't ever have to see each other again. You go your way, and I will go mine." Grabbing Hugo's hand, I tried to lead him out of the alley.

Ian blocked my way. I clenched my teeth.

"I go where you go," he said stubbornly, looking not at me but at my hand that was holding Hugo's.

Before I could start arguing, Hugo intercepted.

"As you wish, but a warning: you will not receive a warm welcome from the X's," he said.

Ian smirked and looked back at me, his steel blue eyes satisfied that he was his getting his way.

"Tell me something I didn't know, warlock."

The three of us made our way back to the X's. I walked side by side with Hugo as Ian trailed behind us. I could feel his eyes on my back the whole time. Nothing had changed as far as my feelings toward him. You would think after all I'd found out about this man, he would be on my prime list of creatures I wanted dead, right along with the queen. But there was something about him, something foreign to me. What that was I was still trying to figure out.

chapter

ELEVEN

"What the fuck is *he* doing here?" Big Red bellowed as Ian came through the doorway. He stepped forward menacingly holding a knife in his hand, his eyes narrowing as he glared at Ian.

"Nice to see you to, Bastian," Ian said, walking in casually, as if he were meant to be there. He looked back at me in warning, turned back, and approached him.

Con walked over to Big Red, grabbing his arm to try to reason with him, but Big Red would have none of it, shoving Con's arm away from him stubbornly. Standing in front of each other, the two men sized each other up. I knew without a doubt that at any moment, a fight was going to break out. I stepped forward to try to stop this pissing contest, but Hugo touched my arm and shook his head. I watched the other X's approach behind Con, their eyes narrowing, looking hungry for a fight. Zayah walked over to Con and whispered something in his ear, and he nodded in agreement, went over to the other men, and talked quietly with them.

Big Red wasted no time making the first swipe at Ian with the knife. Ian quickly moved out of the way and kicked the knife out of his hands. He punched Big Red in the face, and he went down. Now we were all crowding around them as though in a school yard watching two boys fighting. The X's cheered on Big Red to get up, and he got up quickly, tackling Ian to the floor. I could not help but wince. Big Red was on top of Ian, punching him. I started to cringe, biting the inside of my cheek; my first instinct was to go and drag Big Red off of Ian, but I knew Ian had something to prove—to me or the X's I didn't know.

I felt my eyes change and knew they were glowing. I couldn't watch this anymore. I felt Zayah's eyes on me and tried to look away quickly. I didn't want anyone to know that it pained me to see Ian hurt. When I was about to turn and walk away, Ian blocked one of Big Red's flying fists and punched him in the abdomen. Big Red let out a grunt and tried to cover himself, and Ian took full advantage. Like a rattlesnake sneaking up on his prey, he struck. Grabbing Big Red by the neck, he flung him off of him and slammed him to the floor so hard I could have sworn I saw spit fly out of his mouth.

"I could easily kill you, but I am not. I hate you fucks just as much as you hate me, but know we have a common goal. Protect Scarlett and kill the fucking queen. Now are you going to play nice, or do I have to fucking kill you?" Ian growled, his hand at Big Red's neck, his face close to his.

"Fuck you!" Bastian sputtered.

"I take that as play nice," Ian said as he let him go and stood, not bothering to help him up.

The X's makes their way over to Big Red, trying to help him up, but his pride wouldn't accept it. He got up stubbornly on his own and walked away from the men with his head down. Con walked over to Ian with Zayah by his side.

"I won't apologize for Bastian," he said. "You had to know coming here was not wise. I am not the leader of this group, but I take care of my own. I want to know your intentions."

Ian looked at me, and I began to flush. The room fell silent, and it was as if we were the only ones in the room, the electricity between us undeniable.

Con nodded as if Ian has spoken. "Very well. Come with me," he said to Ian.

Ian gave me one final look before following Con into another room.

What the hell just happened? I looked at Hugo, but his expression revealed nothing.

"Hugo, he's staying? Why did you bring him back here? Do you honestly think we can trust him?" I asked.

"I think you have the answer to that question, Scarlett. You saw for yourself; he was going to find a way, with or without me, to get to you. I believe he will protect you from the queen," he said, walking away.

I swallowed. God help me, Hugo was right. For some crazy reason I could not explain, I was drawn to Ian like a magnet. I walked bitterly to what was now my new bedroom, closing and locking the door behind me needing to be very much alone. I leaned back against the door and looked at my room. Beautiful thick burgundy curtains covered the windows. The king-size bed had beautiful antique woodwork. The bedding had the same color scheme as the curtains, and the walls were painted a light gray. I noticed the windows had been painted black to keep the sun out. I switched the light on in another room and found a shower but no tub. *Damn*, I thought. *I would give anything to soak in a tub right now.*

"Oh, well," I mumbled to myself as I started the shower.

The bathroom was already starting to steam as I undressed. I stepped in, closing my eyes and letting the water hit me. I grabbed the soap and just started washing myself, trying to keep my thoughts at bay. After I felt cleansed, I turned off the water and grabbed the closest towel. Drying my body and hair as best I could, I wrapped the towel around myself. I found a brush and started to comb out my hair, slicking it back away from my face. I headed out of the bathroom to find some clothes and nearly tripped over myself because there, sitting on the bed, was none other than Ian.

"What are you doing here? I locked the door," I said, holding the towel more securely in place.

He watched my movement and smiled. "We have to talk."

"Talk about what? I want you out of here!" I yelled at him, feeling my body begin to warm.

"You didn't want me out the other night. In fact, that sweet body practically begged me to be in.," he said.

I sucked in my breath; I could not believe his audacity. "Well that's not the case now. Get out," I said, lying, scared to move.

He licked his lips, my eyes following his movement, my body now radiating heat. My eyes began to glow with desire. I wanted him; by body wanted him. He stood slowly from the bed and moved quickly to me, pushing me against the wall. I let out a gasp and put my hand to his chest, weakly trying to shove him away from me.

"Don't, goddamn you!" I yelled.

He leaned forward, his face so close to mine I could feel his hot breath on my face. "Yes. Goddamn us both," he said as he ripped the towel from my body and kissed me.

I kissed him back with the same urgency, my hands going around his neck. I grabbed the bottom of his shirt and lifted it over his head, my hands now touching his chest. He growled, and I inwardly smiled. *Good. I have the same effect on him as he does on me.* His body felt good under my fingertips. I opened my mouth, his tongue snuck in, and I sucked on it. He tasted so good. His hand went between us, and he touched me between my legs, touching the most sensitive spot on my body, his finger entering me. I threw my head back against the wall, moaning.

"You're so fucking wet for me," he said, breaking our kiss to whisper in my ear.

I heard the faint sound of him unbuckling his belt, and he pulled down his pants and lifted me effortlessly. I gasped in surprise.

"Wrap your legs around me," he demanded.

I did. I was so ready for him. I felt his hard shaft start to enter me and clenched myself around him. My head fell back against the wall as he entered me. This time he did not pause like the first time. He took me roughly, and I welcomed it. I needed this; I needed him. God, he felt so good. He held me up, tightly bouncing me up and down on his thick shaft. I felt myself begin to come, my nails raking his back. I bit his shoulder to keep from screaming out as I found my release. Waves of pure pleasure surged through me, and he was right behind me, pumping into me harder, my back hitting the wall roughly. He grabbed my ass tight against him to take me deeper and groaned against my throat, finding his own release.

We were both breathing loudly, trying to catch our breath, as he withdrew from me and set me down. My legs felt weak, like jelly legs, and he grabbed me up to keep me from sliding to the floor. I hesitated before looking at him; I didn't know what I would see. Would I see him gloating with a smirk? I finally managed to look up at him, and he was looking at me not with a gloat but with desire—and something else.

"Scarlett," he whispered.

He lowered his head and kissed me. Not your sweet, lovey-dovey kiss; he kissed me like he wanted to devour my very soul. I could not help but respond back with the same feverish need, my mind screaming for me to push him away, but my body and heart screaming for him not to stop; the feel of his lips against mine was clouding my senses and, most of all, my judgment. He pushed me back once again against the wall, put my hands behind my back, and held me still to his assault. I moaned letting him take complete control. His lips started to trail to my neck, and then he lifted his head, looking down at me. His steel blue eyes turned black, and he released a growl, fangs protruding from his mouth. I stared stunned. I couldn't speak.

"You are mine," he said and bit down on my neck.

The man walked faster into the forest, his heavy boots digging into the soft, wet ground. It had begun to rain, the droplets soaking his face. He smoothed his long, dark hair from his face, inhaled the scent of the earth, and thought of the plans ahead, of the agreement he had made with the queen. She knew to trust him with this mission. Like the vampires, he too had heard of the prophecy and of the Book of the Undead. It was known to his species, but it was never talked about. After all, *they* were the enemy. It was all propaganda to them. If they wanted to tear each other apart, so be it. And it was true: a child was born of a vampire and a human, a woman who would lead in the war of the undead that the queen was going to lead. No longer did he see vampires as his enemy but as his alliance, his way out. It was time for him to claim his destiny, to be leader of both the wolves and vampires.

Now, with the queen's help, he would succeed, but first he must prove himself to her. He was no fool. He knew this was a test, a test to prove his worth, to prove that he was indeed on her side. He knew the queen used him only for great purposes, and he was proud of that fact. He was good at what he did. He owed the queen. She took him out of that godforsaken pack, the pack that was supposed to make him leader. She saw his greatness. She told him her plan for world order, and while some would think she was mad, he thought she was brilliant. Humans were worthless. She told him to leave with her, and they would rule together.

His ex-pack would never see what was coming, but first he had to put an end to the prophet. Like the queen, he saw her as a block in the way of what was supposed to be his. He would not stand for his brother to be in his way, and he would not stand for the prophet to be. He had two missions: kill Ian and bring the girl Scarlett to the queen. Two tasks that would be easy enough. He smiled for the first time in a long time. It had been so long since he'd had a kill. He missed it. But all that was going to change. Two enemies joined together in an alliance; two great forces they would make. They would be unstoppable.

He could not wait to see the look of dismay on his brother Liam's face. He could almost picture Liam being brought to his knees with the others of the pack, bowing to him with fear in their eyes. The wind began to pick up, making the trees sway to the left and right; the man broke into a run, looking up as the leaves began to fall from the branches. Tearing off his clothes, he ran faster into the night.

"Yes, yes. Victory will be mine!" he shouted. His red eyes gleamed at the full moon, and he howled.

chapter

TWELVE

The sweet smell of her was too much to resist. She gasped as I took my first taste of her, my fangs penetrating her soft skin. I'd never tasted anything so pure, so sweet. I could not get enough of her. Growling, I drew her closer to me, trying to be as gentle as I could as I drank my fill of her. Being gentle was foreign to me, so I surprised even myself when I realized I didn't want to hurt her. Usually when I fed from another, I could care less if they were comfortable or not. My only thought was to feed and feed now, thinking only of the hunger deep within.

But she did something to me. Something I had never experienced. Confusion, possessiveness…and something else I could not name. She let out a moan, her body beginning to respond with pleasure, bringing me back to reality. I lifted my head from her, ready to lick her wounds to seal them, and I watched in amazement as they began to heal and disappear before my eyes. Dumbfounded, I looked down at her. What was she? Her eyes were half open, glowing beautifully with desire, her face was flushed, her lips swollen from my kisses. Jesus, she was the most beautiful, desirable woman I had ever seen. I felt myself get hard again. Shit. I could not keep my hands off of her. The way we were going, I wondered if we would ever have a conversation. Bending my head down for another kiss, I saw realization set in her glowing eyes, glowing eyes no longer filled with desire but with pure anger.

"You asshole. You bit me!" she yelled.

Before I could react, she pushed me away from her and punched me square in the face. I let her go holding my jaw, and she rushed to grab her towel off the floor.

"Get the fuck out of my room," she said, trying to cover herself, her eyes going wide when she looked down at my erection.

My eyes followed her movements, my body burning for hers again, but I nodded in silent agreement, slowly lifting my pants and buckling them. I found my shirt and put it on, watching her as she looked at me with hatred and confusion. Hell, I was as confused as she was.

"Fine. I will leave. Just know that we will speak sooner or later. No door will block you from me," I said softly as I walked to the door.

"Just so you know, I am not yours," she called out to me.

I paused at the doorway, not turning. No one had ever dared challenged me as she had. It took all the power in me not to respond and to instead close the door silently behind me. The desire to march back into the room and prove to her that she was indeed mine was overwhelming. What the hell had gotten into me? She was right; she was not mine. But why did it feel like she was? Shaking my head, I tried to clear my thoughts. This woman confused me beyond belief; fucking human.

I was in a wooded area very far away, a place I had never been before. It was night; the moon was bright and full. I stared at it amazed, mesmerized by its beauty. I could smell a fire burning not too far off. I heard voices to my right, two men arguing, their voices beginning to rise with emotion.

"That is not our way. We protect what is ours."

"Ours? Look around you, dear brother," the long-haired man said, waving his hand around the forest. "This is mine! I was meant to rule and be leader of this pack," he hissed.

"Things have changed, and not to my doing, brother, but your own. If you want to be in this pack, you will have to obey or leave. The decision is up to you," he said, his stare unbreakable.

"You will regret this, Liam. I promise you. You will regret this," The man took one final look at Liam at stomped off.

I looked at the man named Liam. He wore a plaid shirt and fitted jeans. His hair was cut very short, and he had a muscular physique. He looked to be your all-American boy who won the big game in football and was voted prom king. Was he a vampire? I didn't sense that he was. But he wasn't human. There was something different about him, his scent. He hung his head in disappointment at his brother's decision, as if he knew what was to become of him. He cared for his brother. Feeling sorry for him, I turned and started to follow his brother. I saw him talking to someone dressed in a black cloak. She lifted her hood, and I saw that it was none other than Queen Ezarbet.

"Darling, your brother is a fool," she said, coaxing him with her voice. "To go against you and not believe in our domination against the human race is very unwise of him. You were meant to be the ruler of your pack, not your brother. He is weak, his emotions getting the best of him, while you are strong."

She stepped forward and touched his face, her long red nails grazing his beard. He leaned his face into her palm and closed his eyes. I grimaced, disgusted. He was nothing at all like his brother. I could sense goodness, but a darkness loomed over him, just like it loomed over the queen. She had resources everywhere. Her evil plot knew no bounds. This lady was becoming a huge pain in the ass.

I walked over to stand behind the queen, trying to get a look at the dark-haired man who was willing to go against anyone, including his own brother, for world domination. He opened his eyes—red eyes. I gasped. *The wolf.*

The queen smiled at him. "We will rule together, Damian."

They faded out, and I was fast-forwarded into the future. I was *in the castle, looking for the* queen. *Where the fuck is she?* my mind screamed at me. I was by myself, sword in my hand, holding it steady with no fear. I heard a growl—the beast. It came at me quickly. Hastily I ran up the stairs, taking two at a time, the beast right at my heels. I turned right before it leaped at me and blocked its rabid teeth with my sword, its body landing on top of me. He went for my face, and I moved my head to the side. He was growling and slobbering, his claws digging into my flesh. I took a deep breath, remaining as calm as I could, and started to kick out with my legs, waiting for the opportunity, for him to lunge at my face again.

He lunged again for my face, and I kicked him hard, making him let out a yelp of pain and sending him flying back. I got up quickly but noticed my sword lay on the other side of the room. I tried to make a dash for it, but the beast was up again, looking from the sword to me. I could have sworn through that ugly, hairy face of his, he smirked. *Son of a bitch!* My eyes glowing, ready to do battle with him, I raised my hands, my body getting ready for this beast to come at me again. I smirked back at him. He growled, leaping at me. Before he could, a yellow-haired wolf jumped on him, stopping him from lunging at me. The yellow-haired wolf bit down on the side of the black beast, making him growl with pain. I knew who it was. It was Liam.

I woke with a start and sat up. I looked around, almost forgetting were I was. *Shit. What time is it?* I looked at the clock sitting by my bedside: 10:00 a.m. Another vision: Damian, Liam. We had to get to Liam, but how? How the hell would I go about finding a wolf? I walked to the bathroom and examined my neck in the mirror. No fang marks. I took a deep breath and saw myself blush. *I can't believe I had sex with him again and let him bite me, but that's what happened in my vision. It was bound to happen, I guess.* His bite was painful at first, but it turned to something else. I felt myself getting turned on by it, and I had the strangest need to taste him too. I wanted him in every way possible. *This man has gotten under my skin. Why do I have to feel this way for him?* A knock on my door interrupted my thoughts. I opened it half fearing it was Ian or Hugo. I could not face either at the moment. It was Zayah. *Oh, thank God. A female.*

"Come in," I hissed before she could say hello to me, grabbing her by the wrist and pulling her in.

She looked startled. I wondered how long it had been since she'd been up close and personal with a human. Had a conversation without wanting to tear someone's throat out. She looked at me as if reading my thoughts.

"You are safe with us, Scarlett. I do not want to drink from you," she said, smiling.

"Oh, my God. Did you just read my mind? Can you do that?"

"No, but I can hear your heart race as if you are nervous about something," she said with humor in her eyes.

OK. So she didn't want to eat me for breakfast. Feeling a little bit more comfortable, I walked over to my closet. Opening it, I see nothing but black shirts. I opened the draws to the antique bureau and find nothing but black pants. *Geez. Do these people like nothing but black?* Looking at Zayah's attire, I knew my answer. She wore a black tank with black jeans. *What about pink or red? No. No, the color red may make them think of blood. Mental note: no red.*

"So how do you guys feed?" I asked.

"The others go out and feed, but trust me, no one comes to harm. Some humans actually enjoy it."

"Enjoy it?" I couldn't help but think of myself with Ian, of how I was totally aroused by it. "What if you get caught?"

"We won't. We have been doing this for centuries. We entrance our prey after each feeding; they would never know what took place."

"Entrance? There is so much to learn, Zayah. This world was thrown to me," I said.

She walked over to the bed and sat, nodding her head. "I know. Ask me anything. I will try to explain as best I can."

"Why was it that my mother, who was a human, worked for someone who was a vampire? Did she know taking the job?"

"No, she didn't. Not until she became romantically involved with your father. The queen only hired human servants; it was her way of degrading them as much as possible."

"OK. Who are the other members of the X's? How did the X's come about?" I asked as I walked over to a wooden chair and swung it to the front of the bed so we were facing each other. I felt myself so intrigued by this new world that I was now a part of.

"We were all soldiers for the king. The X's were formed when the king passed and Queen Ezarbet took reign. She took full control. She did not care who she had to step on to get there. There was gossip around the castle that she was devising a plan, a plan of world order, a coming-out party to the humans. She hates humans, wants to make them blood slaves." Zayah paused for a moment. "Can you imagine your world as you know it no longer existing? Your family, your job, your hopes, and your dreams taken from you? For centuries we have remained hidden. That is the way of our people. We do this to keep the balance.

"Your father was the queen's foreseer as well as soldier. He saw you in a vision before even meeting your mother. He kept it a secret. He knew he would meet your mother eventually and that their love would bring a miracle. He knew of his destiny and accepted it for what it was. There was no stopping what was to come. Of course, we have all heard of the prophecy, but we just stopped believing, just like you humans with religion. It was as if we had lost our faith. When your father realized that the prophecy was to be, he devised a plan. We came up with a way to secretly get your father and mother out of the castle, and we took off, waiting for you to become of age."

I looked away for a moment, the mention of my mother and father paining me. I wondered what went on in his mind when he did everything he did, knowing this wouldn't end well for him or the woman he loved.

"So that is how the X's were formed?" I asked, trying not to think of my parents.

"Yes. Con worked side by side with your father. He is also a foreseer. Bastian is the youngest of all of us, very pig headed and stubborn, but I assure you he will grow on you. There is Logan, the long-blond-haired one; he is a man of few words but very trustworthy. Derek is our arms specialist. And last but not least, there is Ripley. He is the oldest of us, and he also worked side by side with your father."

I nodded, already trusting them. Then I had to ask; curiosity was killing me.

"Why do you guys hate Ian?"

"Ian was not a solider of the queen, but she hired him to do most of her dirty work. He is very unpredictable; most people would call him a snake. His loyalty lies with himself, making him very dangerous. He was sent here to kill you. The men don't trust him. I guess you can't really blame them. I didn't either until…"

She stopped, looking away as though uncomfortable.

"Until what?"

"Until I saw you two in the club together; I knew we could trust him," she said matter-of-factly.

Holy shit. She saw us in the club together. I opened my mouth and quickly shut it. What else did she see? I felt the blood rush to my face. I didn't know what to say. I quickly tried to change the subject.

"So when do we begin training?" I asked, trying to sound cheerful.

She got up from the bed and walked toward the door. I got up from my chair and walked with her.

"Today. Get dressed and have some breakfast. We went grocery shopping," she said, laughing.

I could not help but laugh with her. I had a feeling Zayah and I would become great friends. As she reached for the doorknob, I noticed a ring on her left hand—a white gold band with diamonds going around it, its simplicity suiting her.

"You're married?" I asked, my eyes going wide.

She looked down at her ring, smiling as her eyes shone with love. I felt slightly envious.

"Yes. Con is my blood mate."

"Blood mate?" I repeated.

"Yes," she said, now smiling at me. "It happens when a vampire becomes enthralled."

chapter

THIRTEEN

Standing outside with Celine, I watched as she nervously looked up at the ancient castle, which loomed over her as if trying to warn her not to come in. I saw her resignation as she took a deep breath and walked up the stony steps slowly. I followed closely behind her. When she reached the door, she fixed her hair, making sure no strands were out of place. She wore a long black peacoat with black dress pants; her hair was tied up in a bun. Knocking on the door, she stepped back as a guard came forth opening it. He looked down at her, and I watched as his nostrils flare in recognition that she was human.

"Hello, sir. I am here for the housekeeper position placed in the newspaper. I was told to meet with Gretchen," she said to the guard, holding up the cutout of a newspaper ad."

"Wait here," he said, not waiting for her response before walking away.

I watched as she took in her surroundings. I couldn't help but look as well. Big, thick black curtains hung from the windows, shutting out any light. A carpet the color of blood lay on the floor, and paintings framed in gold hung on the walls. An elderly woman came rushing down the steps.

"Hello, hello. You must be Celine. I am Gretchen. We spoke over the phone. Please follow me. Master is bringing in his mistress that he is to wed in two days' time." She spoke quickly, not giving Celine a chance to respond as she followed after her, listening.

"Yes, two days' time is the wedding to the master." And she stops, making Celine bump into her, looks around to make sure no one was listening, and whispers, "Yes, the chit is not even the queen yet and she is making all sorts of demands already."

"Queen? I wasn't aware the family was royalty," Celine stated, her eyes going wide.

"Yes, yes my dear. Of course, we were not allowed to put that in the ad."

"No, no of course not. I need the money, but I am afraid I don't have that type of experience. I assure you I am a quick learner and won't be any trouble at all."

Gretchen nodded. "Yes lass, you will do just fine. Now follow me. We have rooms to prepare. I have heard she is bringing her sister."

"OK." Celine lets out a sigh of relief and smiles for the first time since arriving.

I watched as Gretchen trained Celine on the king's likes and dislikes. The castle held over twenty bedrooms and had guards stationed at each corner. As Celine learned the ropes quickly, Gretchen let her go off on her own into one of the bedrooms. She made her way down the hallway holding fresh sheets and clean towels. I followed her into the bedroom and watched as she worked. She was very beautiful and graceful. We did not look anything alike expect for the colors of her eyes. She was blond, and her body was petite and delicate. As she finished making the bed, the door flew open.

"This will be my room," the soon-to-be queen hissed at Gretchen, who came in right behind her.

"Of course, mistress. The room was just not finished yet."

I rushed to Celine, who scurried away from the bed. So this was Queen Ezarbet when she wasn't yet queen and was just human. She was stunning in a lacy ivory dress looking very angelic, expect for the dark cloud that hung over her. In her hand she held a fat black cat with a diamond necklace for its collar. The cat looked just as bitchy as its owner.

"I don't want to hear your excuses. You knew of my arrival since yesterday," she snapped at Gretchen, daring her to argue with her.

Before Gretchen could say anything, Flora entered the room.

"Sister, the room is fine. You must excuse her; she is very tired from her travels," she said to Gretchen apologetically.

"Why would you feel the need to make excuses to a mere servant?" Ezarbet responded, walking further into the room. She stopped once she saw Celine.

"And who are you?" she asked petting her cats head gently, looking at Celine's clothes in disgust.

Flora moved forward to see who Ezarbet was addressing. Once she saw Celine, she tilted her head to the side in wonder.

Coughing, Celine moved forward and bowed her head toward Ezarbet.

"I am Celine, one of the new servants, at your service, madam."

"New are you? Make sure you are going to be at my beck and call. I wouldn't want it any other way; remember that."

"Of course, madam."

"Now run away. My travel has left me tired, and I am of need of a nap."

"Would you like me to turn your bed down, madam?" Celine asked.

"No. You may leave for now."

Celine and Gretchen walked out of the room saying nothing further in fear of upsetting their new mistress. As Celine's day went on, I could tell she had Ezarbet on her mind. She looked nervous as the day came to an end. She said her good-byes and grabbed the new uniform she was supposed to be wearing from then on. She stepped outside into a warm, quiet night; chirping crickets were the only sound. She made her way back down the path to the gate to be let out but heard something behind her, making her turn in fear. The hairs on the back of my neck stood. Vampire! I could hear her heart racing as she tried to walk faster. Then the vampire was before her—the guard who'd let her into the castle. He flashed a sinister smile.

"I've been dying to taste you since you walked in that door," he said, his eyes pitch black and fangs protruding from his mouth.

Celine's eyes widened in fear and she tried to move past him quickly, but he grabbed her, dragging her into the wooded area and covering her mouth. There was nothing I could do but watch helplessly as he brought her further into the darkness and put her down, holding her against the tree. As soon as he let go of her hands, she started to fight, scratching at his face, making him wince with pain.

"You bitch!" he yelled, slapping her.

"Now, now Xavier. Is that any way to treat a woman?"

I looked over into the shadows and saw Edrick come forth.

So this is how they met.

"Stay out of this, Edrick."

"Does the king know that instead of watching your post, you are out stalking the help?" Edrick asked, looking bored.

"I just need one fucking taste of her," he said, turning back to Celine, yanking her small body closer to his.

"No!" Celine screamed again.

Before he could harm her, Edrick was behind him flinging him away from Celine. With no hesitation and before Xavier could react, Edrick took out his sword, slicing his head off and turning him to black ash.

"Thank you, sir," Celine said, stepping closer to the man who'd saved her.

He turned around in surprise, thinking she was already long gone with all that she'd just seen. He stepped forward to get a better look at her, and I watched as his eyes widened in surprise.

"You," he whispered softly.

She said nothing to him; it was as if she was just as captivated by him as he was with her.

"Do I know you?" she asked him just as softly.

"No. I am Edrick."

"Edrick. Do you know what that man was?"

"Yes." He nodded, looking back at the black ash.

"What was he?" she asked, terrified.

"A vampire, just as I am."

Then I was pushed forward into the present time, standing outside with Hugo. It was dark and snowing out, the white flakes melting in his dark hair. He looked frantically about, searching for something on the ground. In the distance the wind is moving rapidly, someone blending in the shadows. *Vampires!* I could hear them breathing with anticipation. There was more than one, at least five of them. I ran to Hugo, screaming for him to hurry. What was he looking for? As if he'd heard me, he stooped down and found what he was looking for. He gently picked up a necklace from the snowy ground, a long, gold chain with a heart-shaped pendant that looked to be a locket. He gripped it tighter in his hand, put it in his pocket, and turned, sensing the approaching danger.

The first ancient struck first, hissing as he plunged out from the darkness, his fangs looking rabid. Hugo wasted no time lifting his palm and whispering a chant, sending a white light shooting out from his hand, catching the ancient in midair and turning him to ash. Another ancient came forward too quickly for Hugo, tackling him to the floor. He punched Hugo in the face, making him bleed, and I couldn't help but wince. I saw the other two ancients come forward.

"Quick. Cover his mouth and tie his hands!" the long-haired vampire yelled at the ancient on top of Hugo. "He is just a human without them,"

The ancient grabbed the bottom of his shirt and ripped it, using it as a gag over Hugo's mouth, and tied his hands together.

"Not so fucking tough now without your magic, witch," the ancient hissed at Hugo, kicking him while he was still down. Hugo let out a grunt of pain.

The three ancients now surrounded him, the smell of his blood enveloping them. I can see their eyes blacken further and their fangs protrude from their mouths. They were on a mission to kill Hugo, but their weakness for blood was getting the best of them.

"I want to drink from him before we kill him," the long-haired ancient said, bringing Hugo to his feet.

"Yes. Let's drink him dry," the other said, licking his lips greedily.

I gasped. This was not right. Before I could figure what to do, from out of the darkness came a scream, a scream of an angry woman. All the ancients turned in fear of the sound coming from the shadows. A huge, bright white light came through the forest in slow motion, making it hard to see. I closed my eyes for a moment against the bright light and heard the ancients screaming as they died in pain. I opened my eyes, and all was quiet. Hugo stood in the same spot, still tied up with his eyes wide, looking just as surprised as I was. I walked over to him looking down at the black ash covering the snow. He was still staring out into the darkness. I followed his gaze and wondered, *What the fuck just happened?*

chapter

FOURTEEN

"You want me to do what?" I asked, feeling everyone's eyes on me—especially Ian's. He sat quietly at the table by himself. The X's avoided him like the plaque.

After breakfast, which was weird enough with me being the only one eating, Con and the others took me to the area of the warehouse with the fighting mat on the floor and punching bags hanging up. He told me to hold out my hands and put gloves on me, the kind you would you see an MMA fighter wearing in the octagon. We walked over to the fighting area, to a huge blue fighting mat. I swallowed hard. Everyone started to gather around, watching us. I felt very self-conscious. What the hell was I doing? I didn't want to look stupid in front of the others, especially Ian. These guys were warriors; they were made to fight, born to fight. *I wasn't made for this type of stuff,* I thought to myself, looking at my gloved hands. But according to them, I wasn't just any girl. I was their prophet, who was supposed to be their leader. Was I a leader? At that very moment, I didn't feel like one, and I sure as hell didn't look like one.

"I want you to go into your fighting stance," Con repeated, breaking into my thoughts.

"Right, right; my fighting stance," I said, blinking rapidly, curling my fingers to make a fist and drawing them up to my face. I could feel my hands begin to sweat under the tightness of the gloves.

"OK. I want you to do a front jab." He held up his hands demonstrating how he wanted it done, his huge arm flexing as he held it out in front of him.

I copied his move, flexing my arm forward.

"All right. Good. Now I want you to use that on me," he said.

I swallowed hard again. *Use it on him?* I stepped forward and moved my arm forward, weakly aiming for his face. He easily blocked my move, moving swiftly to the side. He was fast.

"OK. Again. Use your feet to push forward. Jab faster."

Again I tried and again he swiftly moved out of the way. I quickly began to get frustrated with myself. Clenching my teeth, I moved forward and jabbed again. He moved, and I missed him, stumbling over myself.

"Come on, Con! Who the fuck are we kidding?" Big Red said angrily walking over to us. "She is going to need more than training. She's a fucking human."

"Back off, Bastian," Con warned him.

I felt my anger rise. Fucking human? Who the hell did he think he was? He walked onto the fighting mat, his muscles flexing with his every move, his black T-shirt looking as if it was going to rip at any moment. His stance was every bit as lethal and deadly combined.

"Hey, why don't you put on some gloves, Big Red? Show me how it's done," I said, smiling at him flirtatiously. I nodded to Con, letting him know silently that I had this. He nodded and backed off, folding his arms across his chest and looking at Big Red disapprovingly.

"I don't need gloves, love." He smiled back at me and looked over to Ian, grinning. Purposely trying to piss him off? Maybe.

He came to stand in front of me, smiling all the while, his green eyes now black, looking at me like I was a piece of meat and it was dinnertime. With my peripheral vision, I saw Ian stand up to make his way over to us. Hugo stopped him, shaking his head and mumbling something to him. Ian stood back and crossed his arms over his chest, intensely watching us.

"Love, you don't know what you're getting yourself into. We are faster and smarter," Big Red said softly to me.

I said nothing to this, putting my hands up, ready for him to strike. The hairs on the back of my neck stood, alerting me he was going to make his move any minute. Everything seemed to go in slow motion. He struck out with his right hand, and I quickly moved to my left, his fist swinging past my face. I jabbed him in the jugular hard enough for him to choke, his hands going to his throat. In a sweeping motion with my foot, I made him trip. He fell to the ground with a grunt. I stood over him, his face full of surprise and something else—admiration?

"Not so bad for a fucking human, right?" I said, tearing my gloves off and tossing them down to him. I heard the men laugh in the background.

I walked over to Con, and I couldn't help looking over to Ian. He stared back at me and turned, walking away.

"So what's next?" I asked Con, trying to hide the sting of disappointment I felt when Ian walked away.

Hugo walked over to us. He was wearing the same clothes: dark pants and a long dark trench coat. *Why doesn't he wear leather? He would look so great in it?* I thought to myself. I shook my head. Only I would think of fashion at a time like this.

"Any other visions," Hugo asked softly.

"Yes. My parents' past, you surrounded by vampires, and the beast—err wolf—is a man named Damian."

"Damian," Con says, clearly knowing the name.

"Oh, it gets worse. He's teamed up with the queen. He has a brother named Liam who is also a wolf, who he has betrayed."

Hugo, deep in thought, nodded his head. "We need to find him. He is going to fight with us."

"Vampires and beasts fighting together? It's never been done. Are you sure we can trust him?" Con asks.

"In my vision, he saves me from his brother."

"Yes. A wolf will be in our alliance," Hugo said quietly. "We need all the pieces of the puzzle put together if we're going to defeat the queen."

Con and I both looked at Hugo waiting for him to explain, but he didn't. *Pieces of the puzzle.*

"What aren't you telling me?" I asked, forcing him to meet my eyes. I looked into his soft brown eyes, kind eyes, haunted eyes.

"Scarlett...the prophecy comes from the Book of the Undead. You are part of the prophecy—a huge part. But the other half of the prophecy is missing."

Now I was confused. The Book of the Undead? Part of the prophecy missing? How could this be?

"Who has the other half, and why would it be missing?" I asked, worried.

"I don't know. I was hoping you would tell me."

I shook my head. "No. I had no vision of it."

"OK. We will wait."

I shook my head again. "No. We can't, Hugo. Queen Ezarbet is sending Damian. He was told to kill the X's and send me to her."

"Then let him come," Ian said from behind me.

I turned and looked at him, silently assessing him. He wore a fitted white V-neck T-shirt and washboard jeans, showing off his physique. I silently cursed my wicked body for responding to him.

"Ian is right. We will be ready," Hugo said, nodding.

"I couldn't agree more. Let me let the others know," Con said, walking back toward the X's.

I took a deep breath, suddenly feeling very tired.

"OK. Just stay out of my way," I said to Ian, walking away from him and Hugo.

As I walked toward my door, I could have sworn I heard Ian say, "Never."

The woman crouched forward, squinting her eyes. She couldn't see. It was so dark were she was kept caged, like she was nothing more than an animal. Her dirty fingers grabbed the steel bars as she tried to peek through, praying to God, any god, that there would be light. She swallowed, her throat dry from lack of drink. *Soon,* she told herself. She would wait and wait until she breathed her last single breath to escape this hell she was forced to endure. So much had been taken from her: her family, her power. Time was running out. She needed to make her move and move now. Taking a deep breath, she willed her body to stand, sweat glistening on her forehead. Clenching her teeth, she put her hand on the steel bars and, using her upper body, she pushed up with all her might, feeling her knees begin to buckle, her ripped dress making it hard for her to get up. But she held on, forcing her body to stand.

Shaking, she finally stood on her own, her body beaten and bruised. She knew she couldn't go on much longer like this. For every escape attempt, she was beaten with a leather whip, beaten to a point where they wouldn't stop until they drew blood. Never would she give them the satisfaction of seeing her cry, and she would never beg. When they were through with one of her beatings, she noticed a man with dark hair so long you couldn't see his eyes. He wore no shirt and had black pants on. He showed no sympathy for her and actually looked like he had enjoyed the show. He was neither human nor vampire but something else—something dark.

She'd learned that they had found the prophet, a girl, human, Scarlett, the daughter of sweet Celine. That was when she knew that the man who stayed across the hall locked in a cage just as she was did so willingly. He was a beast. She tried many times to reach out to him, to try to get him to see that this was madness, but he was too far gone in with the queen and her evil plot. His soul was blackened with hate; there was no way of breaking that barrier.

She was alone more than ever now. She felt herself begin to slip down to the floor, feeling tears beginning to fall for the first time since being caged. Was this how it would end? She felt her eyes begin to close and her body slump. As she felt herself begin to give up, a mouse scurried over to her, going in between the caged bars. She sat up as quickly as her weakened body would let her. Was this it? Was this her sign?

"Come, my friend," she whispered, holding out her hand.

The grey mouse made its way to her, going into her hand, his tiny whiskers tinkling her as he searched for food. He was just as hungry as she was. Lifting him gently, she brought him up to her face meeting him at eye level.

"Listen, my friend, we only have one chance and one chance only. You are to get a key from one of the queen's guards, and you must be quick and bring it to me. We don't have much time. Will you do that for me?" she asked softly, her emerald green eyes looking deeply into the mouse's.

He stared back, mesmerized by her voice.

She gently set the mouse down, and he scurried away under the locked cell door, silently promising her what she wanted.

She rested her head against the wall and swallowed hard, hoping this would work. This had to work. There was no room for error. Her body was ravaged and weak from her daily beatings and lack of food. There was only so much a person could take. This would indeed be her only chance. Queen Ezarbet had taken her powers, yes, but she was born a natural witch. No amount of black magic could ever take that away.

Flora closed her eyes and waited patiently for her mouse to come rescue her.

chapter

FIFTEEN

I found myself back with Celine and Edrick. It was like they stood frozen in time waiting for me to return to their story, waiting patiently for me, loving to share this part of them with me.

"Vampire," Celine whispered, shaking her head in denial.

"Yes," he whispered back, stepping closer to her.

She backed away a little. He stopped, looking a hurt by her fear.

"Are you going to kill me?"

He smiled at her gently. "If I wanted you dead, I would have let Xavier have you."

"Well, maybe, you just wanted me for yourself," she said bravely.

He cocked his head to the side. "Are you flirting with me?" He smiled at her again, this time with humor in his eyes. I smiled as I watched their exchange. I saw the horror vanish from Celine's eyes, replaced with embarrassment.

"That's not what I meant at all. What I meant was maybe you just wanted to have my blood, just as he wanted."

"I would never hurt you," he said softly to her, his eyes becoming serious once again.

I could see her doubt and heard her swallow hard. She believed him.

"Oh, my God. My clothes! I just got this job at the castle," she said, looking to the ground for her uniform. Picking it up, she stopped, suddenly realizing something. "Everyone in that castle is a vampire."

"Yes, and you shouldn't come back," he warned her.

"Yes, maybe I shouldn't. But I need the money," she said, walking away from him.

He followed her. I trailed behind them. It was weird to hear my parents' first conversation. I couldn't stop the sadness that overwhelmed me as I watched them together.

"Why do you need the money?" he asked.

She looked at him, clearly puzzled to be having a conversation with a vampire. "I have to take care of my brother."

Edrick was quiet for a moment. "Is your brother disabled?"

Celine let out an uncomfortable cough. "No. He is not disabled. He is an alcoholic," she whispered.

"So he would let his sister work herself to the bone to support his habit?" he asked angrily.

She stopped, raising her chin bravely, her eyes narrowing. "I will not let you speak of my brother this way," she said.

I could see then how we were alike. We may not look the same, but when she was angry, I saw myself. Edrick held up his hands in silent apology.

"I will not speak of your brother, but someday he will not have you around to care for him. What would he do without you?" he asked her softly.

"I haven't thought that far yet. I am just trying to keep a roof over our head."

Edrick nodded his head in understanding. They continued walking in silence as they headed to her small cottage home. It looked shabby, the screen door hanging loose, the windows dirty, and flower pots with no plants in them. She looked away from Edrick as if she was embarrassed. She smiled softly at him.

"Welcome to my castle, sir." She bowed her head toward him, laughing nervously at herself.

He smiled, lifted his hand to grasp her chin, and brought her head up slowly.

"You don't have to be ashamed of where you live."

She shyly met his eyes. Her lips parted, and his eyes follow her movement.

"Who are you?" she asked gently.

"I will tell you tomorrow; tomorrow I will tell you everything. Promise me you will not ask questions in the castle. Do not mention anything that has happened tonight."

"I promise."

He gently leaned down and kissed her. She let out a moan, reaching up on her tiptoes, wrapping her arms around his neck as her body sank into his perfectly. I looked away briefly. I felt like I was not worthy of watching something so precious coming to life. They broke apart, both breathing heavily.

"Until tomorrow night," he whispered to her.

"Why until tomorrow?" she asked, her eyes looking saddened by his departure.

He smiled. "Because I want to make sure you are not just a dream again," he said, and with that he turned, walking back to the path they came from.

She nodded and turned to open the door. As she put the key in the lock, she turned, thinking of something.

"What do you mean *again*?" she called out.

But he was gone, vanishing into the darkness as if he was never there.

My vision seemed to fade, bringing me into the present time. It was dark outside. I felt the heat sting my cheeks, and my forehead felt like it was beginning to get damp. The heat of a summer night. I was with Big Red. He was not dressed for battle. He had on a black muscle T-shirt, showing off his huge arms, and black pants. Something was different about him. His beautiful red hair, cut short, flipped away from his face, but his face looked different. Maybe it was his eyes. He looked angry, his body giving away tension, but most of all he looked lost, like all his emotions were checked out. What the hell was going on with him?

He was walking in a dark alley with his sword hanging loosely from his hand, the tip of it scratching the ground. I sensed further in the alley at least six ancients. I looked quickly behind him for the X's, but there was no one with him. Was he on a solo mission? Where the hell was his backup?

"Big Red, what are you doing?" I asked him, shaking my head and following behind him.

Of course he didn't hear me. He just kept on walking as if in a daze. The ancient's heard him, not that he was making it hard for them to hear him coming. He wanted them to hear. The first ancient came at him with a sword; he easily blocked with his sword, kicking the ancient in the chest and spinning his sword, slicing the head off the ancient. The other five ancients came forth and surrounded him. Big Red released his sword, dropping it to the floor, the metal making a loud clinking sound in the empty alley. He lifted his hands as if he was going to surrender. Instead he raised them into fists before flipping them the bird.

"Come on, you fucks!" he yelled at them.

I put my hand over my mouth. Was he trying to get himself killed? The ancients started laughing at his stupidity and went in for the attack, but Big Red was quick, going in for the first one, uppercutting him and making him fall to the ground with a grunt. The other ancient grabbed him by the arms, trying to hold him while another had a dagger ready to aim at his heart, but he jumped upward, his big, muscular legs going around the ancient's neck, snapping it, making him turn to ash. The ancient that had his arms around him let him go, and Big Red wasted no time turning and grabbing him by the neck with his bare hands and breaking it.

The other three ancients went in for the attack and start beating him, but Big Red was like an animal released from its cage. I had never seen anyone so powerful and reckless—hungry, not for food but for death. He started pounding away at each of them, finally grabbing his sword from the ground and stabbing one in the chest, aiming perfectly at his heart. The other ancient made a move with his sword and missed him by inches. Big Red turned in the nick of time and cut the ancient's arm off. The ancient screamed out in pain, falling to the ground.

The last of the ancients ran toward him. Big Red swiftly pulled out a dagger from his back pocket and flung it at him, turning him into ash in mid-run. The ancient with the lost arm still lay on the ground screaming in pain. Big Red looked down at him, his eyes still looking dazed, and dropped onto his knees slowly.

"What is your leader's name?" he asked quietly.

"Fuck you, traitor!" the ancient screamed at him.

Big Red said nothing, just stood back up and grabbed his sword, cleaning it off with his fingertips. I watched as the ancient froze, his eyes going wide with fear as he sees the sword in Big Red's hand.

"Fuck me, you say?" Big Red asked quietly.

My eyes went wide with fear. What was he doing? I watched as he lifted the sword and brought it down hard, cutting off the ancient's left leg. I put my hand over my mouth to keep from screaming out. The ancient screamed out, almost crying.

"I am going to give you one more chance. Who is your leader?" he asked again, seeming unfazed by the ancient's cries for mercy.

"His name is…His name is Matthias…Matthias is his name!" the ancient screamed at him, flipping onto his stomach, his armed hand reaching up, clawing the ground trying to get away from him.

"Matthias," Big Red whispered. He turned as if he was going to walk away but turned back toward him.

"Too bad for you, ancient, I don't give second chances," he said before raising his sword once more and chopping off his head, turning him to ash. Big Red dropped the sword, spent from battle. He dropped to his knees with his head bent down. I rushed over to him and I went on my knees before him. He was holding his hands in tight fists and pounded on the ground, so hard he drew blood on his knuckles. His body was shaking uncontrollably with anguish. I wanted so badly to reach out and touch him, to comfort him, but all I could do was watch him as his body rocked back and forth. I sat with him the whole while as his scream echoed in the empty alley—his scream of fury and pain.

chapter

SIXTEEN

Walking through the castle, I watched as my servants rushed away, fearing me. I inwardly smiled. *Good. They should fear me. Everyone should fear me. That's the way it is supposed to be, meant to be.* I relished in that. Nothing was going to get in my way. Not even that stupid human bitch Scarlett. Making my way to my quarters, I opened the heavy door and slammed it shut, the hinges rattling. I walked over to the mirror and looked at myself, jealousy and rage overtaking me. What the hell was so special about her? Ian was enthralled; couldn't be.

I was surprised, and surprised is something I was never, but when my solider Alec came to me with the message from Ian, I knew without a doubt he had become enthralled. The man with the heart of stone, enthralled. Ian was going to pay for his betrayal. Still staring at myself, I could not help but want to know more of this Scarlett. What did she look like? I felt my anger begin to rise. I smoothed my corseted green gown. It would have matched my beautiful green eyes perfectly, making me look medieval, which was a look I pulled off like no other. I walked over to my bureau and rang for my servant. The door opened hurriedly. Gloria the human servant bowed to me before she closed the door.

"My queen, how may I serve you?" she asked standing up straight with her arms behind her back.

"You may undress me. I am ready for my bath."

She nodded her head nervously. I could hear her heart beating faster in fear. I could smell her blood rushing in her veins.

"Yes, my queen. I will get your bath ready," she said hurriedly, trying to rush to the bathroom.

"No. Undress me first," I demanded, loving the look of pure terror on her face.

"Of...Of course, my queen," she stuttered, walking over to me.

I turned and gave her my back, letting her unlace my corset. Her hands shook as she began to untie the laces. The gown loosened and slipped off, leaving me naked. My fangs protruded from my mouth as I turned to her. All the color was gone from her face, and she stared at me, tears falling from her eyes and her mouth quivering.

"Please, please my queen," she begged me.

I smiled. "Shhh, shhh. One so beautiful should not cry," I whispered to her, gently touching her face, my long nails following the angle of her face.

I held out my arms, and she hesitantly came into them, hugging me. My arms wrapped around her, my hands rubbing her back gently.

"One so beautiful should not cry," I repeated. "One so beautiful should scream."

I grabbed a fistful of her hair and yanked her head back so hard she gasped and bit down roughly on her neck, making her scream. Taking great pulls of her blood, I think of Scarlett—me drinking from Scarlett. I felt myself begin to get aroused by just the thought.

The door opened, and I released the servant. She fell to the floor with a moan, still alive, her heartbeat now faint. Who would dare interrupt my feeding? Abel walked in, and I smiled. He smiled back at me, his eyes taking in my bloodied mouth and naked body. I watched as he inhaled the scent of blood and saw his eyes blacken with desire and hunger.

"Come, my love. We will share her," I said to him, holding out my hand for him to come to me.

He took off his sword and walked over to us.

"Darling, I have need of you," I said to him as I kissed him. He kissed me back letting out a growl, his tongue flicking out tasting the blood of the servant.

I smiled. "I have need of you to go to Connecticut. Make sure Ian is killed and the prophet comes to me alive."

He looked at me confused. "I thought you wanted the prophet dead."

I narrowed my eyes, the smile leaving my face. "You dare question me?"

"No; never. You know I will do whatever it is you wish," he said. Anything to please me.

I smiled again. "Good. Damian will assist you."

His eyes narrowed at the mention of Damian. Poor fool was like a lovesick puppy.

"Let's not talk about this now. Drink, my love. She is pure." I said, not wishing to discuss it further.

I coaxed him onto his knees with me and lifted the servant's head up, tilting her so that her bloody neck was exposed. He leaned in to get a look at her. His eyes pitch black, he let out a growl at the sight of her blood, bent down to her neck, and drank from her as I watched the life being sucked out of her. I reveled in it. I watched as the servant's eyes rolled back and her body began to shake. I heard the last beat of her heart, and he released her with another growl, his mouth dripping with her blood. He grabbed me, and we began to kiss furiously, the scent of death and blood all around us. I ripped off his shirt and yanked his pants down. I didn't know what I was turned on more by, the fact that we just took an innocent life or the fact that Scarlett would be put on a platter and served to me.

$$\infty$$

The elder man was near death. The boy went to his father and knelt by the bedside. The covers were drawn up and he was tucked in neatly. He grabbed his father's frail, wrinkled hand, once so strong. The boy bowed his head, tears streaming down his face. He felt his father grip his hand tighter. Lifting his head he saw that his father was awake. He tried to speak but started to cough instead.

"Father, don't," he pleaded with him.

Grabbing the water by the bedside, he tilted his head upward and made him drink. Placing the cup of water to the side, the boy stared down at the man who had taught him everything he knew. He was leaving him. He knew it. He felt it. He was going to speak whether he wished him too or not. He was a stubborn man, as was he. He was more like him than he knew.

"Son," he whispered, grabbing his hand and holding it tighter.

"Yes, father. I am here," the boy said, leaning over him so he could hear him.

"You must listen to me. You have been chosen."

"Chosen?" he asked, confused.

"Yes. The Book of the Undead speaks of a prophecy. A prophet, a child, a girl, will be born from one male vampire and one human female. A war is coming, son. She will have a guardian. That guardian is you. You must protect her."

His head was spinning in circles. The prophecy. He was to be a guardian?

"Father, how can you be certain? Why me?"

"Son, you have been chosen. It is not for us to decide or to ask why. You were born to do this. The prophecy speaks of one warlock and one witch who will join forces with the prophet to defeat the queen.

The boy shook his head in denial. Warlocks and witches were enemies. While warlocks kept the balance, witches believed in domination. They spelled with black magic and worked with the dark forces.

"Father, the witches work for the queen. It cannot be."

His father started to close his eyes and began mumbling, shaking his head, trying to sit up from the bed.

"Father, don't," he said, pushing down gently on his father's shoulder.

"Son, listen to me. You must find your witch, before it's too late. She will be in danger. Your prophet will lead you to her."

"Father, who is she?" he asked hurriedly.

His father started to close his eyes again and took his final breath. And just like that, he was gone; gone from this world, full of pain and sorrow, leaving him to face it by himself.

"Father," the boy whispered.

He hugged his father. He didn't care who saw him like this. He felt hands on him trying to get him to stand up. He finally stood and looked down at his father one last time. The old dead man was not his father; his father was full of life and strength. He didn't want to remember him this way. He walked out of the room with his Uncle Rodrick, a warlock as well. They went into the living room, and his uncle left him alone. Having a seat before the fireplace, alone with his thoughts, he put his head in his hands. His mind was at a loss. What was he to do now? He knew nothing of the world his father spoke of. He felt tears sting his eyes again when he thought of his father.

Feeling his uncle's hand on his shoulder, he looked up. He hadn't even heard him enter the room. His uncle was an elder warlock, much like his father. Of course, warlocks could put spells on themselves when they didn't want to age or if they found their beloved. His father found his beloved in his mother, but she died in childbirth. His father was never the same; at least that was what Uncle Rodrick would tell him. Warlocks could see many stars and moons, but, like his father and his uncle, he didn't want to go that route. They always would say, "When it's your time, it's your time."

Uncle Rodrick smiled sadly at him and handed him a book. "Your father wanted you to have this. Guard it with your life. This will lead you to the prophet and your witch. May the elderly sprits be with you on your journey, and let them guide you," he said, bidding him farewell. He walked out of the room, leaving the young man to read the book alone.

With shaking hands he wiped away the dirt that covered the book's lettering, as though it had been buried. His eyes widened. This could not be. How had his family come to have it? The last he'd heard, the book was guarded by the witches. The Book of the Undead. It was a brown, leather-bound book with gold Latin writing. It had a gold clasp on it. Unbuckling it gently, he opened the book that was to be his destiny. He read the page that was folded over: the prophecy. If it wasn't clear before, it was certainly so now. He was no longer a boy playing tricks with magic; he was a man destined to do something great, something that would change the world as he knew it, but was the world worth saving? He shook his head. He was a different person now. He knew what must be done. He would guard the prophet with his last dying breath.

I slowly opened my eyes, the dream fading back to reality. I was with the prophet now. My chest was gleaming from sweat. I got up from the bed and walked barefoot to the bathroom. Turning on the sink, I wet my face, loving the feel of the cold water, and looked at myself in the mirror. I had two-day-old stubble, and my eyes looked bloodshot.

I needed to rest more, but there was no time for that; so much needed to be done. Grabbing the towel I wiped my face, feeling a little better. I walked back into the bedroom and put on my shirt and shoes. Walking over to the door, I let myself out.

I saw that Scarlett was in her room, her light still on. Sitting in one of the lounge areas, I saw Ian sitting there all by himself, like the loner he was, staring at Scarlett's door. Walking over to him, I sat beside him, leaning back on the sofa, staring at him. I immediately felt his body tense. The man did not trust anyone.

"What do you want, warlock?" Ian snapped, feeling my eyes on him.

"Nothing. I just want to know your intentions," I said, shrugging my shoulders, getting more comfortable.

His cold blue eyes looked over to me. He knew what I was talking about. I didn't even have to mention her name. With his cold stare, he tried to intimidate me, but I stared back at him, letting him know that I was not afraid of him and that if I had to protect Scarlett from him, I would in a heartbeat. He may have been enthralled with Scarlett, but I knew how this was going to play out. Ian was a coldhearted bastard. He may not want Scarlett to be killed, but he would break her heart without a second thought. Scarlett was in love with Ian, whether she knew it or not. Was this cold man of ice capable of returning her love?

"Do me a favor, warlock: stay the fuck out of my head," Ian whispered, his body radiating anger. He got up from the couch and walked away to stand in the shadows, still watching Scarlett's door.

Shaking my head, leaning my head back on the couch, I could not help but smirk. I had just gotten under his skin, and I loved it. The man of ice had a warm spot—and that warm spot was Scarlett. My smile quickly began to fade. But could Scarlett break the ice over Ian's heart? Only time would tell.

chapter

SEVENTEEN

The punching bag moved with each of my punches. I kept jabbing and uppercutting, moving left to right just like Con taught me. I felt my thoughts shift. My visions were floating aimlessly in my head. It felt like I had so much information built in that my head was ready to burst. But most of all, I was thinking of Queen Ezarbet and my parents, what she did to them. I wanted to envision them forever as they were when they first met, smiling lovingly at each other, but all I could see was flashes of my mother screaming and my father's beaten face. I felt my anger rise. I started hitting faster, harder, the force of my blows making the punching bag swing furiously. I pictured the queen in front of me. Her pitch-black eyes and evil laugh taunting me. I started to grunt with each of my blows, my mouth tightly clenched. Sand began to pour out of the side of the bag, but I was so angered I didn't bother to stop.

"Easy. You're finished." Ian grabbed the bag from swinging further, his muscled arms wrapping around it.

I wiped the sweat from my face, frustrated beyond belief. "Don't tell me when I'm done," I hissed, unwrapping my taped hands.

"Anger will get you nowhere quickly," he said, letting go of the bag. He came over to stand in front of me.

I swallowed hard. Why did he have to look so good? I quickly thought of how I must've looked right then. My hair was tied up in a ponytail, which was probably nice and sweaty now. I wore black yoga pants and a black tank. My face, without a lick of makeup, was flushed with anger. I quickly tucked loose hair behind my ears.

"Well I can't help it. I'm human," I said sarcastically, walking away. He started to follow me, walking by my side.

Feeling his body beside mine, I felt a jolt of electricity. *Is he trying to make conversation with me?* This was new.

"Yes, you humans do have a tendency to seek your emotions. It is your weakness," he said, shaking his head in disgust.

I stopped walking and looked at him. He was so beautiful but so cold all at once, his steel blue eyes reflecting the cold, eerie presence that surrounded him. What had happened to him?

"You were once human," I whispered to him, my hand reaching for his face.

He flinched back before I could touch him, his eyes turning dark. I quickly pulled my hand back.

"That was very, very long ago. I am everything, but human. Don't ever forget that," he said angrily and stalked away.

I stared at his retreating back. "What the hell is your problem?" I was so tempted to yell back at him. Damn him. No one made me feel as he did. He looked concern for me for a brief moment, and just like a light switch he turned off. I headed back toward my room shaking my head, his words repeating back to me: *I am everything, but human.* I couldn't help but wonder who he was trying to convince: me or himself?

I saw Hugo waiting for me by my door with his arms crossed. Had he seen what just took place between Ian and me? The look in his soft brown eyes as they looked down momentarily revealed my answer.

"Hate that guy," I said with a fake smile, not wanting him to know my true feelings. But what were my true feelings? Maybe Ian was right. Emotion was a weakness. Damn him.

"Scarlett, you don't have to lie to me," he whispered, opening my door.

Entering my room, I felt myself blush. I turned toward Hugo. He was my only friend in this crazy world I was destined to be in. There was no point in lying to him. I let out a deep breath.

"I don't know what I feel for him," I said, shrugging my shoulders. I started to pace back and forth. "The man drives me crazy. I hate him, but there is something about him that draws me in. Is there something wrong with me? I let him drink from me, Hugo. Am I going to turn into a vampire now? But wait. I am half vampire, aren't I?" My confession out, I looked at him.

Hugo shifted a little as though uncomfortable with this subject, putting his hands in his pocket. Thank God I didn't mention our sexual escapades. He would probably put a magic spell on me to shut me the hell up.

"No. You will not turn into a vampire. You do not turn vampire from a bite. You have to have vampire blood in your system when you die to turn. Plus, you are immune to becoming a vampire because you already have vampire blood in your veins. Did you drink from him, Scarlett?

"No, why?" I asked.

Hugo didn't answer and looked at me as if to see if I was telling the truth.

"No," I said again.

"OK. I believe you. Scarlett, drinking and being drunk from between vampires is a sacred thing between their kind.

"What do you mean *sacred?*"

"It's when two vampires become blood mated. The vampire has to be enthralled."

"Enthralled," I repeated. *Just like Zayah and Con,* I thought to myself.

"Well don't worry. Ian hates me," I said trying to act as nonchalant as I could. I walked to my bureau and began opening drawers trying to find something to wear.

"Hugo, I need to go out," I said, changing the subject. "Get some air. You know what would really put me at ease? Really would make me feel better?" I said, closing the drawer and looking at him innocently.

"What's that?"

"I need to get some air, clear my thoughts," I said anxiously.

"I don't think that's a good idea," he said, shaking his head.

"Come on; please? Just for an hour? I just need to get a few things. Please? Pretty please.?" I put my hands together pretending I was begging him.

He laughed at me. *Whoa, Hugo laughing.* He had a beautiful laugh. I beamed at him, grinning from cheek to cheek. He looked almost boyish. Gone was the haunted look in his soft brown eyes.

"Enjoying yourself, warlock?" Ian asked from behind us, his stance overwhelming in the doorway as he stood watching us, his mouth set in a grim line.

We didn't even hear him come in. Who the fuck did he think he was, just coming in here as if he was meant to be here?

"What the hell are you doing in my room?" I yelled at him.

Purposely ignoring me, he walked away from the door still looking menacingly at Hugo.

Hugo smiled at Ian, not looking threaten at all by him; if anything he looked amused by the situation. He looked back at me and nodded his head.

"I was just leaving," he said to Ian, not looking at him. He walked to the door and closed it quietly behind him.

"Give him hell," Hugo's voice whispered softly in my head. He was using his magic. I wondered if he knew what I was saying in my head. Geez, the thoughts that raced through my mind. I hoped that wasn't the case.

"Hello. What are you doing in my room?" I turned toward Ian who was now walking over to my bed and having a seat, putting his elbows on his knees.

The bed looked small with him on it. I felt my body begin to warm, shaking my head disgustedly at my thoughts. I needed to get it together and quick. If I wasn't pissed at him, I wanted to jump his bones.

"I don't want him in your room anymore," he said quietly, ignoring my question again and breaking into my wondering thoughts.

I placed my hands on my hips, his eyes following my movement. *The nerve of this man.*

"Who the hell do you think you are? You have no right to tell me what to do. I will have anyone I want in my room. Matter of fact, I don't recall inviting you in," I yelled, turning toward the door to open it. Before I could turn to tell him to get the fuck out, he was behind me in a flash. With an open palm, he slammed the door shut from behind me, his body against mine. I put my head against the door and closed my eyes.

"I don't want him in your room anymore," he whispered again.

Opening my eyes I slowly turned to face him. His eyes flashed with anger. *Oh my God. He's jealous of Hugo.* I wondered if I should throw it in his face but thought better of it. This looked new to him, as if he didn't realize the look of possessiveness he was throwing my way. It was very human of him.

"If you must know, Hugo is my friend, my guardian. He is named in the prophecy with me. There is nothing going on," I said softly, studying his reaction.

A look flashed across his eyes again. Relief? I heard him swallow. I felt my hands start to lift to reach out and touch him, but I hesitantly put them down. I so badly wanted to touch him, but I was scared of his reaction to me. He took a step back, and I slowly walked away from the door.

"So you said you wanted to go out shopping. I will take you out," he said, opening the door.

"You really don't have to go with me," I said, shaking my head, turning toward him.

"The sun goes down in one hour. Be ready then," he said, ignoring my remark and shutting the door.

And just like that, he switched the light off again. *This man has a problem listening to me. Damn him! We are going to have to work on that.* Walking over to one of my bureaus, I got a towel and headed toward the bathroom. Be ready in one hour? I'll show him. Hugo's voice popped into my head again: *Give him hell.* I smiled as I turned on the shower.

chapter

EIGHTEEN

Two hours later I walked out of my room feeling refreshed, wearing skinny jeans and a long-sleeve black sweater that hung off one of my shoulders, baring my skin. I wore my hair down, falling in waves down my back. Ian was waiting for me. He looked up as I made my way over to him. My heart skipped a beat as soon as I saw him. He was freshly shaven, wearing fitted jeans, a V-neck white T-shirt and a leather jacket that fit him like a glove. Damn he was hot. I felt myself get aroused. I licked my lips and looked away, suddenly shy.

"I said one hour," he said softly, looking me over as if approving. I caught his eyes lingering on my bare shoulder.

I looked at him and smirked, batting my lashes. "Yes, you did, but I never said I would be ready, now did I?"

I watched as he clenched his jaw. Something told me this man waited for no one. *Good!* I kept smirking.

"Let's go. I told the others we would be leaving." He started toward the door, not even waiting for me to follow him.

Rolling my eyes at his back, I reluctantly followed. He opened the door, and the chill of the air hit me fast. *Shit, it's cold out. I have to get a jacket, pronto.* Following Ian to the back of the building, I walked faster to keep up. I saw him reach into his back pocket and press his car alarm. I saw the car's lights flash in response and paused in shock. *Holy shit!* I could not believe it. Ian's car was fabulous. I had never seen one like it before—a luxury two-door sports car painted an unusual blue-silver. I looked closer and noticed the badge of the car. *Holy shit. It's an Aston Martin!* If I could pick any car that Ian would drive, it would be this one. It screamed danger and sex. Walking around to the passenger side, I opened the door.

"This is yours?" I asked, looking at him before getting in.

He looked back at me as he was about to get in. "Yes," he said and got in, offering no explanations.

I got in and was captivated by the inside as much as I was by the outside. *Sleek leather seats. So sexy.* I looked over to Ian as he started the car. I couldn't help but stare at him. He was so sexy. His scent filled the car. I took a deep breath of it, savoring the musky, male smell of him. I felt my nipples harden and an ache grow between my legs. I couldn't keep my eyes off of him. I shifted in my seat uncomfortably. As though sensing my arousal, he looked over at me, desire evident in his eyes. I stared back at him, my mouth open. Did he know of my reaction to him? Did he feel the same for me? I quickly looked out the window, distracting myself.

"So where are we off to?" I asked looking back at him.

Gone was the desire I'd seen in his eyes; he took on a business-like attitude. The light was switched back to off.

"Wherever you want me to take you. Make it somewhere very public," he said, his hand going to the gear and switching it to drive.

"OK. We can go to the mall near here, in Stamford.

"Fine," he said and pulled off into the street.

I looked over at him again, at his beautiful face looking at the road ahead of us. His face was full of concentration, and he kept glancing up at the rearview mirror to check if we were being followed. His body was full of tension, ready for battle if it was going to come our way. Going to the mall with him was going to be weird. Him of all people, going to the mall...shopping? Why did he want to come with me anyway? I opened my mouth to ask him but decided against it. Did I really want the answer to that? My head screamed *Hell no*, but my heart screamed *Hell yes*. Looking back out the window, I concentrated on the road and thought it best to keep my mouth shut and ride in silence.

"We are finally here, Damian!"

I opened my eyes, pretending I'd been sleeping the whole time. The old man named Gary smiled at me. I smiled back, the smile not quite reaching my eyes. I looked out the window, fogged from the cold. Wiping it with my hand, I got my first glimpse of the big city. Lots of bright lights were all I could see in the night. I looked away from the window and waited patiently for the stewardess to let out our aisle next.

"So, son, are you here for business or pleasure?" the old man asked.

"Both," I said, giving him a short answer.

"That's good to hear. I'm here to see my new grand-baby. My daughter just had a baby boy," he said proudly.

I tuned him out. Like I could give two shits. These humans and their useless chatter. They always felt the need to talk. The stewardess called our aisle next, and I waited for the old man to get up. Once he was out of my way, I quickly make my way out of the airport, trying to find the nearest exit. I did not bring luggage, just my carry-on. This was going to be a short trip. I kept my head down. I found it a little strange being out in civilization. It had been so long.

This world was different from the world I once knew. All the bright lights and technology were rather odd to me. Living in the dark was all I knew—until Queen Ezarbet. She taught me that I didn't have to hide, and why should I? Why be ashamed of this great power I held? I was sick of living in shadows. I was the alpha. It was time for the world to know of me. No more living in shadows. The queen and I would reign together. No one was going to get in my way. Not my brother, and not this prophet named Scarlett.

I found it amusing that she was a human female. This would be easy. With her and my brother out of the way, I would see fear in my people's eyes as well as the human race. Sure, there would be those to fight against us, but they would not have a chance. I would see fear in the eyes of the people, whether vampire, wolf, or human, who would dare go against me. I would show no mercy to those who did.

Seeing the exit sign, I turned to the left and made my way out the door. Breathing in the cold, thick air, I closed my eyes. I could smell death in the air. Death was upon us. I smiled, loving that scent. Walking over to where I saw yellow taxi cabs lined up, I saw a Middle Eastern man quickly walk over to me, beating the rest of the men to the punch. His head was wrapped in a black turban, and he wore a matching black shirt and khaki pants.

"Welcome to New York," he said with a thick accent.

"Hello. I need a ride," I said, reaching into my pocket and pulling out a roll of money.

The driver's eyes went wide, looking at the money as if he'd just struck gold. *Humans! They would kneel like a dog if the price was right.* I slowly took out two hundred-dollar bills from the roll of money and handed them to him. His eyes widened further, and his brown hand quickly snatched the money from me.

"OK, OK. Alim will take you where you need to go. Don't worry. I take good care of customers," he said, quickly putting the money in the front pocket of his shirt. He opened the rear passenger door, and I got in. He hurriedly got inside the car and adjusted his rearview mirror. Before pulling out, he looked back at me.

"OK, my friend. Where would you like Alim to take you?"

I looked out the window at the bright lights of the city. It was a shame I was not going to stay for longer. This was an interesting place to explore and to set my sights of a new wolf pack that I will be creating soon. Just the thought of my new pack running rampant through the streets of New York City was enough to make me smile.

I took a deep breath before looking back at him. "Connecticut. Westport, Connecticut."

chapter

NINETEEN

"You have a gun!" I yelled at Ian.

He closed his glove compartment and looked over at me as if I was stupid.

"Of course I do. Now that we have Damian involved, I don't want to take any chances, plus silver can hurt vampires to. This is easy to hide," he said as he got out of the car.

I got out hurriedly after him and watched as he put the gun behind him, tucking it into his pants and covering it with his shirt and jacket.

"You seriously think they would attack in a mall full of witnesses?"

"They want you dead. Yes. I think they would."

I said nothing to this. He was right. Wrapping my arms around me to shield myself from the cold, I walked quickly with him to the entrance. The heat hit me first. It was always hot in the mall, even in the summer. It was filled with people mostly doing their holiday shopping; greatest time of the year for many. Christmas decorations filled the mall. A big Christmas tree stood in the center with different-colored glass ornaments, and front and center was Santa Claus himself with a bunch of kids waiting to tell him whether they had been naughty or nice that year. Wreaths hung on pretty much every wall they could find, and "Jingle Bells" played softly in the background.

Ian stood close to me as we walked through the crowd, his arm brushing mine, his eyes scanning and his body radiating tension, ready and waiting for someone to strike. As we passed the food court, the smell of the food reminded me that I was hungry. I felt my stomach growl, and Ian cast a sideways glance at me, his glare disapproving.

"You should have told me you were hungry."

"I just realized that I was," I said, shrugging my shoulders.

"We will go somewhere after we are done," he said as we went up an escalator.

As the escalator took us up slowly to the second level of the mall, I noticed a young couple in front of us holding hands and felt envious. I wanted that. I wanted to feel that closeness with someone. I wanted it with Ian. I wondered what his reaction would be if I was to hold his hand. I looked away. We made it to the top, and the young couple wondered off blissfully.

"What store do you want to go to?" Ian asked, breaking me from my thoughts.

I knew what store I wanted to go to before we arrived.

"It's here," I said, pointing to the store.

He followed behind me as we entered Armani Exchange. I looked carelessly through the women's section, and then I saw it, the jacket from my vision. *I was in battle wearing this.* It was badass and so feminine. I took it off the hanger, but before I put it on I brought it up to my face and smelled it. There was nothing better than the smell of real leather. I put it on and walked to a mirror, and I knew this was it. This jacket and I would go through many battles together. As silly as that may sound, it was the truth. It fit me like a second skin. I raised my hands to see how I would look fighting. I looked like the woman in my vision, but was I her? Could I take on this great responsibility? Ian came into view behind me in the mirror, and our eyes met.

"How do I look?" I asked.

"You look beautiful," he said softly.

My mouth gaped open and my heart stopped. I didn't hear right; I was sure of it. *Did he just call me beautiful?* I smiled at him and opened my mouth to say something.

"Excuse me, miss. Can I help you with something?" one of the salespeople asked, breaking our moment.

"Um, no; thank you though," I said, taking off the jacket.

I held it out to look at the price tag: five hundred dollars. My eyes went wide. It took me a moment to come to grips with the idea that yes, I could afford this now. This rich lifestyle was so new to me, but I would gladly oblige.

The sales girl's eyes lingered on Ian before she walked away. I couldn't blame her. I couldn't take my eyes off him either.

"OK. This is what I want," I said, walking past him.

I walked over to the cashier, and she rang me up. I took out my wallet and looked for my credit card, but Ian was way ahead of me, taking out cash and paying for it.

"Hey, I got it," I said softly to him, not wanting to cause a scene.

He said nothing, ignoring me.

"Would you like the receipt in the bag, sir," the cashier asked, her voice lingering on the "sir" as she smiled at him flirtatiously.

"No. I'll take it," I said, trying not to let my voice show a hint of jealously. *Mine!* my mind screamed.

I took the receipt and grabbed the bag. We exited the store, and I grabbed him by the arm, stopping him.

"Listen, thank you for buying me the jacket, but I don't need you to buy me anything," I hissed at him.

He looked down at me, his mouth once again set in a grim line.

"You're welcome; now let's get some food in you."

Letting go of his arm, I couldn't help but agree with him. I was starving.

"There's this pizzeria in here we can sit at and eat," I said.

We got there and the place was pretty empty. The smell of the pizza made my mouth salivate. It was an old pizzeria with old black and white pictures hung on the walls of families in Italy. The red leather seating was faded with age. We got seated in the far corner booth. I slid in and watched as Ian did the same. It was a bit comical watching Ian's huge frame being squeezed into a booth, very human. The waitress handed us two menus and told us she would be right back.

"God, I am starving! What are you going to get?" I asked, looking down at my menu, not sure what I was having. Definitely pizza! I looked up at Ian, noticing he hadn't answered my question. Then it hit me. He didn't eat food. God, I had to get use to this.

"Oh, sorry. I forgot," I said, putting down my menu. This was the first time we'd actually been alone together with our clothes on about to have a conversation. I figured this was my opportunity to ask him a few questions, whether I would like his answers or not.

He shrugged his shoulders. Picking it up, he began to carelessly look through the menu.

"I never had pizza," he said, looking at me again.

My God, how old was Ian? He looked to be in his late twenties. What was the story behind those beautiful eyes? There was so much I didn't know about him; physically, yes, but I wanted to know every aspect of his life. I knew if I asked too soon, he would turn off that light again. *Baby steps.*

"You never had pizza?"

"No. I hear it is very well favored to you humans," he said, closing the menu.

"Yes. I love pizza. When was the last time you fed?" I asked, leaning forward a little.

I couldn't believe he was talking to me. He actually looked relaxed, no tension in his body. I wanted him to keep talking. I could listen to the sound of his voice for hours.

"From food or from you?" he asked me, smiling for the first time—very seductively.

My mouth fell open. *Oh, my.* Ian was flirting with me. I felt myself blush from head to toe. His eyes were so intense when they looked at me. I could get lost in those eyes. The last time he fed was from me. I couldn't help but feel pleased that was the case. Was he hungry now? Would I let him feed from me? I knew without a doubt that yes, I would. The thought of his lips on another would drive me crazy.

"OK. What can I get you guys to eat?" the waitress asked us, breaking me from my thoughts. I tore my eyes away from Ian and focused on the waitress.

"Um, can we get a medium cheese pizza with extra cheese and two waters with lemon?"

"Sure. Coming right up," she said, smiling and taking our menus.

"Thanks," I said, smiling at her.

I waited until she left and started with my questions.

"Ian, why didn't you kill me as the queen wanted?" I asked softly.

He looked away from me as though now very uncomfortable.

"I don't know," he said softly, looking back at me with confusion. I believed him. He didn't know—or he didn't want to know.

"You and the queen were lovers." I tried to not sound like I was accusing, but I couldn't help it. I felt my fist knot up. Just the thought of Ian with the queen, their hands on each other and mouths touching, made me want to hit something.

"Yes, we were," he said, offering no explanations.

Damn this man and his short answers. I wanted to ask him, *What are we?*

"Ian, why would you betray her? You have nothing to gain and everything to lose. Why?" I asked again.

"Let's just say I like breaking the rules." He brought hands together, his long fingers intertwining.

I reached out tentatively and placed my hands over his. I couldn't help it. This man was not my enemy. As much as he wanted to be, he was not. He was my savior—and so much more. His hand stilled beneath mine and then moved as though he wanted to pull away.

"Don't," I whispered softly to him, not looking at him but at our hands together.

He didn't move. His hand felt so cold beneath mine. With my thumb I caressed his knuckles, loving the differences in our skin; his was so rough while mine was so soft. I felt the tension start to leave his body. He moved and gently put my hands between his, caressing me back. I stopped breathing in fear that any noise would ruin this spell that we were both under. It was if we were the only two in the pizzeria, the background going dark leaving us both captivated. My hand was so tiny in his, but we fit perfectly together.

"Pizza's here," the waitress said. We broke apart quickly as though caught, the spell broken.

She set a big tray with pizza and drinks on it down on the table.

"Do you need anything else?" she asked.

"No, thank you," I said, my voice shaky. I watched as she exited.

Fearing to look at Ian, I took the first slice pizza, the extra cheese coming off of it and spilling into my plate. I took my first bite and closed my eyes, savoring the flavor. I opened my eyes to find Ian staring at me curiously.

"What does it taste like?"

"It tastes like heaven. The richness of the tomato sauce and fresh mozzarella; there is nothing like it. For as long as I can remember, I've loved pizza!" I said, laughing. He said nothing, but I saw a hint of laughter in his eyes.

"What does blood taste like?" I asked, taking another bite of pizza.

"It tastes like heaven. You taste like heaven. I have never tasted anything so sweet in my lifetime, and if you let me, I would drink my fill of you."

I stopped in mid bite, eyes going wide. That was not the response I was looking for. I was at a loss for words.

"Keep eating. We have to leave soon," he said, all desire gone from his face. The lights turned off again.

I kept eating, in silence this time. The waitress checked on us, and Ian asked for the check. Paying the bill, Ian got up from the table first. I was right behind him, following him out of the pizzeria. The mall was now dead, the huge crowd from earlier thinning out. The employees were closing their store gates, and janitors began to clean up. We headed out of the mall in silence.

He sounded the alarm to his car, and we got in. I took my seat and closed my eyes suddenly feeling very tired. Ever since the visions began, sleep just hadn't been the same. Ian pulled off and we head out into the streets. I must have dozed off. When I woke up, we were in front of the warehouse. Ian parked, and we both sat in the car in silence. I looked over at him, and he was staring at me, hunger in his eyes. We each reached for the other at the same time, Ian nearly ripping off my seat belt. Our lips met hungrily. I moaned, and he took swift advantage, putting his tongue in my mouth. I reacted just as swiftly, sucking at his tongue and shoving my fingers in his hair, making him growl.

His hands were all over me, reaching under my shirt and grabbing my breasts, pinching my nipples through the lacy material. I sucked in breath. My heart was beating out of control, my body tingling all over. I needed to get closer to him. As though reading my mind, he broke our kiss and lifted me easily to the front of his seat onto his lap, my ass hitting the steering wheel making the horn beep. He reached down and pressed a button that brought his seat back a little, giving us more room. Moaning, I started to grid my sex against him, loving the feeling of his hard-on against my bottom, kissing him feverishly.

I pulled at his jacket, trying to get it off of him. Tossing it to the side, I broke away from his kiss and took off his shirt. God, he was beautiful—and he was mine. My hand touched his chest, my fingers tickling from the little blond hair sprinkled there. I leaned down and licked him, my tongue leaving a wet trail on him. He let out a hiss, brought my head up, and kissed me again. His hands grabbed my ass, moving me closer to him, rubbing me harder against him. I felt myself getting lost in the sensation. He broke our kiss and started kissing my neck and lower. He took off my shirt.

"So sexy," he said, looking at my breasts, my nipples peeking through my bra, begging to be put in his mouth.

He yanked down on my bra sending both of my breasts leaping out, eager for him. He molded them in his hands, his thumb lapping over my nipples. I threw my head back moaning. He leaned his head down and took one nipple in his mouth, sucking and licking, all the while shifting himself upward, pressing against me more fully. I grabbed his head, keeping him at my breast, as I started riding his hard length.

"Please," I beg him.

"I know. Let me give it to you," he said.

He reached behind me with his hand and reached into my pants, his hands first touching my ass, caressing me. Moving my thong to the side, he delved deeper, touching me in my sweetest spot, his fingers entering me. I let out a whimper and started to ride his hand, getting totally lost. The windows were starting to get foggy with our hot breath.

"That's it, baby. Take it," he whispered in my ear, encouraging me.

He kissed my ear and bit down gently on my ear lobe. I felt him start to trail kisses to my neck, and I knew what was coming, but I was so lost in what he was already doing that I had no time to think. My nails started to dig into his skin. I was close, so close. My body felt as if it was being lifted and I was beginning to float. He bit down on my neck, drinking from me, and I let out a scream, coming so hard on his manipulative fingers, grinding hard against him, arching my neck to give him better access. I heard him growl as though finding my release brought him great pleasure. I was in a daze, out of breath, my heart pounding in my ears.

He stopped drinking and licked my bite marks, withdrew his hand from me, and put my underwear back in place. He has his head down as though trying to shield his eyes from me. I gently pulled his head up, and his eyes were pitch black, fangs protruding from his mouth and his lips red from my blood.

"You are so beautiful," I whispered to him, my hand caressing his face.

His eyes seemed to darken further, and he quickly snatched my hand off of him, all the gentleness gone from his face, and roughly lifted me and put me back in my seat.

"Put your clothes back on," he said angrily.

I felt tears sting my eyes as I put my bra back in place and bent down, found my shirt, and put it on. I calmed my emotions. Heaven forbid I look human.

I got out the car quickly slamming the door and headed for the warehouse, not saying one word to him. Entering with my head down, I didn't make eye contact with anyone. I walked into my room and shut the door. Leaning my body against it, I closed my eyes, letting the tears flow out of sheer frustration. *How can someone make me feel the way I do and make me so angry at the same time?* Lifting my hand I touched my neck; I could still feel his lips there. With my fingertips I touched my lips, swollen from his kisses. My body still tingled from the aftermath of what we just did in the car, but most of all I felt a deep pain in my heart. I placed my hand over my heart and opened my eyes, realization and dread hitting me full force. I was in love with Ian.

The scent of their arousal was thick in the air. It was intoxicating. Standing in the shadows, he watched as Ian and the girl, Scarlett, got out the car. She smelled so sweet, but she reeked with Ian's scent. She was enchanting. He felt his eyes blacken with desire for her. No wonder Ian was enamored with her. She rushed toward the door as if she couldn't wait to be away from Ian. He was not far behind her, his jaw clenched. Lover's spat? Ian paused as he was about to get to the door and turned, looking into the shadows as if he knew someone was lurking. Abel went deeper into the shadows. After a minute Ian walked in the warehouse.

Abel turned and headed the other way, shaking his head. He knew it was not a great decision to trust Ian, but he knew the queen was sweet on him, even carrying on an affair. Of course she was free to do what she wanted. Nothing bonded them together. But that didn't stop his hatred toward Ian. He'd hated him from day one, with his cocky attitude and bad-boy image he portrayed. The queen took immediate interest in him. He never took orders from the queen, and she would let him get away with it, almost as if she respected him for it. Now that he had double-crossed her, there was going to be hell to pay. No one doubled-crossed the queen and got away with it. Just ask her poor sister Flora.

Now he knew where they were hiding. It was just a matter of time. The queen wanted the X's dead, along with Ian, but the girl alive. He would see that it was done—more like looking forward to seeing it done, now that he has had a caught her sweet scent. He was going to enjoy watching Ian squirm for the first time. He was going to have him put to his knees and make him watch as he took a taste of the girl he was clearly enthralled with. Yes, that was what he would do before turning Ian to ash. He would make him suffer. Taking his cell phone out of his pocket, Abel smiled as he called the queen to tell her they had been located.

chapter

TWENTY

Celine was tidying up her living room in the uniform she was supposed to wear to the castle, a black dress cut just below the knee with a white apron in the front tied tightly around her waist. Her hair was pulled back tight in a bun, and she wore no makeup. Not that she needed any. Even in this ugly garb, she was still very beautiful. I walked over to the window and noticed the sun beginning to go down. Her brother sat on the sofa with a drink in his hand watching television. If it wasn't for the Scotch in his hand, I would have thought he was asleep. His thin body was leaned back; he wore a pair of grey sweatpants and a muscle shirt with holes in it, and his hair looked greasy, as if he needed a shower. I watched as Celine went about her business as though watching her brother drink his life was away was a normal occurrence.

"OK, John. I left the meatloaf in the oven. I have to get to work," she said, walking over to stand in front of the television to get his attention.

"OK, sis. Don't worry. Soon I will look for a job, and you don't have to worry about working," he said, slurring his words.

"John, just get yourself better. That is my main concern. Ever since Mom and Dad died, you haven't been the same. You have turned into this completely different person. You are so much better than this; you just have to realize it for yourself." She moved to sit on the couch beside him.

He looked away sadly from her. "I just can't seem to stop. This makes the pain go away," he said, holding up his drink. "It makes everything better."

"It may make it seem better, but look around you, John. It's not better; it's worse," she said sadly.

She got up from the couch and made her way back to the kitchen, grabbing her coat and purse. At the front door, she turned back to her brother with sadness. He continued to drink as if they hadn't just spoken. She closed the door quietly behind her. As she continued up the trail, I saw the look of fear and excitement as she made her way to the castle. I followed closely behind her. As we got closer, I saw the dark castle overhead. One of the guards at the gate let her in, and Gretchen stood waiting for her impatiently at the door as soon as she opened it.

"My dear, we have to hurry. The mistress is setting up a big dinner with all of the king's friends," she said, hurriedly grabbing Celine's hand and rushing her over to the kitchen. As we entered the kitchen, it was pure mayhem. Caterers and servants with dishes rushed frantically about.

"Come help me set the table," Gretchen said, handing Celine a case of forks and spoons made of 24-karat gold.

We walked into the dining area. It was very medieval looking. A huge crystal chandelier hung from the ceiling. Thick, long, deep red curtains hung from the windows. A beautiful antique wooden dining table that looked like it would seat at least twenty people stood in the center of the room. An ivory linen runner ran across the table beautifully. Gretchen and Celine worked quickly. As Gretchen placed the plates, Celine followed placing the forks and spoons neatly beside them. The doorbell sounded, and they both jumped, startled.

"Come. The guests have started to arrive. We must set up our first course," Gretchen said, smoothing her hair.

They went into the kitchen again and began to prep the first course—your basic garden salad with fresh greens and a balsamic vinaigrette dressing. I heard the guest start to come into the dining room, their chatter carrying over into the kitchen. I left Celine to see who had arrived. I saw Edrick right away. He stood out against the rest of the men, his presence unmistakable. He sat next to Con. All the other X's were there too. The door swung open, and they all rose in unison as the king and his bride to be entered. The king smiled at his guests and shook Edrick's hand.

"I would love to present to you my new bride and soon-to-be queen, Ezarbet."

Ezarbet looked at the king with a fake look of love. I watched as everyone greeted her but noticed how Edrick's eyes narrowed as he looked upon her. Did he also know she was deceitful? They all waited until the king was seated before any of them sat back down. One of the servants came out holding an antique-looking wine bottle. It had a bejeweled gold casing over it. She started to pour the red liquid into each of the glasses. I smelled the air, inhaling the scent of blood. Everyone drank it but Ezarbet, who had water.

The servants started to make the rounds serving the first course, one servant starting on each end of the table. Celine came out holding a tray of salad, and I watched as she and Edrick made eye contact. I heard her intake of breath and her heart beating a little faster. She started on the king's side, placing the salad in front of him and moving to the right, placing the next salad in front of Ezarbet. She noticed no one eating except for Ezarbet. I saw her swallow as she realized they were all vampires.

After her long shift was done, Celine was exhausted, and rightful so. She grabbed her coat and made her way out of the castle. She seemed a little disappointed that Edrick had made no further eye contact with her at the dinner. She started to make her way out of the castle, a solider letting her out of the gate. The night was cold and brisk. She heard a twig snap and turned in fear, but there was nothing. When she turned back around, Edrick stood in front of her. She let out a gasp, putting her hand over her mouth to stifle a scream.

"Oh, God! You scared me half to death! How did you do that?" she whispered to him.

He smiled at her.

"I am sorry; I didn't mean to frighten you. I am not used to being around a human. Vampires are very quick. It's almost like teleporting."

"Do you like being a vampire?" she asked him. They both began to walk again.

"It has its moments. It's a dark world. I got turned by Con. He is my best friend. I was dying from a battle wound. He found me near death and saved me. I was grateful to him; I mean, my God, he saved my life. But he gave me both a miracle and a curse."

She didn't say anything to him, just let him talk.

"It can get lonely, I guess. We live forever. We can run free in the darkness, but the sun would be our worst enemy. I can't even remember what the sun looks like."

"You mentioned last night that you didn't want to think this was a dream again."

He nodded his head. "Yes. When Con turned me, I inherited his gifts."

"Gifts?"

"Yes. Some vampires have gifts. I am a foreseer. We can see the future. I saw you," he said, smiling down at her.

"You saw me?" she asked.

"Yes."

"Well, what did you dream about?"

He paused for a second; I watched as he decided how much he could reveal to her without freaking her out.

"I dreamt that you came into my life and changed everything."

Then everything seemed to go blank as I fast-forwarded in time to the present. I was at a New Year's Eve party. It was not your normal balloons everywhere celebration. This was a sophisticated party. The men wore black suits and ties and the women wore beautiful, lavish ball gowns. There were butlers serving champagne in flute glasses and caviar. I saw myself dressed in a red strapless ball gown with a sweetheart top that dipped very low, hugging my curves beautifully. My hair was down and parted to the side in such a way that it made me look very old Hollywood. I could see that I was wearing my mother's diamond chandelier earrings—the perfect accessory.

I stood next to a man who was chatting away with me. He was very good looking, tall and lean with dark hair slicked perfectly to the side and dashing blue eyes. He had on a black suit with a white collared shirt and black tie. For some reason, I got the creeps from this man. There was just something not right with this picture. I watched, as I was talking with him, how his eyes kept dipping to my cleavage. What the hell was I doing here? These people looked to be high rollers. I looked around and saw Big Red wearing a suit and tie; it was tailored beautifully to his huge body. He looked great, but what the hell was he doing there? He stood in the far corner, looking over at the man and me. It was quite obvious we were on a mission, but for what? What the hell did a swanky New Year's Eve party have to do with the queen?

I watched as the man led me to the dance floor as a jazz band played a nice slow song. My red lips formed a smile as he led me, his hand on the small of my back. Once we reached the center of the dance floor, his hands went to my waist, bringing me closer to his body, and I wrapped my arms around his neck. We started to move to the sound of the music. I watched as I looked over to Big Red, making eye contact with him across the room. He nodded. What the hell was going on?

"OK. We have five minutes before the countdown, ladies and gentlemen," a small man with a microphone announced. "Thank you all for attending New York Bank's Annual Celebration. It is great to celebrate with our VIP customers. To all of our new clients, we welcome you. Please grab a champagne glass and let's toast the New Year together."

I watched as the dark-haired man whispered something in my ear and I threw my head back, laughing. He whisked me away from the dance floor, stopped a butler with a tray, and grabbed two champagne glasses, handing me one. I brought it up to my lips, taking a sip. A man approached and started to talk to him. I watched as I gazed across the room, nonchalantly. I brought the glass to my lips again and then froze, stunned by who I saw across the room.

I followed my other self's gaze and saw Ian. He wore a suit that fit him to perfection with a bow tie. He looked amazing. James Bond, eat your heart out. I looked over to myself and watched my face flush for an instant, and then it was gone. It was as if I'd put up a wall. I seemed unfazed by his presence. The man on the mic came on again and began the countdown. The dark-haired man came back to me, and I smiled up at him as he wrapped his arm around my waist. I looked over to Ian as he stared at me and this man. He was not happy.

"Five…four…three…two…one…Happy New Year!" everyone yelled in unison.

I watched as I looked over to Ian again, arching my eyebrow and licking my lips, taunting him. I turned back to look up at the dark-haired man. His head was lowered as he looked at me with desire clear in his eyes. I slid my hand up the front of his suit, wrapping my hand around his neck, and brought his head slowly to mine as I kissed him—while Ian stood there and watched.

chapter

TWENTY ONE

Sweat was gleaming from my forehead; the sword was heavy in my hand. After practicing with Con for over an hour, I felt like a professional. It all came so naturally for me, as if I'd been doing this for years. Once again Con lunged for me with his sword. I swiftly blocked with mine, our swords slapping together and making a loud clinking sound. I bent down quickly, doing a leg sweep and making him fall onto his back hard. Putting my foot on his wrist hard, I made him release his sword. I swiftly raised my sword and brought it down, pointing it at his heart. He smiled at me in approval and I smiled back, offering my hand to help him up.

"Well done, Scarlett," Zayah said, walking over to us. Smiling, she handed me a bottle of water. She grabbed Con's hand, and he looked at her adoringly. She nuzzled close to him.

"Thanks," I said, feeling a bit awkward as I watched their exchange. I took the bottle from her and started drinking. The water was so refreshing against my dry throat. I looked over to where Ian stood, silently watching. I was hoping to see approval in his eyes, but there was nothing—no expression, blank, giving nothing away. *Damn him.*

"We have to show you how to use a gun," Con said, breaking my stare from Ian.

"A gun? Do you think that's necessary?" I asked nervously.

I'd never used a gun before in my life. The first time I'd actually seen a firearm was the night before with Ian. Just the thought of holding a gun freaked me out.

"Yes. Now we are dealing with the wolves. Silver bullets can kill them, or a chop to the head. Silver can hurt us as well. Wolves are quick and ferocious. They heal just as quickly as we do. They have been our sworn enemy for centuries," Zayah said.

"We have to find Liam. He is the key somehow. I don't know how or why, but he is going to be on our side." I said, nodding my head.

Con nodded, walked over to a huge locker, and opened it. Walking over to us was Derek, the arms specialist. He had dark hair cut very short and green eyes. He was very tall and, like the rest of the X's, built to perfection. Tattoos of skulls and fire covered his huge arms, some looking demonic. He wore a muscle shirt. When he turned, I could tell the shirt hid an even bigger tattoo on his back. He gave off a "don't even try to fuck with me" attitude. Like Big Red, I would give him a nickname. "Skull" would suit him just fine. He held open the door for Con.

"I will let Derek take over from here; I know how to use, but he is better at explaining," Con said, making room for him.

Inside the locker were guns, 9 millimeters to 45 calibers. I walked over to the locker, my eyes widening. Holy shit! I was supposed to use these? Skull grabbed the smaller of the guns and held it out to me. I took it tentatively. I had never held a gun in my hands before, but then again, I'd never held a sword either. Something told me I'd better get used to this. I twisted and turned it in my hand. It felt much heavier than I would have imagined.

"Come," Skull said and led me to the shooting area.

A shooting target hung a few feet away—a white sheet of paper with the black outline of a body.

"The gun you have is a Beretta Px4. There is safety on it," he said, showing me where it was. I clicked it back.

"OK. Now just relax and put your feet apart. Straighten your body and shoot."

I took a deep breath and exhaled. I zoned in on my target and, with no hesitation, began to shoot; I shot until there were no bullets left. Oh, my God. What a rush! There was nothing more badass than that. Skull pressed a button, and the shooting target slid to us.

"How did I do?" I asked, trying to get a look.

Skull didn't say anything. He just held the sheet up to me. I was shocked. All my bullets went straight to the heart. I couldn't believe it.

"Nice work, prophet," Bastian said, walking over to us.

"Thanks, Big Red," I said, smiling at him. Ever since our run-in, we had a silent understanding. He respected me, not as his leader but as his equal. He smiled back as he heard his nickname, and I knew what Zayah was talking about before. He was starting to grow on me. Apparently he could be charming when he wasn't an asshole. Since my vision of him, I felt myself wanting to talk to him more, get to know him better. I felt connected with him.

"OK. Now let's talk business. The queen has resources everywhere—vampires, wolves, and humans," Con said, folding his arms around his chest, his dark face showing anger.

"What do you mean humans? The blood slaves you were talking about before?"

"No. The humans that work for her; we call them sentinels. They work personally for her—lawyers, cops, bankers—anyone who would help her in the daylight," said Skull.

I let out a frustrated breath. *Fuck!* "What do we do?" I asked.

"The queen is always on the move. We either have to find her through her sentinels or make her come to us."

I nodded. *Let that bitch come to us.*

Logan came forward holding a manila folder in his hands. He had long blond hair tied up in a ponytail and razor-like hazel eyes. His nose looked a little crooked—perhaps a few broken noses at one point. He wore a fitted black shirt and leather pants. You would think a man in leather pants would be questionable, but man did he wear those pants. He was a fine specimen of a man. *His nickname will be Razor*, I decided.

He handed me the manila folder, and I opened it. Inside the envelope was a paper with someone's profile: Michael Pearson, age thirty-three, President of New York Bank. Attached was a black and white picture of the guy. I paused as I looked down at the picture. It was the dark-haired man from my vision, the one I practically made out with in front of Ian. This profile had everything on it: his address and social security number, even what restaurants the guy ate at. With the Internet nothing was sacred anymore.

I looked at Razor questioningly.

"This is our sentinel. He handles part of the queen's finances here in the states. This could be our lead to find out where she is," he said, his eyes turning a gleaming black.

"OK. He works in New York Bank in Manhattan. I'll go check it out tomorrow. I could go and act like a customer wanting to do business," I said, putting the papers back in place and closing the folder. I now knew why I was at the New Year's Eve party. But why the coldness toward Ian?

"I will go with you," Hugo said from behind me.

"Great. Then that settles it," I said and looked back over to Con. "Practice over?"

"Yes. Great job." He turns and started talking to Razor and Zayah. I turned toward Hugo.

"Looks like we'll be detectives tomorrow," I said, smiling at him. He started to walk with me toward my room. He was silent. I had a feeling something was on his mind and turned toward him.

"What is it, Hugo?" I asked. I grabbed onto his arm, stopping him from walking. He looked so tired. His soft brown eyes looked inflamed, taking on that haunted look again. What was he hiding?

"Nothing," he said with a fake smile.

"I trust you, Hugo, but when will you learn to trust me?" I asked softly.

"Get some rest. We have a long day ahead of us. We will talk more tomorrow," he said, looking away.

"Promise?"

He looked at me, momentarily stunned. I could tell Hugo had not been around the female population much. I couldn't help but let out a giggle. He let out laugh too. He bowed his head at me as if he was bowing to a queen.

"Yes. I promise."

"OK, buddy. I am going to hold you to that. Goodnight!" I said, pointing my finger at him. I opened my door and went into my bedroom, closing the door behind me.

I turned, my smile vanishing. Ian was in my room, apparently waiting for me, dressed in a black T-shirt and fitted jeans, his hands in his pockets. Never had I seen jeans that looked so good on a man. I quickly got pissed at myself. *Focus. You're pissed at him.*

"What are you doing here? Whatever happened to 'Knock, knock. Can I please come in?'" I asked, annoyed at him for many things—most of all for making me feel the way I feel for him.

"I don't want you to go out tomorrow," he said, his eyes turning dark, shrugging his shoulders.

You would think that dark stare would scare me. It would scare any normal person, but not me. If anything it pissed me off further.

"Funny. I don't remember asking your permission." Walking away from the door, I stood in front of him purposely trying to get something, anything, from him. *Show me you care, Ian,* my mind screamed at him. *Show me you're not this cold person everyone seems to think you are.*

He let out a frustrated breath, yanking his hands from his pockets and roughly putting one through his hair.

"Damn it, Scarlett, it's not safe. You are not trained enough to be out," he yelled at me.

"I can take care of myself. Besides, Hugo is coming with me," I said, shaking my head at him.

He let out a curse turning his back on me. I slowly walked to him, coming to stand behind him. I reached out and touched his back, holding my breath. He flinched but didn't pull away from my touch. What was Ian's story? Why did he feel the need to hide from me? I placed my hand on his arm, turning him toward me, and he turned slowly. His eyes were black. I reached up and touched his face, light beard stubble prickling against my hand. He was beautiful. *Mine! This cold, cold man was mine.* I knew that with every fiber of my being.

"You know, you never asked me how I knew you when we first met," I whispered to him.

He said nothing, so I continued.

"I had a vision of you, before I met you. That's why I knew who you were when you first came to me," I continued.

His eyes turned even darker, lust in his gaze as they focused on my lips.

"You desired me before any other; you worshipped my body. You were gentle, loving, and warm. You kissed me as though it would be your last," I said, moving closer to him, letting him feel the warmth of my body.

"Did I now?" he whispered back. There was lust in his gaze, but coldness lurked there also. It was as if he wanted to prove something.

"Yes," I whispered nervously, not liking where this was leading but not caring.

He roughly grabbed me and yanked my head back, kissing me hard, his hand getting knotted in my hair, tongue invading my mouth. He kissed me so roughly he drew blood. I tasted copper as he had his way with me. I tried to push him off, but he quickly grabbed my hands and put them behind my back. His hands held me still to his assault. I let him have his way until I couldn't anymore. I gasped in pain, and that's when he released me and shoved me away from him. My hands reached my bruised lips, and I watched as he retreated. Before he opened the door he turned and looked back at me, anger in his eyes.

"I am not the man from your vision," he growled and slammed my door shut.

chapter

TWENTY TWO

I was in a cave. It was dark, deep, and damp. I saw light, and I slowly walked toward it, tripping over some rocks. Where was the light coming from? I heard a high-pitch squeak above my head and looked up, but it was too high and dark to tell. Bats? I walked more quickly toward the light. Approaching I saw lit candles forming a circle and a fire going, making the cave luminous. Someone was standing in the center of the circle—a woman in a long black cape with a hood chanting softly. Her voice was beautiful, almost hypnotizing. She was holding a glass and mixing different ingredients. The concoction bubbled up and turned a black color. She poured it into the fire, making the fire rise. Stepping out of the circle, she went to a cage with a beautiful white dove in it. She took it out, gently touched its head, and whispered to it, going back into the circle.

"I am sorry, my friend, but this must be done," she said as she raised the bird above her head in one hand and took out a dagger with the other from the pocket of her cape. She started chanting again, bringing the dove down, and stabbed it, its blood coming out in droplets over the fire. The fire rose and black smoke filled the cave. It made me cough, and I fanned in front of my face to get rid of the smoke. I could not see her face, but I knew she was crying. I heard it in her voice as she chanted.

"Black as night, black as your heart, black as your soul…May your eyes be as black as night," she whispers over and over again, falling onto her knees, rocking back and forth.

The cave began to clear, and I could see her much more clearly now. A wind passed through, and I felt a chill go up my spine. Suddenly a ghostly presence joined us, talking to the witch, guiding her, whispering approval of the spell she was casting. She was powerful. I felt it. The fire went out, leaving black smoke in its wake. With the spell done, she lifted her cape off of her head. Beautiful red hair cascaded out, and I saw emerald green eyes full of tears. I gasped, my hand going to my mouth, my eyes going wide.

"You left me no choice, sister. Now instead of your beauty, people will see the true you. They will see your black heart," Flora whispered.

I was brought into the future. It was dark again. Flora was running barefoot in a dirty, torn dress. The area was heavily wooded, the trees so thick you could barely see where you were going. She was running for her life. She tried to run faster, but she has no strength. I felt her getting out of breath. She looked malnourished and weak. How long had she been running? She was so tired. She tripped over a branch and fell to the ground, scraping her knees and hands. She gasped from the pain but scrambled up, not looking back, not giving up. I admired her. I followed her until we reached a stone wall. She let out a scream of frustration. Her tiny hands balled into fists, she hit the wall in anger.

"No. This cannot be," she said to herself. She leaned her head against the wall, her shoulders dropping in failure.

I walked over to her. I reached out to touch her shoulder and remembered that she wouldn't feel me. I wished I could help her. Who was after her? I felt the hairs on the back of my neck stand. *Vampire.* She was now the queen's enemy. I had to help her, but how? Again I reached out to touch her, and she looked right at me as if she felt my presence, her beautiful emerald eyes full of hope as she saw me.

"Help me, Scarlett," she whispered to me.

I yanked my hand back, surprised. *Oh, my God. She saw me. She can see me!* Before I could ask her where we were, we both heard a sound of someone upon us. Turning she let out a scream at the sight of a vampire right in front of her.

Waking up gasping, I pulled the sheets off of me, got out of bed in a hurry, and began pacing back and forth. What was I supposed to do? Visions were in the future, so this hadn't happened yet to Flora. Had it? *Oh, my God. Flora, Queen Ezarbet's twin sister, cursed her to have eyes black as night forever.* I stopped and smiled. It was a pretty ballsy thing to do, and I admired her for that, but what had it cost her when her sister found out? My smile faded. She looked like she was starved and dirty, her red hair losing its luster and once-beautiful peach skin going pale. Her sister must have had no mercy to her, but why keep her alive? Why not just kill her? Was it to make her suffer?

Feeling a headache coming on, I sat on the bed, putting my head in my hands. Raising my head I looked at the time: 10:00 a.m. It was time to go to the bank and find out more about this Michael Pearson. Maybe he was the key to finding Flora. Walking to the bathroom, I turned on the shower. I headed to my bureau and took out a cute, fitted beige sweater and some skinny jeans. Zayah had gone back to my apartment and gotten a few of my things. Thank God for that. Wearing full black on a daily basis was making me feel like I was going to a funeral.

Going into the steamy bathroom, I took off my clothes. Opening the shower curtain, I let the warmth of the water hit my face. So much was going on in my head. Queen Ezarbet, Damian, Flora, and most of all Ian; he was always on my mind. Watching him walk out the door yesterday made me want to march out after him and prove to him he did care for me. *Damn him!* I showered and washed my hair quickly. Turning off the water, I wrapped one towel around my head and one around my body. Stepping out of the shower, I walked in front of the fogged mirror and wiped it, undoing my hair, letting it cascade down my back. I grabbed the blow dryer and started to blow dry my hair, combing my fingers through it. I then started to apply my makeup, using lip gloss and black mascara.

Going into my room, I put on my underwear and matching bra, choosing the sexy matching one and thinking to myself I'd picked it not because of Ian but just because, which I knew deep down was a lie. After putting on my beige sweater and skinny jeans, I found a pair of flats and put on my leather jacket. I looked in the mirror and smiled, satisfied. Walking out the door, I found Hugo waiting for me. He smiled softly. He looked better no longer having bloodshot eyes, looking more rested and freshly shaven. He was also wearing that hideous trench coat again. I promised myself we would go shopping. Hugo was in need of a makeover, and as soon as I could I was going to put that damn coat in a fire.

"You look beautiful. Would you like some breakfast before we go?" he asked, walking over to me.

"Thank you, and no. We can get something on our way," I said. From the corner of my eye I saw Ian. He looked pissed, his eyes dark. His stance was also telling, with his arms folded over his chest. I was getting used to this look of his. I smirked.

"*Give him hell,*" Hugo's voice whispered in my head.

I looked over at Hugo, and he winked at me.

"Shall we go on our adventure?" I asked. Taking him by the arm, we made our way out, not looking back. I smiled as I heard Ian growl.

The crisp, cold air hits me first as we headed out of the warehouse. The sun was out, bringing little warmth, but it was beautiful. Even though I didn't love the holidays, I still loved winter.

"Ian says we can use his car," Hugo said, tossing me the keys.

I quickly caught them with one hand, beaming. *Holy shit. I get to drive this!* I tried to hide my excitement as I rushed over to the driver's side. This was going to be fun.

"Get in," I said, giggling.

Sliding into the seat, I was automatically engulfed with Ian's scent. My body started tingling. Hugo got in and looked at me. I wondered how much he really knew about Ian and me. I was sure everyone knew by now.

"Well aren't you going to start her up?" he asked, smiling.

"Yes." I started the car, and I couldn't control my girlish squeal.

Hugo laughed. I laughed with him; his laugh was infectious. I loved the playful Hugo.

"On second thought, maybe I should drive," he joked, buckling his seat belt.

"Unless you want to get your nose broken, hands off, buddy," I said. We headed for New York.

The hop onto I-95 was pretty decent, with surprisingly little traffic. I knew I was speeding, but I couldn't help it. It felt so great in this car; it felt great to be out of the warehouse, period. Using the signal light, I quickly passed a white BMW, its male driver looking at the car admiringly. I glanced at Hugo, who looked a little nervous. I smiled. My Hugo, always the worrier. We passed the Triborough Bridge and I went a few exits before exiting the highway. Getting off the ramp I was stopped at a red light. I started to explore the car. First was the radio. It looked like it hadn't been turned on at all, ever. There were no CDs, no playlist. Turning on the radio, I put it on my favorite station. Adele was playing, her beautiful voice surrounding us.

Taking another left, we drove a few more blocks before I saw the bank. There was nothing like being in the heart of the city—taxi drivers everywhere, the hustle and bustle of city workers, the sidewalks filled with people either going to work or shopping. Finding a parking spot was going to be an issue. I made a quick turn into a parking lot. Rolling down my window, I paid the parking attendant twenty-five bucks, which was a rip-off, but I wasn't about to argue now. The lot was filled; I drove up to the third level and found an empty space. *Thank goodness.* Parking in the spot, I put the car into park and took the keys out of the ignition. I looked over at Hugo, and he was no longer Hugo the man but was now Hugo the puppy.

"So, yeah, what's the plan?" I asked, starting to get nervous about our grand scheme.

Hugo barked at the glove compartment. Cocking my head to the side, I reached over and opened it. *My savings account, of course. Good one. This is how I will talk to Michael Pearson.* Putting the booklet in my purse, I looked down at Hugo.

"OK," I said, patting his head. "Oh, honey, I don't have a leash for you. Mommy will have to pick you up," I said, teasing him. Hugo let out a warning growl, and I laughed.

Getting out of the car with Hugo in one arm and my purse in the other, I made my way out of the parking lot. I had to walk a few blocks before I saw the bank. "The New York Bank of Investments," the sign said in bold gold letters. I walked in through the big glass doors and was even more impressed. Beautiful brown and copper tile work covered the floors and a huge art-deco statue made of porcelain stood in the main lobby. It looked more like a modern hotel than a bank. The architecture was exceptional.

Looking around the place, I noticed it was very busy with customers. Business must be good.

I watched as a balding man came out of his office, straitening his tie as he approached me eagerly. He had on a gold name tag with black lettering: George Prescott, Investment Coordinator.

"Hello, miss. Welcome to New York Bank of Investments. How may I assist you?"

"Hi. I need to open an account, and I would love some help on how to invest," I said, smiling and petting Hugo's head.

"Great. I would love to help you. Please follow me," he said cheerfully.

I quietly follow behind him. His office was moderate in size with a cherry-colored wooden desk and high-tech computer system. On his desk stood a picture of who I assumed to be his wife and kids in a black frame.

"Please have a seat," he said, standing behind his desk and putting his arm out to the black leather chair in front of it.

Smiling and putting my purse down, I sat, placing Hugo on my lap; He automatically lay down, his head resting on my knee.

"OK. First I need you to start filling out these forms," he said, having a seat and handing me a clipboard with paperwork and a pen.

"I would need to transfer funds. Would that be a problem?"

"It shouldn't be. What type of funds?"

Bending down, I reached into my purse. Finding what I needed, I handed him my bank book. He took it, smiling, and I watched as his eyes widened. *Yeah, I was shocked too, buddy,* I thought to myself.

"Um, well, yes. This will not be a problem at all. Do you have identification with you? This just has to be verified first," he said, coughing and clearing his throat.

Holy shit! ID? The only ID I had was the one with my foster care name. Hugo let out a little whimper and sat up a little, looking down at my purse.

"Ah, yes, identification. Of course. Never leave home without it," I said, trying to buy time.

I bent down grabbing my purse, putting down Hugo, and fumbled through it. There in the front pocket was my Identification card with my real name on it: Scarlett *De Laurentiis.* My finger gently ran across the name. It seemed unreal. This was who I really was. George let out a cough, trying to get my attention. Letting out a breath, I looked up and handed it to him, picking up Hugo once again.

"OK. I will be right back," he said, beaming at me.

I waited until he left and looked down at Hugo.

"Shit that was close. You're a lifesaver," I whispered, scratching his ear. I picked up the clipboard and looked at all the forms I needed to fill out. A thought crossed my mind. I looked down at Hugo again.

"Do you mind?" I asked him.

I placed the clipboard at eye level with Hugo, and he placed his little paw on it. I blinked, and it was completely filled out. I looked at it amazed, my eyes widening. This was great; I loved having a warlock as my sidekick.

"OK. All has been verified, Miss De Laurentiis," George said as he walked in a few minutes later, but he was with someone. I recognized him right away; it was Michael Pearson. He was much better looking in person than in my vision—blue eyes, chiseled chin, hair was slicked to the side, and tan skin, as if he'd been on vacation recently. I wondered if it was for business or pleasure. *Sentinel!* my mind screamed.

"Hello, Miss De Laurentiis. George just informed me we are going to have you as one of our VIP clients. It's a pleasure making your acquaintance. I am the president of New York Bank of Investments, Michael Pearson," he said his eyes flirtatious as he held out his hand for me to shake. I placed my hand in his and pretended to be charmed.

"The pleasure is mine, Mr. Pearson," I said, smiling flirtatiously.

"Please, call me Michael," he said, holding my hand a little longer than needed. I felt a chill go up my spine. This man gave me the creeps. Hugo let out a growl, and Michael let go quickly in fear of getting bitten. I snatched my hand quickly away.

"It's OK, honey. He's so protective. Sorry," I said, petting Hugo's head, smiling down at him.

"Of course. I would be too if I were him," he said, looking a little annoyed. "George, we have other clients. Go see if Beth needs assistance, please."

"Of course, Mr. Pearson," George said hurriedly and rushed out of the room.

I stood, not liking being in a room alone with this guy, even though technically Hugo was here. Suddenly the office seemed too small.

"Well, here are my forms. I have to go, but I am looking so forward to hearing about my different options of investments."

He smiled again at me, fished a business card out of his pocket, and handed it to me.

"Yes. I am looking forward to helping you. Now here is my business card. My cell phone is on there. Please do not hesitate to call me whenever you wish," he said softly, his eyes hinting at something more. Hugo let out another growl.

I smiled back trying very hard not to roll my eyes. I always hated the guy who knew he was attractive, and knowing he was a sentinel didn't help matters. I had to use what little acting skills I had not to seem totally repulsed by this guy.

I took the business card and looked down at it briefly. It was ivory linen stock paper with gold embossed lettering.

"Thank you. You will be hearing from me soon," I said.

"Sooner rather than later?"

"Perhaps," I said, shrugging my shoulders. As we walked out of the office, I felt his hand on the small of my back, leading the way to the exit. It took everything in me not to flinch from his touch.

"I look forward to hearing from you, Miss De Laurentiis," he said, holding the door open for me.

"Please, call me Scarlett," I said, turning to look at him briefly before walking away. I felt his eyes on me the whole time. I was getting good at this. Inwardly I smiled. *Sucker.*

In the parking lot, I set Hugo in his seat, putting my purse on the floor of the passenger's side, and started the ignition. As I started driving, I looked over and watched in amazement as Hugo transformed himself to…well, himself. *Holy shit. Did that really just happen?*

"Does it hurt when you do that?" I asked, focusing on the road again.

"No. It's a spell. I can turn into pretty much anything. I choose dog more often because people like dogs," he said, shrugging his shoulders.

"Whoa, how perceptive of you," I said, laughing at him. I made a sharp right, making him buckle his seat belt.

"Hey there are a bunch of boutiques in Westport where I worked. I need to get a few things," I said, looking at Hugo sideways.

He looked as if he was about to argue but nodded his head. I smiled. *Smart man. He chooses his battles wisely.*

chapter

TWENTY THREE

Walking side by side with Hugo was just as weird as walking with Ian. Of course, with Ian, everyone was captivated by his amazing looks and great body, especially the females. But with Hugo, there was something mysterious about him that could not be overlooked. He was the type of man who'd obviously had to grow up quick. He looked wise for one so young. *He must be in his, what, late twenties?* His hair needed to be cut, and that damn trench coat. I didn't even want to think about the trench coat. Reaching our destination, I opened the door, holding it open for him, and we walked into my salon. Looking around for Fernando, I spotted him talking to a client he was finishing up with. I waved my hand at him and he smiled, holding out his hand, letting me know he would be with me in a minute.

"You're getting your hair done?" Hugo asked, confused.

"No. I'm not. You are," I said, beaming at him.

His eyes narrowed. Oh boy, he was pissed.

"Look, it will be a quick trim. No big deal," I said, reassuring him.

He let out a breath, and I knew I had him. Fernando walked over to us.

"Scarlett. What brings you back? Your hair is looking great, mi amore," he said, giving me kisses on each cheek.

"Fernando, I have a friend that I need you to give your special touch to," I said, grabbing Hugo by the arm and pulling him forward.

Fernando eyed Hugo up and down, clearly checking him out. Hugo shifted uncomfortably.

"OK. I will see what I can do," Fernando said, leading Hugo to follow him.

Hugo reluctantly took off his coat and sat in the chair. Fernando and I stood behind him, both of us studying him. He met our stare in the mirror.

"I really don't see why I would need a haircut."

"Men," Fernando said, shaking his head.

I let out a giggle and started to cough when I noticed that Hugo was not laughing or smiling.

"It's going to be fine; I promise. Do you trust me?"

He gave a long pause before answering me. "Yes. Yes I do."

Nodding my head, I put my hand on Fernando's shoulder and whispered to him.

"OK. I will be right back," I said to Hugo.

Before he could argue with me, I stepped outside and walked to a men's clothing store nearby. The sales clerk greeted me right away. I smiled and told him I was just browsing. I saw a leather jacket that I knew would be perfect for him. I grabbed some other items that would look good on him. Thank God I knew about clothes. The great thing about my line of work was that I could look at someone and know right away what their size was. I walked over to the jean rack and picked a few fitted pairs for him and some T-shirts. Going over to the shoes, I picked a basic black shoe that he could either dress up or down. Walking to the counter with my hands full, I set the items down.

I thought that was all I needed, until something caught my eye. Looking at the accessories, I saw a rosary necklace. It wasn't your standard rosary chain. It was encrusted with black crystals and had a medium size cross with the same black stones on it. I took it down from the small rack it hung on and knew I was finished. The cashier rang me up and handed me my receipt. He wished me a Merry Christmas. *Jesus, what's today's date?* Looking at my receipt on my way out, I realized it was Christmas Eve.

Holy crap. I hadn't even noticed. I'd been so caught up in everything, I couldn't believe it had only been a few days since my life was turned upside down. Trying not to get in a depressed mood, I walked quickly back to the salon. Hopefully Hugo hadn't put Fernando under some type of spell. Walking in, my hands full of bags, I stopped in mid-stride, dropping the bags. There he stood with his hands in his pockets, waiting patiently for me. *Oh, my God.* Hugo looked hot. His hair was cut short on the sides, but long enough on the top to give a nice flip in the front. It wasn't like he didn't look good to begin with, but whoa; this haircut did wonders for him.

"I know, I know. I am a genius," Fernando said, fanning himself.

"Yes, you are," I said, laughing. "You look great," I said, walking over to Hugo smiling.

He smiled uncomfortably and shrugged his shoulders. "OK. So you trust me, right?"

He looked at me questioningly but nodded his head.

"I have a gift for you." Going over to the bags, I took out the jeans, black T-shirt, and shoes. "Here. Put these on. The bathroom is over there."

He took the clothes from me and headed to the bathroom. It seemed like forever before he came out, holding his old clothes in his hand and looking uncomfortable with his new look. He looked great. Fernando let out a squeal of delight and clapped his hands.

"Oh, my, Scarlett…Where did you find him? He is muy caliente," he whispered to me, batting his lashes at Hugo.

Smiling, I walked over to Hugo.

"I have this as well." I reached up on tiptoes and placed the rosary over his head and around his neck. It looked perfect on him.

He touched it momentarily and smiled. Even though he didn't tell me, I knew he liked it.

"Thank you," he said softly to me.

"You're welcome. Now come on. I am starving," I said, rushing to pick up the rest of the bags.

Hugo went to put on his trench coat, and I almost let out a scream.

"No!" I yelled, startling him. "I got you this too." Taking the leather jacket out of the bag, I handed it over.

He set the trench coat down and put it on. It fit him perfectly.

"Let's go," he said, leading the way out of the salon.

I bent down and grabbed the rest of the bags, following him out the door. Before we walked out, Fernando called out to me.

"But Scarlett, what do you want me to do with this?" he asked, holding the trench coat away from his body as if in fear he would catch something off of it.

"Burn it."

Outside, Hugo grabbed the bags from me. *The proper gentlemen*, I thought to myself.

"Hey, you want to grab a bite to eat? I am starving. We can go to Martins; we can sit and eat there."

"Sure," Hugo replied, letting me take the lead.

I had been to Martin's maybe twice since I'd been employed at the W. It was a cute little café that sold home-made soups and sandwiches. The décor was very homey, with comfortable sofas in the center. It was a place where you could get good food, read a good book, and relax at the same time. My stomach growled as soon as we walked in. I could smell the different varieties of soup they were serving from the chicken stock of the chicken noodle to the fresh onions of the French onion soup. I looked up at their bulletin where they had their specials written and decided I was going to get a panini with grilled chicken, fresh moz-zarella, and basil with a side of their chicken noodle soup.

I placed our order with the cashier, and Hugo stood waiting for the food while I went to get a table for us to sit at. I picked a table by the window. It was so pretty outside with the sun shining in. I sat down, closing my eyes, savor-ing the warmth on my face. The door jingled open and a cold gust of wind came in. Opening my eyes, I watched a woman with a baby walk in. The baby boy was about six months old, his chubby cheeks red from the cold. He wore a navy blue coverall; his big blue eyes almost seemed too big for his small face. I waved my hand and smiled at him. He smiled back, showing off his two front teeth.

I couldn't imagine the world that Queen Ezarbet wanted. Were there blood slaves already being held against their will? As I looked outside, I tried to imagine the world overturned by vampires and wolves. Wolves would rule in the daylight, and vampires would rule the streets in the night. Families would be stripped away from each other, never to see each other again. I felt a heavy weight on my shoulders. I couldn't let this happen. I would find a way to stop her. I was confident in that. But at what cost? I would never get the chance to live a normal life. But as I looked back at the mother and child, I realized what my sacrifice was for. Hugo came with a tray of our food, and I dug in right away, happy to get away from my thoughts.

"Hugo, tell me about yourself," I asked, biting into my sandwich and looking at him curiously.

"There's not much to tell. I am from a small town in England. No brothers or sisters. My parents are dead," he said, his soft brown eyes looking haunted as he took a sip of his soup.

"How you did became a warlock?" I asked softly.

"Every warlock is born with a marking."

"Marking? As in birthmark?"

"Yes."

He stopped eating and took off his jacket, pulling his arm toward me. I saw it there on his forearm, a black mark that looked like a moon. I reached out and touched the mark. It felt like it was tattooed there. The mark of a warlock.

"So you said you were in the prophecy with me. How?"

"Before my father passed, he said I was to be your guardian. He said the guardian with the moon marking would come to aid the prophet." He stops talking, his voice trailing off as though there was more.

"What else does it say, Hugo?"

He looked away deep in thought, but he answered me. "It says the one with the moon marking and the one with the star marking will form as one to aid the prophet."

"Star marking?" I asked, confused.

He looked back at me, his soft brown eyes haunted.

"Yes. A witch."

My mouth shot open. Oh, my God. I couldn't have heard him right. A witch...and my vision. Was this the way I was supposed to help her?

"A witch. Hugo, I just had a vision of her," I whispered to him.

"What?" Hugo hissed as he leaned closer to me. "Who is she, Scarlett?"

I watched as his face paled, and he looked as if he was going to be sick. I felt like he knew my answer before I said her name.

"It was Flora that I saw...Queen Ezarbet's twin sister."

chapter

TWENTY FOUR

Everything seemed to blur for me after that last sentence with Hugo. I felt myself drift. I was in a bedroom with a fireplace crackling, illuminating the room with a romantic glow.

"What will she look like?" Celine whispered to Edrick.

I stopped breathing and froze in place. I was sharing a very intimate moment between my parents. They were under the covers. Celine's hair was down, and her creamy, pale shoulders were exposed. Edrick's chest was bared as he lay on his side looking down at her, his hand smoothing the hair from her forehead, his eyes black as he gazed upon her with love. It was a beautiful picture to capture of the two of them. I don't think I will ever forget how beautiful they looked together.

"She will be stunning. Long, dark hair, from me of course." He smiled. "She will have pale skin, and her eyes will represent who she is. She will be strong and brave, just like you."

"She sounds beautiful," she said, placing her hand on her stomach.

"Yes. Just like her mother," he said, leaning down and kissing her.

"Tell me more, please," she whispered.

They lay there in bed as she asked many questions concerning the prophecy, but Edrick only knew up to a certain point. He told her of how Ezarbet, who was now the queen, was going to reign and of the world order that was supposed to take over the future, and how I was the key to put an end to it.

"Will she miss us, Edrick?"

He smiled sadly and nodded his head. "Every day," he whispered.

I felt tears sting my eyes as I watched them. There was not a day I didn't think of them.

"I wish she could see us now," she said, tears beginning to roll down her face.

"She will. I promise you that. She will know how much we both loved her. Don't cry." With his index finger, he wiped at her tears. "If you stop crying, I will give you a present," he said. Reaching back to his nightstand, he grabbed a black velvet box with a white bow on it.

"Edrick, you didn't have to get me anything," she said, her watered eyes widening, shaking her head as she grabbed the box from him.

She untied the bow from the box and gently opened it. She gasped as she saw her gift. I didn't come closer to see it. I already knew what it was—a pair of diamond chandelier earrings.

"Oh, my. I don't know what to say. They're beautiful," she said as she touched them.

"Here. Put them on," He said as he took the box from her. She lifted her head a little as he put one in each ear.

They looked gorgeous on her. With her pale blond hair down and the white brilliance of the diamonds, she looked like royalty.

"I want to share myself with you completely," he said to her as she lay her head back down. He smoothed the hair back from her neck, and I saw the tell-tale mark of his bite.

"As soon as you let me drink from you, you became mine," he said to her.

She smiled up at him and touched his face.

"Yes," she whispered.

"The moment I envisioned you, I became enthralled. You have captured a part of me like no other. I want to become yours in every way possible. Will you be my blood mate?" he whispered to her.

"Yes," she said with no hesitation.

He smiled down at her, satisfied.

"Do I have your trust?" he asked softly.

"It is yours," she said.

"Do I have your love?"

"Always," she whispered.

He brought his wrist to his mouth and bit down. He tilted her head up, bringing it up to his bleeding wrist. She drank from him as he looked down at her, smoothing her hair back, encouraging her. As she finished, she leaned up and brought her body closer to his as he leaned down and kissed her, completing the ritual. I couldn't watch this anymore. I walked over to the window, crying silently, wrapping my arms around my midsection. Everything they would be going through, everything they would endure, was for *me*. I would never get a chance to say thank you. Looking up, I noticed that the windows were painted black so no sun could come through. *This must be Edrick's home.* The phone started ringing, breaking them apart and making Edrick growl with frustration as he leaned back and answered the phone.

"Edrick," he answered.

His face hardened as he listened to the caller.

"Are you sure?" he asked, his angry voice making Celine sit up, pulling the covers up as she looked at Edrick, worried.

"OK. I will be there as soon as I can." He waited for the reply and hung up, silent for a moment.

"Edrick, what is wrong?" Celine asked, clasping his hand.

"The king is dead," he said after a moment.

"Dead? How?" She gasped, putting her hand over her mouth.

"I don't know yet."

"It's begun, hasn't it?" she asked, but it didn't sound like a question.

"It's begun."

Everything went black, and I zoomed forward. Liam was there, and he was trying to reason with me, our voices rising with outrage, especially mine. He wore a flannel shirt with stonewashed jeans, his face looking angered and turning red. I seemed unfazed by his anger, not showing a glimpse of fear. Standing beside him was a woman that worked for the queen, Maylina. I looked around and noticed we were in a building that was not the warehouse. We seemed to be in another training center, but this was more high-tech with computers and monitoring devices set up. *What training center is this?* The X's came forward to see what all the commotion was.

"You don't understand. Things are not what they seem!" Liam yelled at me.

"I can't believe this. You have the balls to tell me that this is not what it seems! You shouldn't have brought her here. She cannot be trusted!" I yelled at him, pointing at the her angrily.

"Listen, I don't have to be here. Without me, you are fucked. I know everything there is to know about the queen. I knew this was a mistake coming here," she said, looking at Liam.

"Your goddamn right this was a mistake. Without your ancient buddies around, it seems you're the one that's fucked," I said softly to her, my eyes glowing bright.

She cocked her head to the side, arching her eyebrow, glad to take on the challenge I was silently giving her. She stepped forward. Liam quickly tried to get between us, but I stopped him with my stare. Her hair was jet black, her face so pale, and her blue eyes almost looked white. She wore leather gear. Her eyes began to go black as we began circling.

"This is going to be good. My money is on Scarlett," I heard Big Red say in the background.

Something told me this was going to be an epic battle. Not waiting for words, we went right at it. She took the first swing, and I caught her fist in my hand quickly, squeezing it. Her eyes widened, looking momentarily shocked as I showed her a brief glimpse of my power. To her astonishment I took complete advantage, front-kicking her right in her abdomen, making her hit the wall with a grunt. But with lightning speed she came back at me. I swung and she quickly blocked me, grabbed my arm, turned, and flung me over her shoulder, slamming me to the floor. *Holy shit!*

I quickly put my hands behind me and did a kip up, facing her off. She came at me again, jabbing and kicking. I easily blocked her, punching at her face and grabbing her long hair, twisting it around my hand. I turned, flinging her over my shoulder and making her hit a wall. I walked over to her sliding out a dagger from the sleeve of my pocket, ready to turn her to ash. I looked up to see Liam's reaction, and his eyes were an even brighter red, as if he was going to make his transformation to protect her, but Big Red was quickly at his side, shaking his head. What was his relationship to the woman I thought of as an enemy?

Turning my attention back to the fight, I saw that she sensed me walking toward her. She got up and kicked the dagger out of my hand, tackling me to the floor. She sat on me, and I kicked up with my legs, making her fall onto her back, and got on top of her quickly. As soon as I was on top, she rolled so she was once again on top. From there, the fight began to get sloppy, both of us exhausted. We began to roll back and forth until I get her onto her stomach. I grabbed her by the neck , one of my hands at her chin and the other at her head, twisting it, ready to snap it.

"*No!* Don't hurt her!" I heard a child scream. A little girl, maybe three years old, stood at the doorway with curly brown hair and tears in her big brown eyes, looking at Maylina like a child would a mother.

chapter

TWENTY FIVE

In the distance I heard a voice calling my name. Someone was gently shaking my shoulder. My vision started to fade. The little girl's eyes, filled with pure terror, were pointed straight at me, as if I was the bad guy.

"Scarlett, wake up," I heard Hugo's voice say in the distance.

I opened my eyes, rubbing them. *Where am I?* Sitting up I realized we were in Ian's car, and Hugo was sitting right next to me. *What the hell just happened?*

"You blacked out in the café," he said, reading my thoughts.

"Oh, God. I feel like I have the worst hangover ever," I said, even though I had never experienced a hangover in my life. "How did you get us out of there?"

"I used a shield, making us invisible. Your eyes just rolled back, and I knew you were having a vision," he said.

"Invisible? Will these visions come to me like this all the time?"

"With time I am sure you will come to control them."

"With time," I repeated. I grabbed the car keys out of my purse and started the car.

We didn't have time. With each vision, it felt like time was not on our side but on our enemies'. I told him every-thing—Flora cursing the queen for upsetting the balance; how she was locked in a cage, beaten and starved like an animal; how she was going to find a way to escape; and how she had communicated with me through my vision.

Hugo became quiet, totally withdrawn, deep in thought. I couldn't say I blamed him. The witches were the enemy, and to top it, off Flora was Queen Ezarbet's twin. *As if this shit couldn't get any more complicated.* I knew I should be thrown off with them being identical twins, but she was different. While her sister was cold and dark, she was light and warm. Pulling up by the warehouse, I grab Hugo's arm, stopping him from getting out.

"Hugo, are you OK?" I asked, worried.

He smiled, reassuring me, nodding his head, but I could still see the shadow of doubt in his eyes.

"Yes. I will be fine. We just have to find out where she is."

"Don't worry; we will," I said, promising him.

"Come. The others are waiting for us," he said, open-ing his door.

Nodding my head and letting him go, I opened my door. We headed into the warehouse silently together.

Con and Big Red were the first to greet us. I looked around for Ian, but he was nowhere in sight.

"What the fuck happened to you, warlock?" Big Red said as he checked out Hugo's new look.

Hugo let out an embarrassed cough.

"What? He looks great," I said, now pissed.

Big Red held up his hands in mock innocence as if he'd said nothing wrong. It was just like him to try to ruin the mood.

"What have you learned?" Con asked.

"Nothing solid yet, but I am sure we will find something out sooner or later," I said, still giving Big Red the evil eye.

"Yes, it seems that Mr. Pearson is sweet on Scarlett," Hugo said, teasing me.

"And who wouldn't be? What, love? You must know you are ravishing," Big Red said, giving me a wink.

I rolled my eyes at him, and Con let out a grunt.

"Where is Zayah?" I asked. I was in much need of some girl time.

"She is in our sleeping quarters."

"OK. If you guys would excuse me," I said. Passing by Big Red, I slapped him playfully on the shoulder. I heard his laugh as I walked away.

Making my way over to Zayah and Con's room, I knocked. She opened the door and smiled as she saw me.

"Hi. Can I come in?"

"Of course," she said, opening the door wider to let me in.

Right away I noticed she was wearing the silk blouse from the W, the one I told her she would look great in when I thought she was a customer. She was wearing it with, of course, black pants. And I had to say I was right; she looked beautiful in it, and the crisp white color of the blouse brought out her beautiful dark skin tone. Her thick black hair was pulled back, showing off her amazing cheekbones. She did not need one lick of makeup. Her skin was flawless. She reminded me of a ballerina, very tall and graceful, her posture always straight.

"I couldn't help but go back to your job and get this blouse. I have to tell you, Con is saying you are having an effect on me," she said, laughing.

I laughed as well, thinking of Hugo and his new look. "I guess I have a way of rubbing off on people."

Looking around their room, it looked like your normal bedroom, with a bed. *Don't vampires sleep in caskets?*

"Do vampires sleep?" I asked.

"No, we don't," she said, shaking her head.

"Oh…so, why the bed?"

She smiled shyly at me, and my eyes widened. *Oh, my God. What a stupid question. Idiot!* I wanted so badly to slap my forehead. Letting out an uncomfortable cough, I noticed that their bed was king size with a cream duvet. It was a little awkward being in the room they shared. I felt like I was invading their personal space.

"Zayah, I hope I'm not bothering you, but you are really the only one I can talk to about this. Of course, there is Hugo, but he is nowhere near female," I said quickly.

She looked at me curiously.

I coughed nervously again, pulling my hair behind my ear.

"Well, I am sure it comes to you as no surprise that Ian and I are involved, and, um, we have never used protection, and I am not on the pill…" I trailed off, embarrassed, my face flaming red. "I know what you're thinking. My God. A girl my age should know about these things…" I trailed off again.

Zayah smiled a knowing smile. "You have nothing to fear. A vampire cannot breed, and we carry no viruses."

"Yeah, well, how do you explain me?" I asked, pointing to myself.

"Yes, but you are part of a prophecy. Your mother and father were special. They were meant to have you. It's hard to explain and understand. One day it will all make sense to you," she said softly.

Taking a deep breath, I felt a little better. One day it would make sense to me, but that day was long from here. I was growing more confused by the minute. What was I going to do about Ian? Was he part of my destiny? My visions told me yes, but what about the queen? My vision also told me Ian would die. *Do I risk showing him how I feel and live in the moment with him, or do I let him walk away from me?* Closing my eyes, I felt that same pain in my heart.

"You are in love with Ian," Zayah said to me softly, breaking me from my thoughts.

Opening my eyes, I knew they were filled with tears—tears of frustration, hope, and most of all, uncertainty.

"How can you tell? Am I that obvious?" I whispered.

She came over to me and touched my face gently.

"I can see it in your eyes," she whispered back, her arms going around me to pull me in for a hug.

I quickly went into her arms; I wanted to be comforted so badly. I was never this emotional wreck; I was so closed off for so long. Even with Jewels, she would sometimes make fun of me saying I was an "Ice Princess." If only she could see me now. I missed her. I wondered what she would think about this whole situation. I was sure she would give Ian a cent or two. That exchange would be hysterical. I now had Zayah and Hugo. Zayah was a woman of this world; she knew exactly how I was feeling. Was it this hard for her and Con? I doubted it; he couldn't take his eyes off of her. I broke away from her before I had a total melt down.

"Thanks. I totally needed that," I said to her, wiping my eyes.

She smiled and said nothing.

Walking toward the door, I turned back to her and asked her a question I'd been dying to ask her since our last chat.

"Remember when you said you knew you could trust Ian when you saw us together at the club? What did you mean?"

She smiled that knowing smile again. "That's because your Ian is enthralled with you."

My heart slammed against my chest. Could it be? Could my cold-hearted man feel? I smiled sadly back at Zayah and closed her door. Walking back to my room in a daze, I opened the door to find Ian waiting for me. He was wearing the white shirt and fitted jeans again. I was coming to know this as his signature look. His blond hair was getting a little long, but it was nicely in place, coming off like a wave in the front. His mouth was set in a grim line, and his arms were folded over his chest, his beautiful eyes dark.

"Didn't we have this discussion before about you being in my room?" I asked, closing and locking the door.

I knew why he was there. I could see it in his eyes, and I didn't care. I wanted him as much as he wanted me. No, he wasn't the man from my dreams, but I loved him so much more. I was in love with this cold, damaged man. At that very moment, I didn't care of the consequences. To hell with them. I was so sick of playing it safe and closing out life. I wanted to live. I wanted to live in this very moment with him for as long as I could. He walked over to me, not saying one word, and I held my breath. He stood in front of me, still saying nothing. I tentatively reached up and touched his face. He closed his eyes briefly and let out a breath of relief.

It hit me then. I tilted my head in wonder at him. He was worried for me when I was out; I felt it. This was his way of telling me. *My cold man.* I inwardly smiled. Feeling braver, I took a step closer to him, moving my hand to the nape of his neck, bringing his head down for a gentle kiss. His lips closed over mine so softly and tenderly. My body melted into his as he pulled me closer, his strong arms going around me. I could feel his hands going under my jacket, gripping the back of my shirt as though he was using all of his self-control not to rip it from my body.

The kiss turned hungry, our hot breaths mixing together, tongues intertwining, making passionate love to each other, his hands now in my hair. I moaned. God I needed him, and I needed him now. Feeling his hard-on, I pressed myself more fully against him. He growled in agreement and started taking off my jacket. I started pulling on his shirt, bringing it over his head. My God, he was beautiful. He took my breath away. He had a flat stomach rippled with muscle. He was perfect. *He is mine!* As he took off my shirt, I started to feel self-conscious, raising my hands to cover myself.

"Don't," he whispered, shaking his head.

My hands dropped away, and his eyes darkened even further as he looked at me with pure want. It made me feel sexy. I was sexy, and I was his. I wanted to explore him. I placed my hand on his chest, feeling his coldness, and followed the trail of blond hair sprinkled there. He didn't stop me. My hand went lower to his belly, my fingernails grazing him, making his belly quiver from my touch. I heard him growl. I looked up at him and smiled. His eyes were pitch black, and his fangs were out, long and sharp. The ache between my legs was growing further. *My God, I have never seen anything sexier in my life.*

Unbuckling his belt I pulled down his pants, very slowly, teasing him. I loved how his eyes narrowed and his breath came out as though he was running. Watching his response to me brought me so much pleasure; I wanted to make him feel every bit of pleasure as he gave me. I smiled wantonly at him. He was wearing black boxer briefs, his hard-on straining against the thin material. Licking my lips I knew I wanted to explore him further. How far would he let me? I wanted to taste him. Going on my knees before him, I started to kiss his stomach using my tongue and teeth, playfully biting him. His hands were in my hair, encouraging me. Pulling down on his briefs, I found his cock hard and wet. Licking my lips again, I was desperately trying not to rub my achy thighs together.

"Go ahead; touch me," Ian said softly, looking down at me.

He grabbed my hand, putting it around his cock, showing me how he liked to be touched, setting up a rhythm. My hand squeezed tighter, and he growled, his head falling back. Getting more brazen with my exploration, I leaned forward and started kissing the head of his cock, my tongue flicking out, licking the beads of wetness forming there. His hands went into my hair, again moving me more forward, and I took his cock in my mouth.

"That's it," Ian said, groaning.

Opening my eyes I looked up and saw that he was looking down at me, enjoying the show I was putting on, his breathing coming out more harshly. He tasted so good. I couldn't get enough of him. I was consumed with his taste. I began to take him more fully into my mouth, using my tongue all the while. He started to reach down to touch my breasts, pinching my nipples. I felt myself quivering with want for him; I was so wet. Moaning with want of him, I felt him getting harder in my mouth. He pulled my head back, and I looked up at him questioningly. Was I doing something wrong?

"I was about to come in that pretty little mouth of yours. I want to fuck you," he said, pulling me up and rubbing his thumb against my lips.

My body was out of control with want for him. He pulled me closer and kissed me. I loved the feel of his naked chest against mine, his little hair tickling me. Feeling his hands on my jeans, I heard the sound of a zipper and he yanked them down. I quickly stepped out of them, leaving me in nothing but my bra and underwear. My hands went to his shoulders, up his neck, my fingers in his hair. Next thing I knew we were on the bed. He was over me, his hot breath on my face. Breaking our kiss, he started kissing my neck and went to my breasts, pulling them out of my bra.

"I can't get enough of you," he said, looking up at me.

He didn't wait for my reply. He took my nipple in his mouth. I moaned, lost in the sensation. I felt his hand go between my legs, touching me through the lace material; I arched up needing him to touch me there so badly.

"You are so wet for me," he said, smiling up at me deviously.

He moved my underwear to the side, and his finger entered me. I moaned again, feeling very close. I felt his hand still, and I groaned in frustration, my hips arching upward, willing his hand to move. My hand gripped the sheets under me, my nails digging into the fabric. His arm went over my belly, holding me still.

"Please," I moaned to him. He looked back up at me.

"Not yet. You will come on my mouth first," he said, trailing kisses to my stomach.

I let out a gasp, and my eyes widened with shock and anticipation. Hearing a tear, I looked down as he ripped my underwear with his fangs. *Holy shit!* I could feel his hot breath on my thighs.

"Touch your breasts for me while I pleasure you," he growled.

My hands covered my breasts, cupping them gently and pinching my nipples, lost in everything he was doing to me. He took his first kiss of me, and I nearly jumped off the bed, but he held me down to his assault, not wanting to be denied. His tongue swirled and sucked. I felt myself floating, my hand now in his hair, pulling his mouth closer to me, arching myself to his greedy mouth. Moaning, I had an overwhelming feeling come over me and I was flying, coming hard and screaming his name, not caring who heard me. He came over me, his mouth wet from me.

"Fuck, you taste so good," he said as he opened my legs wider and positioned himself over me.

He entered me roughly, and we both moaned from the pleasure of it. Wrapping my legs around him, I felt myself getting lost again, my body accepting his and arching my hips to take him in more fully. His eyes were closed, and I put my hand gently to his face wanting him to look at me. He opened his eyes, and we looked at each other. He started to slow down his body, now moving in me gently, loving me like no other could. He combed the hair stuck on my forehead away.

"You are mine," he whispered.

I closed my eyes, my body building up again. I felt myself beginning to come again.

"Yes, I am yours. I love you Ian," I whispered back, my mind and body lost.

I felt his body automatically stiffen. I opened my eyes and gone was the gentle Ian I just saw briefly. Lights off. He looked away, no longer making eye contact with me. He started to pound into me roughly, my mind screaming but my body helplessly reacting to his. I moaned, coming hard, my nails digging into his back drawing blood. I heard him grunt, spilling himself inside of me. He pulled out of me quickly, making me wince, nearly jumping off of me. *Shit! I can't believe I just told him I loved him.* I shook my head at my stupidity.

He got up from the bed not looking at me. I watched as he got his things, putting them on quickly. I grabbed the covers, covering myself, feeling very much cold even though my body still burned for him. He walked out of my room, slamming the door behind him. I threw myself back on the bed, tears rolling down my face. I didn't know who I cried for—him or myself.

I was with Ian, watching as he came before a steel gate and opened it, the gate making a loud creaking sound. We were at a cemetery. It was dark out, the fog making the cemetery look as if we were in a horror movie. It was hard to see through. I followed beside him. I looked over to him and knew this was his past. He was wearing a navy suit, and his vest was black velvet, his blond hair slicked back, and he carried a bouquet of lilies. He seemed so much younger somehow, even though I knew he was a vampire. His steel blue eyes looked vacant, almost empty. There were tombstones everywhere, from children to elders. Making our way over, we both saw an older man with a long blond beard wearing a suit that was too tight for him standing beside a tombstone. Unlike Ian he was holding a bottle of liquor. The man looked over to us as we approached and looked at

Ian disgusted, his eyes narrowing. Who was this man? I felt Ian stiffen next to me, his body radiating tension. Going closer to the man, I saw the resemblance right away, the same eyes. This was Ian's father.

"I knew you would come. You're still the same boy who would cry over his whore of a mother," his father spat at him.

I flinched. Why was he talking to Ian like this? I watched as Ian took a step toward his father.

"I would be very careful what you say, Father. I am not the same boy you once beat."

His father laughed and walked over to Ian, tripping over himself and dropping his bottle. He was drunk. I could smell the liquor on his breath. If he wasn't so drunk, he probably would have noticed how Ian's eyes blackened.

"You are just like her, weak," he spat, lifting his hand to strike Ian.

Ian grabbed his hand stopping him, dropping the flowers, and twisted his hand. His father screamed with pain, falling to his knees. Ian bent down so he was making eye contact with him. He could now see Ian's eyes that were pitch black and his long fangs. His eyes wide with terror, he was too scared to speak.

"Never again," he growled to his father.

He lets go of his father's hand and watched as his father scrambled up.

"What...What are you?" he asked stuttering, rubbing his eyes as though he was not seeing clearly.

"I am the devil, coming to take you to hell."

As his father's eyes widened even further in fear, he tried to run. Ian caught him quickly, grabbing his father by the collar of his shirt and biting his neck hard. His father screamed, swinging his arms trying to get away. Ian brought his head up and spat his father's blood in his face, dropping him to the floor and letting him bleed out, suffering. Bending down he picked up the flowers, dusting off the dirt, trying to make the lilies presentable. He started walking toward the tombstone, his face bloodied as well as his clothes.

It was a small granite stone with a name engraved on it: Annalisa. He sank to his knees before the tombstone with his head down. I got on my knees next to him wishing I was really there at that very moment comforting him. He looked numb. *Cry, Ian*, I silently begged. *Cry for your mother. No one is watching.* But he didn't. I saw the regret in his eyes. What happened to her? He set the flowers down and gently touched the engraved lettering of his mother's name.

I felt myself start to cry for him. We had more in common than I thought, both of us coming from broken homes. It seemed like forever before he got up, taking one final look at the burial spot of his mother. Still on my knees, I watched him walk away, not taking a final look back at his dying father, the tombstone, or the life he once knew.

All the little children were tucked in their beds nice and cozy, ready for Santa to drop off the presents under the tree. Parents already done with their Christmas shopping were doing last-minute wrapping with the fireplace going and listening to Christmas music in the background, totally oblivious to this dark world, a world they could never imagine; this world that was now mine. The night was dark and the wind was still, the smell of death enveloping me. The cold weather made the sun go down sooner. We had no idea of what chaos was about to ensue.

They surrounded the warehouse ready to strike—in the back, front, on both sides, and the roof. There were at least twenty of them—ancients. Ready to be given the orders that the man with the scarred face, Abel, was quietly giving. He looked to be the leader of this strike. They were all dressed in black and thirsty for death. They had guns and swords, all of them vicious and hungry, making them even deadlier. They could all smell the human that was inside the warehouse, and that human was me.

"Remember, the girl is not to be harmed. Kill Ian and the X's. The queen wants her alive and well," Abel whispered to the others, warning them silently that they were not to feed from me.

The queen wants me alive? Why? Wasn't the whole purpose was to have me dead? What game is she playing now? Well, they won't take me without a fight. The shit is about to hit the fan, I thought to myself. Looking around anxiously, I couldn't find Ian. I had to warn him and the others. I heard in the distance a howl of a wolf. Damian. He was here. I watched as Abel held out his hand to the ancients and began a countdown: three, two, one…

I woke gasping, moving the covers away, and quickly got up from the bed, immediately looking at my nightstand for the time: 9:30 p.m. The hairs on the back of my neck stood. Turning on the light I went over to my bureau and found a fitted white tank and put on my skinny jeans I had worn earlier. Going into my closet, I found a pair of boots and put them on quickly, tying the laces, all the while looking at the time. Finding my jacket on the floor where Ian had tossed it, I put it on, zipping it all the way to the top. Going to the mirror, I combed my hair back and tied it up in a ponytail. Swallowing hard, I tried to calm by adrenaline.

Was I just being paranoid? I couldn't stop my heart from beating so hard; my hands were shaking. I went back to sit on my bed, putting my head in my hands. *Shit.* I couldn't shake this feeling. I could hear the sound of my breathing. It was quiet—too quiet. Closing my eyes, inhaling a deep breath in, I could smell something. I could smell death. Something was not right. Shaking my head I got up to let the others know of my vision, and boom, the lights from the warehouse went out leaving dead silence. They were here.

chapter

TWENTY SIX

My door swung open so fast I thought it was going to be knocked from its hinges. Prepared to attack, I realized it was Ian and Hugo.

"They're here!" I screamed at them, running back to my closet and taking out my sword, preparing to do battle. I started to head to the doorway, and Ian blocked me from going out.

"Get her the fuck outta here, warlock!" Ian yelled at Hugo, ignoring me.

"Wait!" I yelled, watching his retreating back. *Damn him.*

Hugo began to take my arm, and I shoved him off, running after Ian. They wanted to kill him and the others. I refused to run like a victim. That was not how this was supposed to work. I was the fucking prophet. This was my battle, damn it! Hugo was right behind me. I sensed he respected my decision to fight with the X's, even though I felt his body was tense. He was ready for battle, as was I. I stood in the middle of the X's. There was dead silence, as we waited. I could picture Abel with his ugly, scarred face counting down the seconds as he had in my vision. Three *seconds, two seconds, one second.*

The door bust open and windows shattered everywhere. I looked to my left and right. They were coming in through the doorway and windows. The ancients ran in screaming, head first. I watched as Zayah took the first one out swiftly, her sword swinging rapidly, stabbing the first ancient in the heart turning him to ash. Then chaos broke loose. I ran swiftly to my left, an ancient right at my heels, and took out my sword. Eyes glowing, he moved to kick me quickly. I easily moved to my right. He missed me by inches, and I hit him in the face with my elbow and kneed him in the groin. He fell to his knees, and I raised my sword and chopped off his head. I didn't even get a chance to enjoy watching him turn to ash. Another ancient was coming my way. Before he could get to me, Ian blocked him and snapped his neck, turning him to ash.

"I thought I told you to get the fuck out of here!" Ian yelled at me.

"I don't take orders from you!" I yelled back, ignoring him and going in the other direction.

"Not a good time to have a lovers' quarrel," Big Red yelled at us both. I watched as he took on a huge ancient, countering him swiftly with no weapon, and grabbed him by the neck, breaking it easily, smiling as though he loved every minute of it. Another ancient came at him and he axe kicked him in the chest, making him fall to the ground. He grabbed the sword that the ancient lost his grip on and stabbed him in the heart.

Hugo was walking toward two ancients as if bored. He put his hands together, palm to palm, and started to whisper words. He held out his hands away from his body open palmed, and two big blue flames shot out from them at the two ancients, making them scream from pain before turning to ash.

Someone else was coming in the doorway. I watched as Abel entered. His was even uglier in person, and someone was right behind him—a naked man, Damian the wolf. *Shit.* We made eye contact, and I watched as he turned from man to beast. His transformation looked painful. He stomped forward, bones seeming to break as he went through his change, growling in the process. He lifted his hairy face, and his gleaming red eyes were focused on me. I screamed, "Wolf!" to alert my X's.

Running to the gun locker, I got my Beretta and my dagger, placing it in the sleeve of my jacket and putting extra clips in my pocket. I quickly loaded the gun and clicked back the safety lock on it just like Skull taught me and started shooting like my life depended on it. Damian quickly started running in the other direction, clawing up the walls. I shot until I was out of bullets. Grabbing another clip from my pocket, I reloaded.

I raised my gun to shoot again, but Abel was in front of me. He knocked the gun out of my hands, knocking it to the other side of the room. He backslapped me hard, making me fall to my knees. He grabbed a fistful of my hair and brought me up wincing so I was facing him. I saw Ian coming toward us behind Abel, but Damian blocked him. Ian quickly tackled him, but Damian was quicker, rolling on top of him with a howl.

"So you are the prophet?" Abel asked, his head tilted, pitch black eyes looking at me with wonder.

"Hello, Abel," I said, gritting my teeth. *This is it. I am finally face to face with one of the monsters that helped capture and kill my parents.*

"Oh, so you know me. Don't even think about it, witch," he said to Hugo, behind him. "I will snap her neck before you can let out a spell."

"He's a warlock," I quickly corrected him. "Don't, Hugo," I said, not wanting him to get hurt.

Hugo stopped, his eyes meeting mine, and was grabbed by an ancient pressing a sword against his throat. Hugo held up his hands in silent surrender.

"Cut off his hands if he so much as talks. Now back to business. Come look at your lover," Abel said as he turned me, my back against him and his hand still around my neck, forcing me to watch Ian, who was still battling the wolf.

Ian momentarily looked up at us, distracted, and Damian seized his opportunity, taking swift advantage, clawing Ian's side, making him growl with pain. I watched Ian's blood cover his shirt, and he dropped to his knees in pain. Damian pounced, holding Ian by the neck, forcing him to watch Abel and I. His eyes were focused on us, and I could see his anguish—and something else. I looked around and noticed all the X's were now being held, all becoming distracted now that their leader was being held by one of their fiercest adversaries.

"Ian, it looks like you're in a predicament," Abel said sarcastically, laughing.

He moved my hair to the side, smelling me. I could feel is arousal behind me. I swallowed hard, disgusted.

"Mmmmm. I can see the obsession, Ian. She smells delightful. I wonder if she's as delightful in the bedroom," he said, pressing himself hard against me. He put his hand to my mouth, his finger grazing my lip and taking the blood there. He put it to his mouth, tasting me.

I heard Ian growl, trying to get up and holding his bleeding side, but Damian held him down easily.

"You taste just like your mother," he whispered in my ear.

I briefly closed my eyes. I envisioned my father and mother, his ugly, scarred face grinning as he watched the queen mutilate them. This was my chance for vengeance. I felt something overwhelming come over me—a buildup that was so great I couldn't control it. Closing my eyes, I concentrated.

"Hugo, get ready," my mind whispered to him. I peak at him at him and I see his eyes widen in surprise. I focused harder.

My body was being overtaken, and something told me to close out everything, keep my mind completely focused.

"X's, get ready," my mind whispered to them.

Opening my eyes, I looked to my right, making eye contact with Big Red. He winked at me. *My God. They can hear me.*

"Your powers are just beginning, Scarlett," Con's voice shot back at me. We made eye contact, and he looked back at me fiercely, understanding. Slipping the dagger from my sleeve into my hand, I stomped as hard as I could on Abel's foot. I could hear his bones breaking beneath my foot, and he screamed with pain as he let me go. As quickly as I could, I flung my dagger toward Damian, hitting him right in the side. Letting go of Ian, he howled with pain and took off running in the other direction.

The X's took advantage of the ancients getting thrown off, quickly getting their weapons and attacking, turning the last of the ancients to ash. They all started to form a circle around us, watching the last battle that was to take place between Abel and I, none of them daring to get involved. They understood this was my right; this was my battle—my destiny.

I turned, and Abel was right behind me. He moved to punch me and I blocked him with both hands, front kicking him in the chest. He went down. I saw my sword in the corner and started running for it. He grabbed me by the leg, making me fall. I tried to scramble up, but he was on top of me. I dug my fingers into his eyes, making him scream. I pushed him off of me and got my sword. I turned, and he had a sword as well.

We both charged each other at the same time, our swords hitting together so hard the metal sparked. I quickly turned to my right as he made another go for me with his sword, but I was too quick for him and he missed. I sliced the other side of his face with my sword, matching his scar. He howled with pain from the silver, his hand going to his face, and dropped his sword. I pointed my sword at his heart. He raised his hands in surrender, knowing he was finished.

"Stupid human, bitch. You think this is over? This is just the beginning. You are going to pay!" he yelled at me.

Big Red and Con got a hold of his arms, making him go onto his knees before me.

"Where is your queen?" I asked.

He had the nerve to spit on the floor and smile at me.

"You think I will tell you? The queen will show you no mercy. You're just a weak human. You're no fucking prophet!" he yelled.

I kneeled quietly before him and made eye contact with him. This man, this ancient, helped share in the death of my parents. He showed no mercy, no remorse. I would show him the same.

"You and your queen can go fuck yourselves," my mind whispered to him. I watched the look of surprise on his face, his eyes widening for the first time in fear. I got up and raised my sword, and with one swift move I cut his head off, screaming in anguish as I did so, watching him turn to ash. Dropping my sword, I sank to my knees, out of breath. Hugo was on his knees beside me with his hand on the small of my back. He was talking to me, but I couldn't hear him. It was as if I was having an out-of-body experience. Shaking my head, trying to clear it, I looked up trying to find Ian. Where was he? That's when I noticed he was still on the floor where Damian had dropped him.

"Ian!" I screamed. Scrambling up I ran over to him. He was lying still—too still. Sinking onto my knees next to him, I turned him over gently. His eyes were closed, but he was still alive, barely. His shirt was soaked with blood. Lifting the shirt gently, I bit my lip trying not to let out a scream of horror as I looked at the damage Damian had left behind. The wound had big, jagged claw marks that were deep, still oozing blood and pus.

"Oh, God, Ian," I whispered, tears in my eyes.

Con walked over and knelt down. "A beast's bite can be poisonous to us and can be deadly. He needs your blood, Scarlet; When one vampire male is enthralled, only *her* blood can heal him quickly," Con whispered to me. He took out a knife he had in his pocket and handed it to me. *Is it true?* Taking the knife from him, I cut my hand, wincing. I lifted Ian's head gently and brought my hand to his mouth, the blood drops falling into his mouth. I saw his nose twitch, recognizing my scent. His head started moving from side to side and he began to drink from me.

"That's it, baby. Drink," I whispered, encouraging him, gently touching his hair.

I watched in amazement as his wounds started to heal, the jagged claw marks closing up leaving no trace of a scar. I looked at Con, surprised, and he smiled, got up, and walked toward the X's. Ian was enthralled, whether he wanted to admit it or not. He opened his eyes and pulled my hand away, sitting up and looking around.

"Abel is dead, but Damian got away," I said, getting up. I tried to help him up, but he would have none of it, growling when I tried. Frowning at him I clutched my bleeding hand. He would not meet my gaze. The X's all came forward, battered and bruised but looking as if they could go for another round.

"We have to split up for the time being," said Razor. "The sun is coming, and we have to clear out of here. We all have cell phones to reach each other, and when the time is right we will reunite."

All the X's nodded in agreement, even Hugo. I looked over to Ian, and he said nothing, showing no expression and still refusing to look at me.

"Split up?" I asked.

Zayah looked over to me. "Yes. Just for a short while. We will now need a new location. The queen is going to hear about what just happened, and she will send more ancients."

Of course. The new location I had envisioned. *That's why we were there.* At least that part of the vision made sense.

"OK. Let's be out of here in twenty minutes," Con said, and the group broke apart.

I stayed silent as I watched the X's take off in different directions. When would I see the people I now considered my friends again?

"I will wait outside until you are ready," Hugo said to me. I looked at him and noticed his stare was on Ian, his eyes narrowing at him. I looked back and forth between the two. Tension radiated between their bodies. Hugo stiffly walked away toward the doorway.

Nodding my head I quickly walked over to my door, Ian silently following me. I closed the door behind us, headed to the closet, got out a duffle bag, and started packing as much as I could, grabbing handfuls of clothing at a time. Ian stood silently by the bed, watching me, his face expressionless, cold even.

"Don't you have anything to pack?" I asked, looking over at him while stuffing the clothes in the bag.

"I am not coming with you," he said simply.

I inhaled sharply and swallowed hard. I didn't know what to say. There was an eerie coldness about him I had never seen before.

"What do you mean?" I asked. I stopped packing and turned toward him, folding my arms around my chest.

"You know exactly what I mean. I was never going to come with you." He shrugged as if I should have expected this. Hell, maybe he was right, but that didn't make it any easier.

"What about us?" I asked, trying not to let my voice quiver.

He let out a harsh laugh. He was actually laughing at me. I didn't know this Ian; this was the Ian everybody was talking about, the Ian they silently warned me of.

"Us? There is no us. Never has been," he said incredulously, shaking his head smiling at me evilly.

I shook my head in denial. "You can't mean that. You're lying!" I yelled at him.

He turned to leave the room, and I followed him, grabbing him by the arm, forcing him to turn to meet me in the eyes.

"You love me as much as I love you. I know you're enthralled with me," I said bravely to him.

"In love with you?" he said, disgusted. "Jesus, Scarlett, don't confuse great fucking with love," he yelled at me, yanking his arm from my grasp.

I flinched back as if he'd slapped me, putting my hand to my mouth, tears beginning to roll down my face. My vision of his beautiful, cold face began to blur. I turned away from him, not wanting him to see how much his words ripped my heart in two.

"You're a fucking human caught up in some fairytale of happily ever after. Grow the fuck up. The world doesn't work that way," he said, opening the door and slamming it shut behind him.

As soon as the door slammed, I fell to my knees crying. I should have expected this, should have wanted this, but it hurt all the same. He didn't love me. The door quietly opened, and it took me a while to realize Hugo was in the room with me, on his knees with me. His hand was on the small of my back, and he brought me in for hug. I went into his embrace, my head resting on his shoulder as my tears flowed even more, his hand gently moving up and down my back, comforting me. I couldn't seem to stop crying. I was broken.

"Scarlett, we have to go," he whispered to me.

Nodding my head and wiping my face, I felt myself beginning to become numb. I couldn't meet Hugo in the eyes. We both got up, and I went over to my bureau and got the jewelry box my father left me. Putting it in the bag, I zipped it shut.

"Ready," I said softly.

We headed out of my room, and the X's had already departed, taking most of the weapons. As soon as we were outside, I watched as Hugo whispered some words and snapped his finger. The warehouse went up in flames, the windows filling up with black smoke, getting rid of any evidence of the battle that just took place.

"Come. We will walk a block, and a taxi will come get us," he said, leading the way out of the lot, walking fast.

Saying nothing, I followed him. It was cold and rainy. I lifted my face, letting the rain hit me. My hair and clothes were getting soaked. It felt great even though it was freezing. The weather was imitating my mood. Before we walked away, I took one final look over at the burning warehouse, feeling a little sad that we were forever leaving it. This was where my journey began. Swallowing I turned and followed Hugo. I could hear in the distance the sound of fire truck sirens.

As we walked a little further, just as he promised, there was a taxi waiting for us. Hugo slowed down, waiting for me to catch up to him. As I opened the passenger's side door, I looked over at Hugo and watched him transform into Hugo my puppy. Smiling down at him, I got in and he hopped in after me. The taxi driver was an African American male with long dreadlocks.

"Where are you headed, miss?" he asked me with a strong Jamaican accent.

"Take us to the best hotel in New York City," I said, looking not at him but out the window.

"Yes, miss," he said and pulled out into the street.

I looked out onto the streets of Westport. The streets were pretty much dead, not a car in sight. Would this be the last time I would be here? We went past downtown Westport, past Martins and the W boutique. I saw flashbacks of me when I was first hired at the W, Jewels and me going over to Martins for lunch to hear about her latest relationship drama. Life was so simple then. I couldn't help but feel a little resentment for this new world that I was now to be a part of.

Ian flashed through my mind, and I felt tears come to my eyes. So, this is what heart break feels like? I felt like my heart was ripped in two, and Ian took a piece of it with him when he walked out on me. I heard Hugo whining beside me. I looked down at him, and he rested his head on my lap. I gently pet his head, reassuring him I was OK, even though I wasn't. Leaning my head back in the seat, I took a deep breath as I closed my eyes, feeling myself doze off as we headed to New York City.

The beast ran in the wooded area on all fours, his body hurt and injured, running as fast as he could in the darkened forest. His hands clawed at the branches in his way. He blended in well into the darkness; the darkness was all he knew. Growling with pain, he turned into human form, looking down at the bloody dagger in his side. She made a perfect shot. He put his hands around the dagger, gritting his teeth before he yanked it out. He let out a roar of pain. With shaky hands he examined the dagger and then looked back down at the wound that was seeping with blood and smoke. It burned like hell; only a silver dagger would do that. *Fucking bitch!*

Dropping the dagger, disgusted, he put his hand on his wound. If the dagger would have been longer, it would have probably killed him. The prophet was powerful. She had glowing eyes and was as quick as a vampire. She was not to be underestimated. He watched her in fascination from the shadows as she killed Abel, slicing his head off with powerful purpose. Abel was such a stupid fool. He thought he was the all-powerful and mighty, but in fact he was the weakling. He was actually glad to be rid of him. His love for the queen had made him lose focus on the real plan, his anger and jealousy of Ian overtaking him and clouding his judgment.

Finding his clothes where he'd left them, he quickly put them on, wincing from the pain in his side. Leaving out of the wooded area, he walked into the abandoned streets with his head down. The smell of the morning sunrise was in the air, filling his nostrils. He needed to get out of here and quick. He saw a car approaching and stuck out his thumb. It was an old, beat-up red Honda Civic in desperate need of a wash. The shabby car came to a stop in front of him, and the window rolled down. Smiling, he leaned forward and saw a man perhaps forty years of age. He smelled of cigarettes and beer.

"Hey, buddy, do you need a ride?" the man asked, slurring his words, his eyes glazed over as if he was about to fall asleep at the wheel.

"Yeah. My car broke down; do think you can give me a jump?"

"Sure, buddy. Get in."

"Stupid human," he said to himself.

He got in, giving the man directions to where his supposed car was. He could never get over how humans were so quick to trust. Of course, they thought their world was perfect. If only they knew—and soon they would.

"It's right over here," Damian said, pointing over to the area of forest he came out of. The stupid human was so drunk, he didn't even notice there was no car there. He swerved the car to the side of the embankment and came to a stop.

"OK. Let me get my jumper cables, buddy." He opened the door and almost fell out of it, heading toward his trunk.

Getting out of the car, Damian felt himself stalking his prey, taking in his scent, remembering it. He was desperate for a kill. He felt himself shaking for it, needing it. He felt the saliva build in the back of his throat. The beast wanted out to play. Grinding his teeth, he held him at bay.

He wanted to enjoy this kill without feeling the pain of the transformation.

"OK, buddy. I got it," the man said, turning, unaware that he was about to meet a terrible fate.

He caught a glimpse of the striking red eyes before him and dropped the jumper cables, ready to let out a scream, but Damian struck before he could. Grabbing him by the throat and cutting off his scream, he dragged him into the woods. Letting the man go, he let him run—run for his life. That was part of the sadistic pleasure he took from it. The beast let loose, transforming him, tearing his clothes off, making the human in him scream in pain from the transformation. From man to beast, he sniffed the air, smelling his prey's fear. Setting off in a run, he began his chase. There was nothing better than the chase. Playing a cat-and-mouse game with his prey was always something that pleasured him before his kill. He watched as the drunken fool tripped over a branch and fell onto his belly. He turned over quickly and lifted his shaking hands.

"Please, please!" he begged.

Damian slowly approached, taunting him.

"Oh, please. Oh, please, God," the man began to pray.

Damian struck, catching the man by surprise, jumping on top of him and going for his throat. The man tried to wrestle him off, but he was too strong. He easily ripped out the man's jugular. Blood was everywhere, and he loved it. He imagined the queen watching and became aroused by the idea. Once the kill was done, the beast let out a howl of satisfaction. Going back to human form and falling onto his knees from exhaustion, he realized he'd torn his clothes during the transformation.

"Shit."

Looking at the drunken man's clothes, he got up and started removing the pants and shoes from the dead man's body. Putting on the stolen clothes, he walked back to the abandoned car, not bothering to look back at the human body he'd destroyed. He found his torn clothes and the cell phone in his pants pocket. Picking it up and dusting it off, he put it in his new pocket. He got in the car. Catching a glimpse of himself in the rearview mirror, he noticed the blood all over his face and neck. "Fuck." Seeing a bottle of water in the car, he grabbed it, got out of the car, and cleaned off all evidence of his kill. Getting back in the car, he looked in the backseat and noticed a grey hooded sweater. Walking around bare-chested in the winter was going to look strange to the humans, even though the cold did not bother him one bit. He put it on.

Before turning on the car, he reached for his cell phone. It was time to give the queen a review of what had taken place. She was not going to be happy about this. The fact that Ian and the X's were alive and Scarlett would not be sent to her was a message he would gladly deliver over the phone and not in person. There would be hell to pay. He was just happy he would not be on the receiving end of it. Soon, with Abel out of the picture now, he would see that no more errors were made. He would see that Scarlett was sent to the queen by him personally, and he would finish off Ian, if he hadn't already. But first, she would have to hear the bad news.

chapter

TWENTY SEVEN

I was with Celine as she worked nervously in the castle. It was pure mayhem; everyone was talking about the death of the king. There was no sign of Edrick in the castle, but I felt his presence. The elder servant came into the kitchen as Celine was setting up dishes.

"Have you seen the queen?" Celine asked her.

"No. No one has. She has barricaded herself in her room. No one is allowed in. She even sent her dear, sweet sister away," Gretchen said as she helped Celine set up her dishes.

"What do you mean?" Celine stopped what she was doing.

"Well, they said that she just up and sent her sister away. Something is not right here," Gretchen said very softly to her.

Celine nodded her head but said nothing. She knew of the queen and her plot. I saw the look of something in Celine's eye. What was she thinking? Edrick warned her of the danger, but the look on her face was telling me she was going to do something, whether he approved or not.

"Gretchen, you must leave here and never come back," she said.

"What?" Gretchen asked, stepping back from the dishes.

"The queen is not what she seems. She is very dangerous, and I feel we are all in danger. She killed the king," she whispered to her quickly, looking over her shoulder to make sure she wasn't heard.

Gretchen's eyes widened in fear. Just then the bell rang.

"Oh, my. The queen is summoning. What will we do?" she asked, wiping her hands on her apron.

"Gretchen, I will go. You must leave," Celine said, blocking her from going further.

"But, my dear…" she pleaded with Celine.

"Promise me you will leave this place, Gretchen. Don't come back here. Pretend you never worked here," Celine begged her.

"OK," Gretchen promised her. She took off her apron, heading out of the kitchen, looking back at Celine one final time before heading out. *Oh, God.* What did Celine have planned? That was a pretty ballsy thing to do. I wondered what Edrick would do if he found out. Just then the bell rang again, making her jump. She took a deep breath in and out, heading up the stairs quickly. Once at the door, she took a deep breath again before knocking. I followed right behind her. She shut the door quietly behind her and bowed at the queen.

"My queen, how may I serve you?"

The queen's back was turned away from her, and she was staring into the fireplace deep in thought. She wore a red laced gown with a low back, revealing her pale skin. I was coming to learn this was her signature look. She seemed fond of sexy medieval attire.

"Didn't you hear my first ring, servant?" she demanded angrily, her back still turned.

"I am sorry, my queen. I am also sorry for your loss. To lose your beloved must be a terrible feeling."

The queen let out an evil laugh. Turning, she revealed the new look she was now cursed with—eyes as black as night. I watched as Celine's eyes widened and she stifled a gasp of fear.

"Beloved? There are many ways I could describe the king, and beloved would not be one of them."

Celine said nothing to this. I could hear her heart racing in fear.

"Come here, servant."

Celine slowly made her way over to her, coming to stand in front her.

"Do you fear me?" the queen asked.

Celine didn't speak at first, looking away. The queen grasped her chin roughly, making her meet her in the eyes.

"Answer me, servant."

Celine swallowed hard, bravely meeting her in the eyes.

"No," she said softly.

The queen's eyes widened at her response. She grabbed Celine by the back of neck, making her tilt her neck, her fangs protruding, her mouth ready to have a taste of her, and she paused, noticing the bite marks on her neck. She let out a vicious hiss.

"Who bit you?" she asked, looking back up at Celine, grabbing her by the hair, twisting it.

"I don't know what you're talking about." Celine winced with pain, trying to shake her head in denial.

She grabbed her by the shoulders so they were now meeting eye to eye, and I saw how the queen's eyes began to dilate, just like when Ian was trying to get me to calm down. *She's going to entrance her,* I thought with dread.

"I am going to ask you again: Who bit you?"

I watched in fear as Celine swallowed hard.

"One of the guards that opens the doors, he bit me. I tried to stop him, but he was too strong. I was so scared."

Holy shit! Celine somehow, some way, was not entranced but was pretending to be. She was looking at the queen as though in a daze and talking like she was drugged.

"One of the guards?" she asked again.

"Yes, one of the guards. I don't know his name or what he looks like. It was too dark."

A knock came at the door in the nick of time, distracting the queen.

"Come in," she practically yelled.

The door opened and one of the guards came in. He bowed before the queen before speaking.

"My queen, I apologize for disturbing you, but you did say to let you know if any issues arose with our captive."

"Celine, you may go. You will not remember this conversation at all. Do you understand me?" she asked, still looking deeply into her eyes.

"Yes, my queen." Celine turned to go, looking down. She shut the door behind her, letting out a breath of relief.

She quietly stood by the doorway listening to the conversation between the queen and the solider.

"What issue?" she asked, irritated.

"She tried to escape; of course she was caught right away."

"Every time she tries to escape, I want her beaten. Do you understand?"

"Yes, my queen."

"She is powerless without her magic, but she is desperate, which makes her dangerous. I don't want her fed tonight. Make sure that is done. Sooner or later she will go weak, and I want to watch her rot."

Celine then stepped away from the doorway in fear of being caught. She went down the stairs and made her way to the kitchen in a rush. I watched as she put bread and pieces of meat in her pockets. She put Clorox into a bucket with hot water and grabbed a mop. What the hell was she doing? She went into the long hallway of the castle, walking toward a doorway protected by the guard.

"Where do you think you're going, servant?" the huge ancient asked, blocking the doorway from her.

"The queen has advised me to clean up the dungeon for our soon-to-be guests."

"Guests? What would you know about the guests?"

"I am the queen's blood slave," she said, exposing her neck to the guard, showing off her bite marks.

He looked at the bite marks, and I watched as his nostrils flared. *Oh, God. What if he smells the food she has hidden in her pockets?* I watched as Celine lifted the bucket.

"Can you please let me pass? This is getting heavy," she said, showing him the bucket.

I realized what she was doing; she was trying to break his scent with the smell of the Clorox. She was not only ballsy but a genius.

"OK. Fine. You have twenty minutes."

She smiled at him sweetly. "That's all the time I need."

She headed down the stairway slowly. There was not much light. She set the bucket and mop down, beginning her search for the captive the queen had mentioned.

She peeked inside many doorways and found nothing. By the far end of the dungeon, she came across a room with steel bars. There, lying on her side on the ground, was Flora, her back turned. I could see the bloody rip marks on her dress from where she'd been whipped. Celine noticed as well and put her hand over her mouth in shock as she realized Flora was the queen's own sister. Putting her hand on the steel bar, she tried to open the gate but found it locked.

"Flora, can you hear me?" she whispered.

Flora weakly turned her head, her eyes widening as she saw Celine. She sat up, wincing with pain, moving her long hair out of her dirty face.

"What are you doing here? Don't you realize the queen will have your head if she finds out you are here?"

"I brought you food," she said, ignoring her questions as she took the food out of her pocket.

Flora got up slowly and walked over to the gate.

"Why would you do this for me? You don't even know me," Flora said.

Celine shrugged her shoulders.

"It just felt like the right thing to do. The queen mentioned about you losing your powers. What is she talking about?"

Flora looked away suddenly.

"I am a witch—or was a witch. She took my powers with the help of Opal."

"A witch," Celine repeated, nodding her head.

Flora looked at her curiously, raising her hands, her fingers curling around the bars, holding onto them.

"Why are you not surprised? What do you know of our world, servant?"

"Let's just say fate has a clever way of working."

"Only if you let it," Flora said to her.

"Fate and destiny are inevitable," Celine countered.

That fact left her speechless. She blinked twice, seeming satisfied and bewildered by this human who spoke such words so strongly.

"Why did she take your powers?"

"I cursed her."

"Cursed her?"

"Yes. By killing the king, she sealed her fate. She will have eyes as black as her heart forever. I guess you are right, fate and destiny are inevitable," she said sadly, looking down.

Celine swallowed hard and reached into the gate, holding out the food to her. She took the food with one hand, their skin making contact and her emerald green eyes opened wide in shock. She dropped the food to the floor and grabbed Celine's hand quickly, taking a closer look at her palm.

"Hey! What are you doing?" Celine hissed at her, trying to yank her hand back.

Flora couldn't speak; she just shook her head in denial. "Oh, my God. It's you," she whispered.

"What are you talking about?" Celine whispered back.

"You are carrying the babe of a vampire."

Celine took her hand back and placed it over her belly protectively.

"How could you know something like that? I thought you didn't have any powers?"

"You have to leave here. You don't have much time. The babe will be born soon."

"What do you mean soon?" she asked, her eyes widening with fear.

"You probably have a week or so. I don't really know," Flora said, shaking her head. "You must prepare and be ready to leave."

"OK, but what about you? I can't just leave you here."

"Don't worry about me. You just take care of that baby," Flora said to her.

"I will," Celine said, backing away from the gate, picking up the bucket and mop.

"Servant, what is your name?" Flora asked her.

"My name is Celine. Why?" she asked, turning back toward Flora.

"I just wanted to know the name of the brave woman who would aide in the death of my sister."

My vision began to black out, taking me into the future, but I refused to let it. I wanted to know more, more of my mother and father. I didn't want any part of a future that could wait. I felt it pulling me out, but I fought against it. I closed my eyes and concentrated. I wanted to be able to see what I wanted to see. I willed it not to take me away from the past; I felt tears spring to my eyes, silently begging it to leave me here a moment longer. I felt my body begin to float as if I was in a time machine, images floating around me like pictures. I kept seeing my parents' picture flashing by me. I reached up, trying to not let it escape. Again it circled around me. Focusing hard, my mind began to grasp it. I let out a scream of frustration, shattering all the images all around me.

Opening my eyes I found myself outside. It was dark out, the moon shining brightly. Edrick and Celine were together in the backyard of his home. They stood in a gazebo. It was once white but now looked gray, giving it a rustic look. His hand sat protectively on her stomach. My heart screamed with joy as I realized what I'd just done. My visions were now in my control, no longer controlling me. I would see what I wanted to see when I wanted to see it. Celine looked beautiful under the moonlight. Her long blond hair was down, and she was wearing a cream-colored dress with long sleeves. The dressed did her justice, showing off her petite figure and highlighting a glow to her beautiful pale skin. While she was dressed romantically, Edrick was the complete opposite, dressed in dark pants and a sleeveless shirt with a protective vest made out of steel, his sword was hanging loosely by his side. He was every bit as magnificent as he looked.

"I cannot believe that after I warned you, you went ahead and put yourself in danger. You are lucky we are blood mated. She could have entranced you," Edrick said to her.

"I know, but you warned me, remember? I was safe." She smiled, touching his face gently. "I love you," she said, reaching up, she kissed him gently.

"I love you too," he said, abruptly lifting his head. "Are you trying to distract me?"

"No, but is it working?" She kissed him again. "I don't want to fight. We don't have much time…" she said, her voice trailing off.

"I know, my love. Do you wish that we could be married? As in the traditional sense you humans like? I hear it is every woman's wish to be married."

She smiled sadly at him, shaking her head. "I suppose it is. I never really gave it much thought," she said with wonder. "But it doesn't matter. I have you, and that is what is important."

"Let's say that I can. Would you?" he asked.

She pulled away from him, looking puzzled by his question. "Would I what?"

He paused for a second as if he was nervous. I felt tears well up in my eyes as I saw his hidden intention. I found it a bit humorous to watch a man of his size look upon a small woman with fear.

"Would you marry me?"

She smiled softly, still clueless to what was going on.

"Of course I would."

I heard Edrick swallow hard as he went slowly on one knee before her. She gasped with surprise as her hand went to cover her mouth. He looked up at her, his expression serious.

"Celine, you did me a great honor when you became my blood mate. I want to honor you in every way humanly possible. Will you marry me?" He took out a beautiful antique diamond ring from his pocket, grabbed her hand, and slipped it on her finger. The ring had a round center stone with red rubies going all around, forming an eternity band. It fit her perfectly.

"Yes. Yes I will marry you!" she said, practically throwing her body at him. He captured her in his arms hugging her tightly, standing up and twirling her around. He set her down, her small body sliding down his body gently, her arms wrapped around his neck.

"Are you sure?" he whispered to her.

"I have never been more sure about anything in my life," she said looking up at him, her green eyes wet with tears.

He nodded his head and let her go. He walked out of the gazebo, leaving her waiting impatiently. I stood waiting with her, wondering, like she, what he was doing. He went inside his house for a few minutes and came out with someone behind him—a man wearing the cloth of a priest. He was a small, balding elderly man . He held a Bible in his hands as he walked behind Edrick. Celine's eyes widened as she saw the priest. Edrick smiled at her mischievously as he took the steps into the gazebo.

"How do you know Father Daniel?" she whispered as she took Edrick's hand.

"This evening, I went into the church just before sundown and entranced him to come and marry us," he whispered back.

"You what?" she said, trying to sound angry but failing when she let out a giggle.

I sat on the hard ground in front of the gazebo, watching as the priest began the ceremony. I looked on, bearing witness to the marriage of my parents. This would be another beautiful picture, forever captured in my mind. They were not in my life, no, but I was in their life, their past. I got to share in this moment with them.

"You may now kiss your bride," the small priest announced.

Edrick grabbed her face between his hands, kissing her ever so gently.

"My wife," he whispered.

"My husband," she whispered back.

Edrick turned toward the priest, looking deeply into his eyes. "You will go back to the church and return to your room," he told him.

"Yes, of course. Thank you, sir," the priest said in a daze. He took the steps carefully off the gazebo and headed back obediently toward the church. As they watched him leave, I watched as Edrick's body stilled. He closed his eyes briefly, his expression sad.

Celine looked up at him. "Are you OK?"

"Yes. Let's go inside," he said to her after a minute. Smiling, he grabbed her hand and they walked together down the steps of the gazebo. I got up and watched them walk away. My vision was beginning to fade, but I willed it to stay. I didn't want to leave just yet. *One more minute. Let me watch them just a little longer.* As my vision began to pull me out, I watched as Edrick turned, looked straight at me, and smiled sadly.

chapter

TWENTY EIGHT

"Abel is dead. Ian and the X's live."

Queen Ezarbet stood very still. She could not have heard right.

"What did you say?" she whispered.

"The prophet killed Abel."

She hung up the phone, not wanting to hear anymore. Letting out a furious scream, she heaved the cell phone against the wall, shattering it to pieces. The prophet killed Abel. Ian and the others were alive! She felt her hand clench into a fist, her long fingernails digging into her palms drawing blood. This could not be. Screaming for her guards, she paced back and forth in her bedroom, her anger overtaking her. Alec and Gavin entered the room and closed the door behind them, going on one knee and bowing before her.

"My queen, you have summoned us?" Alec the young vampire spoke first, looking up at her earnestly.

"I want you both to go find the prophet and bring her to me. If you don't, don't bother coming back. Consider yourself dead!" she yelled at them.

"But my queen, where shall we start looking?" Gavin asked, standing.

The queen cocked her head to the side, smoothing her red silk gown, and walked over to stand in front of him.

"Are you asking me a question on how to go about looking for someone? Should I show you how to hold your cock while pissing too?" she hissed, coming closer to him.

"No, no, my queen. I simply meant…" He didn't get to finish. She yanked out his tongue and sliced his neck with her sharp fingernails.

Blood splattered everywhere, dripping down her face. She licked her finger, tasting his blood, watching as he turned to ash. She looked over to Alec, slowly coming to stand before him, getting aroused by his fear as he looked away from her.

"Do you have any questions for me?" she asked, her face looking almost demonic, her voice sounding child-like.

A wide-eyed Alec simply shook his head in fear of speaking.

"Good. Leave," she said, turning away from him.

Walking over to her bathroom quarters, she took off her gown, walked naked to the sink, and grabbed a towel, wetting it. Taking a seat at her vanity, she cleaned off her bloodied face and neck. Once cleansed she grabbed her brush and started combing her beautiful, lustrous hair, deep in thought. Scarlett was going pay for what trouble she had caused already. The X's most likely ran, that's what they were good for, but soon they would come together again. It would only be a matter of time before they would seek their precious prophet. She would wait patiently, and when the time was right she would strike. With Abel now dead, he would not stand in the way of the next plan she had in mind. She did not need a troublesome male in her way. The next phase, he would not have been happy with.

Damian was a huge part in this plan. He was the key to what was to come. Finding her lipstick she applied it, the luscious red color complementing her pale skin and red hair. Looking at the label, she almost laughed out loud. How ironic that is was called Scarlett Red. Putting the gold cap back on it, she tossed it to the side. Getting up from the chair, she went over to her walk-in closet. She looked at the many gowns she owned, all designer of course, nothing but the best silks and satins from all over the world.

She took out a red gown and pulled it over her head. The gown fit her perfectly, the fabric almost like water over her skin. Looking in the tall mirror in the closet, she was pleased by her appearance. The dress had a deep V, revealing the curve of her ample breasts, and with the sheerness of the fabric, you could see the outline of her nipples. The gown was long with a long slit on the side, showing off the pale smoothness of her leg, and the back of the gown was almost nonexistent. Putting on her diamond earrings, she walked out of her bedroom. Soon she would consult with her foreseer, but it was time she tended to another matter.

Walking to another part of the castle, she headed toward where she kept them. In front of the doorway stood Maylina, one of her most trusted ancients. Maylina was as cruel as she was. There was not one ounce of emotion in those pale blue eyes of hers. She bowed her head to the queen and opened the door. The dungeon was dark and filthy, letting in little light. Walking through each door, she peeked inside and saw her human blood slaves, all being kept feed and healthy. There were at least a hundred of them so far. Some of them were sedated, hooked up with IVs, tubes of blood being taken from them.

This was the whole purpose of the war. This was what was supposed to happen. Humans were worth nothing.

They idolized God, religion, money, and celebrities. *I will be their God,* she thought. *They will worship my religion. They will have no money. I will be their celebrity they will fawn over.* No one was going to stand in her way. She closed her eyes and started to chant, summoning an elder witch named Opal. Opal was one of the most powerful witches, a witch who played with the blackest of magic. She had helped her remove her sister's power, and she would be a key to the next phase.

"It's time we raise the stakes."

The queen started to smile as she began to think of the new plans that waited. She twirled the diamond and ruby ring on her finger that had been Celine's, letting out a vengeful laugh. Dear, poor Scarlett had no idea what was to come.

❦

The grey mouse came out from his hiding spot and started to make his way up the grand staircase. Reaching the top he watched as the queen left her room with an evil smile, eyes as black as night and a red silk gown. Quickly scurrying to the corner trying not to be seen, the mouse waited until she closed her door and walked away. He crawled under the doorway and into her room. The room was big with lots of furniture and artwork on the walls. He carefully went into the room further, seeing a pile of clothes on the floor with black dust around them. Finding the pair of pants, he went into the pockets and came up with a key. Holding the key tightly with his tail, he scrambled out peeking out of the pocket first to make sure he was he was still alone in the room. He ran out as fast as he could, the key trailing behind him, making a faint clinking sound.

Squeezing himself under the doorway, he looked from right to left before crossing the hallway, once again sticking to the corners. He heard a hiss of a cat and turned. It had huge green eyes and black, fluffy hair. It wore a diamond necklace around its neck for a collar. The cat made a leap for him, baring its claws, but the mouse quickly ran down the stairs, the cat not far behind him. Seeing a table, the mouse climbed up its leg to the top. The cat jumped up after him, knocking over a glass vase in the process, the glass loudly shattering everywhere. He gave another of his hisses, catching the mouse by the tail with its claw, making him let go of the key. The mouse gave a small squeak of pain and faced the cat, ready to meet his fate. The cat licked its lips, ready for dinner.

"Alvah, look at this mess!" the queen yelled, looking at the shattered glass on the floor.

Alvah jumped, startled by his mistress's voice, and released the mouse. The mouse quickly took advantage of the distraction. Gripping the key with his tail, he ran to the opposite side of the table. Noticing that his meal was getting away, Alvah started to run after him, but not before his mistress picked him up.

"Alvah, what will I do with you? Maybe I will cook you and feed your remains to the blood slaves," the queen said to the cat. Petting his furry head, she walked up the stairs with the dark cat in her arms. Loving his mistress's touch, Alvah began to purr, closing his eyes, his meal forgotten.

The mouse breathed a sigh of relief. With his tail and the key intact, he made his way toward the basement.

chapter

TWENTY
NINE

As the vision of Edrick smiling at me sadly began to fade, I knew he'd just had a vision of me watching them. I waved my hand at him, knowing he couldn't see me anymore. I felt myself being pulled again, this time to the future. I once again tried to fight against it. I didn't want to see the future. I wanted it to be unknown. With all the visions I'd had of the future, I felt as if it all led to my own personal doom. What good could come from all of this? Everything seemed to turn white around me. I felt a pair of warm hands on my shoulders, coaxing me into this future that I dreaded. I felt useless against it. It wanted me to see this, and there was no way I could deny it.

Opening my eyes, I felt the warm hands that were guiding me release. Going into the future, I drifted into a big castle, where I saw myself dressed in my gear, sword in my hand. My hair was longer, sitting softly in waves against my face. I looked different. My appearance was the same, but I somehow looked wiser, experienced. I heard doors burst open, and my head went up in alert. I watched myself go down the stairs, running. I ran after myself with urgency. Ancients and wolves were everywhere. What the hell was this? The whole place was surrounded. I paused and stood frozen in the doorway. I watched as I ran into the room, powerfully and with purpose, jumping so high, catching one of the beasts by the back. Grabbing it by the hair, I yanked his neck back, slicing off its head. I saw my X's, all in battle with beasts and ancients. I saw Hugo and Flora together holding hands, chanting magic, making the vampires against us turn to ash. I saw Skull with two big rifles in his hands, shooting at the beasts, aiming perfectly at their heads.

"Scarlett!" someone shouted.

I saw myself turn to the voice, that familiar voice, of Ian. I watched myself acknowledge him. It was as though we were talking to each other without words, the fierce stare between us undeniable. Someone began to move in the shadows, making me break our stare. I watched as a man, shirtless in fitted jeans, fought. He went over to Zayah as if he was going to attack her, but he blocked an ancient from attacking her from behind, grabbing him by the neck easily and snapping it with his bare hands. Who was he? He was very tall and had dark black hair. His body was rippling with muscles, and he looked like a true warrior. I couldn't take my eyes off of him; he was fascinating. Like a moth to a flame, I was drawn to him. He was vampire, not just because I saw his fangs protruding from his mouth but because he had the quickness of a killer instinct. He must have been an ancient, but there was something very different about him.

A beast let loose a howl from the ceiling above, crawled its way down the walls, and jumped straight at him. My heart instantly froze, fearing for him, but the man was too quick. One minute he was in front of the beast, and the next he was behind him. His arm went around his neck and he grabbed him by the mouth, prying it open with his bare hands. The beast howled again, swaying this way and that way, trying to swing him off of his massive body. The man was too strong and with one forceful tug, he spilt open the beast's mouth, tearing it to the neck. Blood gushed from the dead beast and he drops its body onto the floor, disgusted, blood gleaming off of his naked chest. My God, who was this man?

"Chayton," Big Red yelled at him.

The man looked over to Big Red, who tossed him a sword. Catching it, he grinned at Big Red, running in the other direction.

"Not a good time to show off," Big Red called out after him.

I followed the man named Chayton. Three ancients were right at his heels, all chasing him. He smiled again, knowing they were onto him. I followed them, knowing this man named Chayton was going to lead them to their deaths. I watched as he led them into a long hallway running at full speed. I as well as the ancients found it hard to keep up with him. The ancients growled their frustration at being outrun by this young vampire.

"Come and get me, you fucks!" Chayton screamed at them.

They growled again at his taunt, picking up their speed. I watched him lead them into a doorway that led outside. He checked his watch and waited until the ancients were standing before him. The morning sun was coming. What the fuck was he doing? I wanted to scream at him for his stupidity. The three ancients raised their swords. Chayton smiled at them. His smile looked familiar to me somehow.

"You guys have one minute," he said softly to them.

"We die, you die; Dominick will see that you are dead," one of the ancients spit out at him.

"See, that's where you have a problem…" He trailed off looking up at sun that was starting to rise.

I watched as the ancients' skin started to smoke. They dropped their swords and fell to their knees before Chayton, who seemed unfazed by the sun's effects. They simultaneously began to turn to ash, before the one who'd spoken to Chayton looked upon him with shock.

"I am not that easy to kill," he whispered to him as he kicked him, sending his ashes crumpling to the ground.

He stood there looking up at the sun that was beaming brightly down on his muscular body. I put my hand over my mouth in awe. A vampire that can go into sunlight. Who was this man?

chapter

THIRTY

My vision of Chayton standing there with the sun gleaming down on him as if in approval began to fade. Something was nudging me, but I didn't want to wake. Hugo. *"No, no. Just a little longer,"* my mind screamed. I wanted to stay with this man who intrigued me. I didn't want to wake up and face this reality, or maybe I wanted it all to be a dream.

"Excuse me, miss," the taxi driver said, looking back at me.

Groaning, I opened my eyes, rubbing them. They felt swollen. My hand went to my neck. It feels stiff from the way I'd slept.

"You're here," he said, looking at me suspiciously.

"Right. Thanks," I said, my voice raspy. I let out a cough and went into my purse, handing him money.

I pick up Hugo and my duffle bag and got out of the cab. The morning sun was bright, stinging my eyes momentarily. It was freezing out, the type of cold where you find it hard to catch your breath. I looked up to see what hotel we staying are at—The Plaza. Whoa. Maybe I was being a bit dramatic when I told the driver I wanted the best hotel in New York. Looking up at the tall building made me feel a little intimidated and underdressed as I walked up.

I was automatically greeted at the doorway by the doorman, smiling at me and welcoming me to the hotel. It was beautiful with high ceilings, floral arrangements everywhere, and lavish artwork on the walls. The guests walking out were dressed to the nines. All most likely were very rich and living a privileged life. If they only knew of this other dark world, one that didn't require money, didn't require social status, only required your blood.

"OK, buddy. You know what you have to do," I whispered to Hugo.

I headed to the front desk, where the receptionist Laura greeted me, looking at my appearance and down at Hugo. She was a middle-aged woman wearing a navy suit with a white, collared shirt underneath. She wore her hair pulled back tight into a bun, making her face look as if she was uptight about something.

"Hello. Welcome to The Plaza. Do you have a reservation?" she asked, narrowing her eyes and pursing her lips, looking at me as if I was lost and not meant to be there. I started to feel like Vivian from *Pretty Woman*—minus the prostitution.

"Yes, yes I do. Scarlett De Laurentiis," I said in an equally snobby tone, batting my lashes at her.

"OK. Let me take a look for you," she said as she examined her computer, her long fingers pressing down on the keyboard making a loud, annoying tapping sound.

Hugo let out a little whine, and I pet his head gently, smiling at the receptionist.

"Um, yes." She lets out a cough, looking uncomfortable. *Good. Serves her right.* "It looks like you have one of the best suites our hotel offers. The Royal Palace Suite," she said, plastering a fake smile on her face as she looked at me.

"Of course. Nothing but the best for us; isn't that right, honey?" I said to Hugo, kissing his head.

I was shocked. Really, Hugo? The Royal Plaza Suite? He must not have liked her tone of voice with me, or he was just feeling sorry for me. Either way it was a genius idea. She handed me the keys, and we walked through the hotel to the elevator. There was an actual elevator person to take us to the floor we needed to be on. Even the elevator was beautiful, with big gold doors and gold buttons with the floor numbers. He escorted us to our room. Taking the key from me, he opened the door.

"If there is anything you need, Ms. De Laurentiis, please do not hesitate to call upon me," he said before exiting the room.

"Thank you," I said softly. Watching him leave, I turned to the room.

Oh, my. The suite was something celebrities would stay in. The décor was rich with gold and cream colors. A grand white piano stood in one corner, and a beautiful fireplace was already burning with wood. Walking over to the big windows, I took in the view overlooking Manhattan. I leaned forward against the window, letting the cold touch my skin. I closed my eyes. I was so tired, so tired of feeling. I was on the verge of tears again.

Turning I looked at Hugo, who was transformed. He wasn't wearing his jacket, and his back was toward me. He stood by the doorway and put his hands on the door, open-palmed, and began to chant. I watched, mesmerized by him and his beautiful voice. Blue light came from his palm, forming a barrier around the door. I blinked, and just like that it was gone.

"What are you doing?"

"Casting a shield around the doorway. No vampires are going be able to get through here," he said, finishing up.

He turned to me with worried eyes. I said nothing to him.

"Are you OK? Do you want to talk about It?" he asked softly, coming toward me.

I held out my hand, stopping him. I knew if he came any closer, I was going to crumble.

"I think I will be fine, and no, I don't want to talk about it," I whispered, folding my arms across my chest.

He stopped in his tracks, nodding. I knew he was trying to find the right words to comfort me.

"I want to show you something," he said, walking to the gold-colored sofa and having a seat. He grabbed his jacket and reached inside the pocket. He produced a rock.

"Have a seat," he said softly to me.

Curious, I walked over, sitting beside him. The rock was small and brown with gold flecks in it.

"Hold out your hands."

I did, my palms open. He placed the rock on my hands and began to chant. I looked at him, confused at first, but I felt my hands begin to warm. Something was happening to the rock. It began to move, shifting in my hand. With eyes closed, he put his hand over the rock and I watched in amazement as a bright white light came from his hand. The bright light made me blink rapidly, and I felt weight on my hands as the rock transformed into a brown, leather-bound book with gold lettering on the front and a thick clasp securing it closed. What was this? It must have been important for him to feel the need to disguise it. I looked up at him with the question in my eyes.

"It's your destiny, the reason why you were born. The reason why you are what you are today. It's the Book of The Undead," he whispered to me.

I stared down at the book that was not only heavy on my hands, but also represented the heavy weight I'd felt on my shoulders since turning twenty-one. So this was it, the reason everyone wanted me dead. With shaking fingers, I opened the clasp, opening the book and going to the page that was folded over. My finger skimmed through the page. It was handwritten in what looked to be Latin.

"What does it say?" I asked softly.

He took the book from me and read:

A child will be born, a miracle, from two species, from a male vampire and a human female. This child will become of age and with this age will have amazing strength and power. A new era is coming, a coming of evil and a coming of war. A queen will rise. Rivers of blood will spill; death is inevitable. The prophet will have the aid of her guardian, a man with the marking of the moon. The man marked with the moon will meet his full potential when he comes together with a star. Together they will be one. Lost brothers will be in a crossroad of a point of no return. The decision has been made. Sides will be taken; rules will be broken. The prophet will lead in the war of the undead, and anyone against her will be defeated.

As Hugo finished reading, I got a chill up my spine. Hugo and Flora, Liam and Damian, Queen Ezarbet and I. It read as plain as day. I looked again at the book and stopped Hugo from closing it. The other half of the page was ripped, just like Hugo told me earlier.

"Why would someone rip the other page?"

"It is said that when one prophecy is fulfilled, another comes to light."

"But why take it? Unless it has something to do with now," I said, grabbing the book from him, my finger touching where the page was torn. I wondered what the next prophecy was. I felt certain that it had to do with the prophecy I was now living. I felt drawn to know. Something was not right about the page being missing. I felt this deep knot in the pit of my stomach.

"Hugo, who is Chayton?"

"I don't know anyone by the name of Chayton. Why do you ask?" he said, looking at me intently.

"I had a vision of a man named Chayton."

Hugo just nodded his head, not saying anything.

"We have to find out who has the other half," I whispered, closing the book gently. I got up from the sofa. Picking up my duffel bag, I started to make my way to my bedroom.

"I am so sorry it had to end badly for you and Ian. He is a fool, Scarlett. Whether he wants to admit it or not, he is enthralled with you," he called out to me.

I turned smiling sadly at him. "Some things have to end badly for it to end, right?" I said, leaving it at that.

I walked into my room and closed the door behind me. The room was beautiful and bright, its décor white, crisp, and clean. Beautiful floral artwork hung on the walls and big windows overlooked the gorgeous view of Fifth Avenue. The bed was covered with beautiful pillows and silk sheets with an opulent gold pattern. Dropping my duffel bag, I walked right away into the bathroom, seeing a big whirlpool-style bath tub. "Oh, thank God," I said to myself. This was just what I needed: a nice, long, hot bath. I quickly began to take off my shoes and peel off my shirt. Turning on the faucet, I left it on warm, watching the steam start to build up. On the side of the tub I saw complementary bath salts. As soon as I opened the jar, the sweet scent of French vanilla hit me. Pouring it in I watched the water start to sizzle.

Getting up I removed the rest of my clothes and put my foot in, testing the warmth. Satisfied I got in, letting the water hit my body, letting the warmth ease my achy muscles. I inhaled deeply, taking in the relaxing aroma of the sweet scent, my body beginning to relax. Lifting my foot, I turned the knob, turning off the water. Sinking my body further into the water, I really tried not to think of him, but I couldn't control it. *Ian,* my mind whispered to me. I looked at my hand where I'd cut myself to feed him; it was almost healed now, leaving a faint hint of a scar. I wished I would have reacted differently instead of acting hurt. I should have yelled, kicked, threw something at him instead of looking so hurt, crying, practically begging him.

Sinking my head into the water trying to escape my thoughts, no longer did I feel hurt. Yes, that was still there lingering in the back of my heart, but now that my mind was involved, I felt anger. I threw myself shamelessly at him and for what? For him to say I was weak, because I am human? *Damn him.* I hoped I never saw him again, even though my gut was telling me I would. My visions told me so. But what if they were wrong? What if everything I envisioned of him was wrong? He was incapable of love, and any emotion was a weakness. Opening my eyes under the water, I started to feel myself getting lost with my erratic thoughts; I was drifting, my mind staying focused and concentrated on pushing forward. I wanted answers, and I wanted them now.

I felt myself free fall into a home, falling hard on the floor with a loud thump. Standing I noticed the home was dark and old. A big black cross with thorns hung on a wall in the living room. Walking closer to it, I noticed blood on it. I felt a chill go up my spine. This was no religious cross. Where the hell was I? Whose house was this? I heard footsteps. Someone was here. I tried to listen carefully and realized whoever was in the home was downstairs in the basement. Slowly I walked to where the sound led me. Passing the hallway, I saw paintings on the wall, all of children. The children looked as if they were lost and being lead somewhere. In the background, it looked as if they were being led by someone—by a man with red eyes.

Swallowing hard, I found the door and hesitantly turned the knob. There were steps, and I started to descend slowly, the old wooden steps creaking under my weight. The basement was dark and smelled of mold. Reaching the bottom of the steps, I saw a dark figure dressed in a black cape. I knew it was a woman from her slender frame. I followed her as she made her way through her basement. She came to another doorway and unlocked it. Following her,

I felt a sense of pure evil drift my way. Inside the room was a round wooden table with a black lace cloth over it. On a bookshelf sat jars, neatly lined up. Walking over to it and looking inside a jar, I saw eyes—human eyes! Putting my hand over my mouth, I looked at the other jars and saw other body parts in them. *Witch!* my mind screamed at me.

She walked over to one of the other shelves and took down a black book. The book was old, the spine looking like it was about to unravel. On the front of it was an engraved carving of an angel, but not your typical Angel with beautiful wings and a cherub face. This was a dark angel with fangs and red eyes. It looked demonic. Coming closer to her, I watched as she opened the book and took out a folded paper. She unfolded it gently. Her hands were dark, her long, pointy fingernails painted black. Swallowing hard, I looked at what she was looking at and knew the handwriting right away, even though I could not read it. It was the other half of the prophecy. I watched as she read it, smiling evilly. She stiffened momentarily as though she sensed me, lifted her cape off her head, and looked straight at me. I gasped. This witch's eyes were white, and she stared at me as though she saw me.

My body came out from the water in a rush. I started coughing from the water that got into my lungs. Bringing my knees up, I laid my head on them and closed my eyes, trying to steady my breathing. "Opal," I whispered her name out loud. The woman who helped the queen take Flora's powers. What did she want with the other half of the prophecy? What could the queen possibly gain from it? Who was Chayton? There were so many unanswered questions. Once I reunited with the X's, I would make it a point to corner Big Red and ask him about it. They looked like they were friends.

Opal posed another problem. There was no way we could kill her physically. The only way she would be defeated would be to fight magic with magic. Hugo and Flora were the key to all of this, and what a powerful duo they would make. I noticed the water had turned cold and my hands were wrinkly. *How long was I out for?* Sighing with frustration, I stood up quickly, splashing water onto the floor. My wet feet touched the cold marble flooring. Grabbing two towels, I dried my hair with one and wrapped my body with the other. A beautiful white terrycloth robe hung on a hook on the inside of the bathroom door. I put it on, not caring if my wet hair was going to soak the robe.

Leaving the bathroom, I walked over to the window and admired the beautiful view of Fifth Avenue. I bet it would look even more beautiful in the spring, when all the leaves were on the trees and flowers were planted. Even though we were high up, I could still see the people walking back and forth on the busy streets. I wondered enviously if they were all meeting up with family to open presents and have a huge dinner. Leaning forward against the glass, I felt the coldness of the outside touch my skin. I'd never had that and probably never would. I felt tears sting my eyes as Ian's words shot back at me. "Jesus, Scarlett, don't confuse great fucking with love." I angrily wiped my tears away. My visions were all screwed up. Maybe I was dreaming of him, and they were not visions at all.

Pulling the curtains closed, I made the bright room dark. I felt drained emotionally and physically. Throwing myself back on the bed with a huff, I thought of Zayah and Con telling me Ian was enthralled. I was now more convinced than ever the man was not capable of loving, let alone being enthralled with anyone. I closed my eyes, and all I could see were his cold, steel blue eyes looking back at me. As much as I tried to deny it, I knew our paths would cross again. This time I would be ready, showing no emotion toward him. *Enthralled!* I let out an exasperated sound. *I have two words I would say about that. I would say, fuck you.* This was just the beginning of our story. *Whoever said this was a fairytale?*